THE CHEMIST'S SHOP

BY RICHARD BRUMER

THE CHEMIST'S SHOP

Limitless Publishing, LLC
Kailua, HI 96734
www.limitlesspublishing.com

Formatting: Limitless Publishing

ISBN-13: 978-1-68058-179-9
ISBN-10: 1-68058-179-1

For my wife

First they came for the Socialists, and I did not speak out...
Because I was not a Socialist.
Then they came for the Trade Unionists, and I did not speak out...
Because I was not a Trade Unionist.
Then they came for the Jews, and I did not speak out...
Because I was not a Jew.
Then they came for me...and there was no one left to speak for me.

—**Martin Niemoller, Protestant pastor**

Chapter 1

Szentendre, a small village near Budapest -April 1944

Miklos Rosen stared out his bedroom window, hypnotized by the large fluffy snowflakes floating down under the bright street lamp. He focused on one of them, following it as it drifted downward to rest with those that had already fallen. He never lost his sense of wonder. The snow would be gone by morning with the onset of the sun and warm spring air, but winter was giving one last shout before its demise.

Ilona lay in bed, her head pressed against the pillow, and watched her husband. Miklos knew she thought he was a dreamer. Their three young daughters were asleep in their rooms, already tucked in with kisses and hugs. Ilona closed her eyes and sighed. She seemed content.

At thirty-four, Miklos felt blessed to have Ilona and their three lovely daughters as his family. The youngest was Eva, age five. Their identical twins,

1

Roza and Magda, were eight.

The Easter and Passover holy days had recently passed and, although the Rosen's were Jewish, they shared some of the spring festivities with their Christian neighbors. The children loved the egg hunts with their friends and getting their baskets filled with goodies. Family and friendships were valued above all else.

"Miklos, come to bed. My feet are cold," Ilona called.

He stepped away from the window, abandoning his wandering thoughts as he slid under the thick feather comforter and snuggled up to her. She was so beautiful. In all their years of marriage, it seemed she hadn't changed a bit. Her fair skin, jet-black curls, and sparkling brown eyes had first attracted him, but it was her tender, inner feelings that made him love her.

Ilona's eyes fluttered open. Miklos heard a soft moan hum through her lips as she turned and stretched her arm around his neck to draw him closer. His heart raced in anticipation of the passion that would follow. They held each other's hands in front of their lips, gazing at each other as they kissed the gold bands that encircled their fingers.

Short kisses followed as Miklos moved his hand under her nightgown and along her slender body to feel her breasts. She trembled beneath him.

"I love you," she whispered. "I could never live without you."

He felt her tender kisses on his eyelids...so soft, so light.

"I love you too, Ilona. So much."

Miklos remained motionless as her moist lips traced his face with soft kisses. He pulled her closer until he felt her heart beating against his chest.

A hard tapping on the bedroom door broke the moment.

"*Apa, Anya.* Papa, Mama," a young girl cried.

Ilona rushed to open the door. Little Magda stood there with her face crinkled up, wet with tears. Ilona knelt on the bedroom floor, rocked the child in her arms, and kissed her tears away.

"Shh, shh, little sweetheart. You're with Mama now."

"*Anya*, Roza hit me and called me a bad word," she said, sobbing and pulling on her mother's white night dress.

A minute later, her twin sister, Roza, dashed into the room and shouted, "*Anya*, Magda is telling a lie. I knew she was going to wake you. She's mean and always lies. I never used a bad word."

"Shh, be quiet. Don't wake Eva," Ilona whispered as she took them to her bedside. "Did you hit her, Roza?"

"*Nem, nem, Anya*," Roza shouted.

"She's lying," Magda yelled. "She hit me on my arm."

"Girls, girls, I love you both. Roza, just tell me if you hit Magda."

"Well," she said, looking down at her feet. "I didn't mean it. It was an accident, and I only *touched* her arm with my little finger."

"Apologize to your sister," Ilona said, then kissed each girl on the forehead. "If you did say a bad word, Roza, don't use it again."

Roza took a deep breath, rolled her eyes, and frowned as she stood in front of Magda. Then she put her hands on her hips, looked at the ceiling, shrugged, and said in a low whisper, "I'm sorry."

Magda cried out, "Mama, can we sleep with you and Papa?"

Roza chimed in, "Please, please."

Miklos and Ilona exchanged a glance, sighed, and nodded as the girls climbed in and nestled under the warm blanket.

***

Miklos was the first to wake the next morning. He looked at Ilona and the girls sleeping peacefully, a stark contrast to the violence going on in most of Europe. His little girls knew nothing of it. They lived in the world of fairy tales, only aware of the pleasures of childhood and the love they felt for each other in their country home. The young girls awakened to the chirps of birds and the sweet fragrance of their flower garden, which were much more peaceful and pleasant than the noise and odors of the city.

Miklos sat at the edge of his bed, alone with his thoughts. He was aware that anti-Semitism had been prevalent in Hungary for many years, and, since his country had allied with Nazi Germany, he felt the inevitable was near. The Nazis and Hungarian authorities were brutal. He had listened to shortwave radio reports of the killings and conscription of people in villages and farms in countries throughout Europe, where the Holocaust was in full force.

His family meant everything to him. He had to protect them but didn't know how. Ilona depended upon him to keep her and their daughters safe, and he felt guilty for being powerless.

Miklos was glad that, for now, his family was unharmed, but he believed they would be safer in their Budapest apartment, where they had lived when he taught at the university. He was thankful he had a home to go to in the capital. The Jewish community in Budapest was secure, but he knew it would not last. The oppressive anti-Semitic laws made the lives of the Jews difficult, and, although his neighbors seemed to be out of harm's way, the Hungarian authorities recruited them to clean up debris and dig graves for the dead after air raids. They did whatever was necessary to appease the authorities and stay alive.

Moving to Budapest might buy us time, but why? Are Budapest Jews privileged? Is what's happening an illusion? Soon, no Jew will be safe anywhere in Hungary. How could the world allow this?

Miklos's sense of security evaporated when German troops occupied Hungary. Everything happened so quickly, there was no time for Hungarians to organize any significant form of resistance. There was talk that Jews were being forced into a ghetto and kept under guard behind a high fence and a stone wall. Thus far, the Rosen's had not been arrested or disturbed, but Miklos had already been relieved of his position at the university, where he was a pharmacology professor. His crime was being a Jew. His parents were among those who were missing and his inquiries went unanswered. Germans occupied Ilona's family vineyard and forced her parents to accommodate them under threat of arrest.

Miklos knew that time would not be on their side and he tried to keep Ilona optimistic. It was no longer safe to stay in Hungary, and he made plans to move back to their home in Budapest in a few days. He was fortunate that his family had their apartment in the capital, but the idea that they would be part of the few Jews left in Budapest made him uneasy.

Maybe the fact that I was once a prestigious professor will protect us. The Germans are part of a high culture and always showed respect for those in the world of academia.

Many of their neighbors and friends in the countryside had mysteriously disappeared, including Miklos' best friend, Laszlo Radnóti, a poet, and János Schwarz, a historian and author. The village streets were barren except for the ominous presence of Nazi troops marching on cobblestone. Times had changed drastically. He thought it could be a matter of weeks before they, too, would be arrested.

Miklos had to take his mind to another place to escape his thoughts and find serenity. He created an illusion that everything would be all right in the end and his family would live, but the truth was that it was a dangerous time, and they were in an unsafe place. He could not afford to daydream.

We are safe now, but I can't anticipate what is to come, just like unexpected snowfall on a spring me to tell you something."

"Tell me now."

"No, it's a surprise for the whole family."

Magda's excited cries interrupted them. "Look at me, look at me!" She skipped barefoot along the hardwood floor, spinning, turning and bowing to her audience.

"Wonderful!" Miklos shouted as he clapped in rhythm to the music.

"Look at me too," Roza yelled as she jumped up and down on the sofa.

Then little Eva caught her breath and performed her solo. "Look at me, Papa. I'm the swan queen."

She twirled her young body around until she was dizzy, but continued to dazzle her audience. At the end of her dance, her black curls were wet with perspiration and she bowed to everyone as they applauded. Her eyes widened and sparkled when Miklos presented her with a red rose he had taken from Ilona's birthday bouquet.

"Oh, Papa, thank you!" she said, taking in the delicate scent of the rose.

"You're welcome, Eva. Every ballerina should have flowers when she takes her bows at the end of her performance."

Miklos squeezed his wife's hand. "Did you ever think that when our girls were born, they would provide us with so much entertainment?"

"Never," Ilona said with tears of delight. "We were given a gift, a wonderful present," she said, her dark brown eyes glistening.

"We're blessed," he said with a deep sigh, but his thoughts were troubled.

"Will we be all right, Miklos?" Ilona asked. "I'm worried about the girls. They're so young, just babies."

"Everything will go well. I was a professor. The Nazis will show respect and find some use for me. We will be safe, Ilona. I promise you."

Little Eva was out of breath. She sat on the couch, her chest heaving in and out, but Roza and Magda continued to dance with the little energy they had left. They loved each other in a special way, as twins do, but had distinctive personalities. Magda was a bit of a complainer, but good-natured. At the dinner table, she would scrutinize the food carefully and either eat it or give it a "yuck." Her dream was to be a singer, and she constantly hummed and whistled her tunes.

Roza was the resident introvert. She read books and loved to write poetry. She was sensitive, like her mother.

Miklos thought that when his girls grew up, they would be a gift to the artistic world. They had so much ahead of them and were lucky to be at the beginning of their lives.

The dancing and music continued. *Everything will work out all right.* He and Ilona continued to be an enthusiastic audience. They clapped and sang through their daughters' performances.

Until...

The sound of marching boots and loud banging on the door brought the festivities to a halt.

Chapter 2

Post World War II

Miklos survived the concentration camp in Auschwitz and felt there was no reason for him to remain in Hungary. The Nazis had taken everyone he loved and Soviet communism dominated Hungary's post-war government, thus trading one oppressive political system for another.

In 1946, he immigrated to the United States, anglicized his name to Michael Ross to sound more American, and worked to perfect his spoken English. He did what was necessary to familiarize himself with the American educational process and secure teaching credentials. Eventually, he accepted a post as a professor of pharmacology and pharmacy at a private university near Oneonta, New York. He bought a house from the estate of an elderly former policeman who had passed away. The officer had no family and the house was sold "as is," including the furnishings and the officer's personal belongings.

It was a comfortable house set far enough away from neighbors to afford privacy. The detached two-car garage was impressive with a built-in workbench along the back wall, a deep sink, and an assortment of manual and electric tools, neatly hung on a wall. An exhaust fan circulated hot air to the outside, and a duct, connected to the house furnace, provided heat when needed. The right wall was bare except for several exposed pipes leading back to the sink. There was also a shelf holding a cardboard box filled with miscellaneous items.

Professor Ross taught at the university for twenty years. He was only sixty, and, in anticipation of leaving the world of academia, he opened a community pharmacy called The Chemist's Shop in January 1970. He hired Dan Berman, his former student and now an experienced licensed pharmacist, to manage and operate the store. There was a need for an independent pharmacy in the area, one that provided compounding services and personal attention, and it wasn't long before the shop had many customers passing through its doors. In April, after his retirement from the university, Michael joined Dan at The Chemist's Shop.

***

The Rosen's homes in Budapest and the countryside had been damaged beyond repair and their contents confiscated either by the Nazis or the Red Army. As a result, the only pictures Michael had of his wife and daughters were in his mind. At Auschwitz, he remembered his little girls skipping and playing with the other children as they made their way to the gas chamber, thinking they were going to a playground for fun and games. Tears came to his eyes when he imagined little Eva carrying what was left of her red rose.

Even after all these years, Michael could never get his last glimpse of his girls out of his mind. He had been upset because the twins, who were rarely apart, were separated in the initial lineup at Auschwitz. It was an ironic twist of fate that enabled them to elude Dr. Mengele's depraved, horrific experiments on twins to improve the Aryan race. Michael tried to find solace with thoughts that his girls' deaths were quick and painless.

***

Still in his pajamas, Michael turned on the TV. Sesame Street splashed on the screen in glorious color. He watched the Cookie Monster puppet as it ranted, "Me want cookie, me eat cookie." He imagined his young daughters sitting next to him, spellbound by the big eyes of the blue-furred monster.

He turned the TV off and prepared to leave for The Chemist's Shop. The pharmacy prided itself on offering a high level of customer care and attention to detail. They filled prescriptions, prepared sterile solutions, and compounded medications when no commercial product was available. Michael was proud of the reputation his shop had developed as "the pharmacy with a heart."

He and Dan regularly engaged in patient

counseling with their prescription customers. It included in-depth medication reviews that gave patients a better understanding of the purpose of their drugs and how they worked in the body. Dan was an excellent pharmacist, a young man of high personal integrity who took pleasure in classic literature and music. He enjoyed live theater and fishing in the mountain streams, and the customers appreciated his pleasant smile along with his quirky sense of humor. He would be a good catch for a girl with the same interests. When Michael asked him why he made himself unavailable, he answered, "I'm available, all right. I'm just waiting for the right girl."

***

Michael showered and soaped himself as he hummed the music from *Swan Lake*. As he rinsed off, the blue tattooed number on his forearm became more visible. It reminded him of a time long ago. He had looked at it every day in Auschwitz, when he told himself there would be a better life ahead. The warm water glistened on the tattoo, bringing the number A11328 to life.

He was glad when people asked him the meaning of the number. It gave him an opportunity to explain that it helped prevent people from forgetting that tragic time. Some children asked if it helped him remember his phone number, others thought it was a design, but Michael always explained that it represented a terrible time in his life.

One little girl asked, "Why was it so bad?"

"Because it was a time when millions of innocent men, women, and children were tattooed with a number like mine and then killed by evil people. It was called The Holocaust, and the world stood silent."

"So, do you keep it there to remember that terrible time?"

"No," he answered. "I keep it there for you to remember that whenever evil raises its ugly head, you must never be silent."

***

Michael dressed, walked a short distance to his two-car detached garage, and drove his ten-year-old 1960 Chevy Bel Air to work. It was a lovely spring day in early May and he had been working steadily in the pharmacy for a few weeks. When he arrived, he greeted Dan and the two technicians, then went into the office to retrieve his long-sleeved white lab jacket.

The staff was busy typing labels and filling prescriptions for several waiting people, a few of whom chatted with neighbors while others mulled about the shop, perusing new cosmetic items. One of the medications was for Hilda Sanders, a customer of the pharmacy since opening day. She was waiting for her prescription for eye drops to treat her glaucoma. Her husband approached the counter to pick it up. At first, the man's slight accent drew Michael's attention. He thought nothing of it, until he turned and stared into the man's icy, steel-blue eyes, eyes he could never forget.

Hans Stern.

Michael's lips tightened and his hands trembled at the sight of the Nazi officer.

He recognized Stern at once. The man's cold eyes and downturned, thin lips were a dead giveaway. *It's him!* Stern's face was wrinkled, his blond hair almost white, but there could be no doubt. Stern glanced back at Michael for a moment, but showed no signs of recognizing him. How *could* he make a connection? Their eyes had met only twice, briefly, more than twenty-five years ago.

Michael boiled inside at the sight of him, but forced himself to remain calm and say nothing. In that instant, he felt two opposing but related feelings—one was anger, the other exhilaration. He would have his revenge at last.

night. But I fear Jews are as fragile as snowflakes and will soon disappear. Maybe Budapest is not safe either. Once we are there, I will arrange for us to leave Hungary and go far away...to America.

He smiled at that idea.

***

Miklos and Ilona protected their daughters from worry and harm so they could live in their sweet world of innocence. He was delighted to see his girls play dress-up as they danced around the house, like little ballerinas, to the music of Swan Lake. Little Eva was the best dancer of them all.

"Go, go, Eva," he shouted and clapped with his hands over his head.

She turned and spun, like a prima ballerina, the star of the show. She had her own graceful style and expressed her emotions with her small, delicate hands, dancing and turning, with her arms arched above her. In his mind's eye, Miklos saw her grown-up, in her ballet costume, on point and on stage.

The twins skipped and danced until they were breathless. They were all dressed up and fancy, painted with their mother's makeup and wearing colorful outfits sewn together by Ilona from scraps of material. Roza and Magda had their own sense of grace. They lived in the moment, *their* moment, as they twirled their young bodies, attempted pirouettes, and leaped into the air.

Ilona turned toward Miklos and whispered in his ear, "When the girls are finished dancing, remind

Chapter 3

After the pharmacy closed, Michael stayed behind in the dim light and silence. He sat in his leather swivel chair in the office and thought back to his time in the concentration camp, when rare moments of solitude became his best friend.

Today was not one of those times. After seeing Stern in his store, the image of him laughing as he threw Ilona's bleeding, naked body onto a pile of jagged rocks ate at his insides. Trembling and overcome with anxiety, Michael tried to steady himself. He nestled his head between his arms on the desk and closed his eyes, struggling to erase that horrible image from his mind. Nothing helped. The nagging image persisted, and the memory of Stern's high-pitched, diabolical laughter inflamed Michael's anger further. Stern had been invading Michael's dreams since the Soviets liberated Auschwitz in 1945. The evil SS officer was always in the recesses of Michael's mind and he could not escape the tormenting visions of Stern using Ilona as his plaything, his sexual toy.

His nightmares plagued him. He saw Stern ripping Ilona's clothes off and smacking her until blood poured from her nose.

One vision tormented him like no other. It was when he saw Ilona lying on the rocks with her arms stretched out toward him, begging for help, and he was powerless. He was never able to erase it from his mind, and it made sleep impossible.

Michael thought back to a few hours earlier, when he'd laid his eyes on Stern. His face was wrinkled and worn and he appeared vulnerable. For Michael, it was a dream come true.

A different picture entered his mind. This time, Michael was in control and imagined himself with his hands wrapped around Stern's throat, tightening, squeezing until the SS officer's face swelled. He imagined Stern's face turning blue as he gasped for air, his bulging eyes erupting from their sockets and hanging along his cheeks. Strength surged into Michael's hands. Pure joy coursed through his body as he continued to squeeze Stern's neck tighter until it was crushed and his body fell to the floor. Michael looked at him lying dead, his face still and gaunt with his mouth open and blood gushing out of his eyes. It was over. Michael lifted his head from the desk.

Have I become him?

He rubbed his eyes. Killing Stern by choking him would be too easy. He had to know *why* he had to die, an option never given to tens of thousands of his victims. Most of the prisoners killed at Auschwitz, in their sweet innocence, could never have imagined that the unthinkable was about to occur. To be murdered *just because they were Jews*. Michael knew he had time on his side. His plan for Stern had to be carried out slowly.

Like the Jews in concentration camps, Stern would never know what was coming next.

Michael examined Stern's family prescription records, which were under the name of Harry Sanders, and made a mental note of the details. Stern's profile showed that he used sleeping medication and drugs to treat congestive heart failure.

Hilda's record revealed that she took medication for depression and eye drops for glaucoma. She also used sleeping capsules for her insomnia.

The compounding room at The Chemist's Shop was an area filled with chemical apparatus and a hood with an exhaust fan for preparing capsules, troches, and sterile products.

Michael took a bottle of grain alcohol off the shelf and brought it to the office, where he poured it into a glass and added orange juice. He sat at his desk, sipped his drink, and allowed his mind to wander. He thought of how much he loved Ilona and his little ballerinas, who were going to change the world of dance, literature, and music.

The image of Ilona lying on the ground, half buried in the rocks, was burned into Michael's mind. He remembered her pained expression as he ran to cover her with his striped shirt. In the background, he heard Stern's drunken ranting. The Nazi laughed and cursed, pointing to her and calling her a *schlampe,* a bitch, as he stood in the doorway of the barracks. Miklos held Ilona close, her blood on his bare chest.

She whispered in his ear, "He raped me, Miklos. Why didn't you protect me? Our daughters died. Our little babies are dead."

Michael looked into her sorrowful eyes begging him to rescue her. His tears fell upon her face as Ilona touched them and brought them to her lips. He comforted her as best he could. They looked at each other in what they knew would be their final gaze. Their fingertips drifted apart as Michael fought to hold on to her. Crying silently, he let out a scream when the pain of a Nazi's boot against his back and the butt of a rifle brought him to the ground.

It was the last time he saw Ilona. Shortly afterward, she was moved to a different part of the camp. Many months later, he learned that she had found her freedom by running into an electrified fence.

I should have searched for a way to save my family. Maybe it was possible, even in a concentration camp. I should have tried.

Michael continued to feel the pain in his back after he was attacked by the Nazi. He was assigned to work as a janitor, where he saw Stern's face close-up. They glanced at each other for a moment as Stern passed him. Even with Miklos's head tilted downward, he saw the Nazi's eyes, cold as ice. He wanted to learn more about him, and in a rare moment, when Michael was alone, he discovered several original documents of Stern's history in a filing cabinet folder. Each one had a photo of him in his SS uniform and his signature on the bottom. He took one and concealed it in his pants.

Michael's thoughts returned to the reality of The Chemist's Shop. The pharmacy had a different feel for him in the darkness. He was used to the sound of the cash register ringing up sales, used to seeing activity buzzing around him and the staff busy with people who had questions about their medication. He fixed himself another drink, then another. The alcohol took him to a different level in his mind. It didn't make him sleep but brought him to a quieter place, where he was able to think clearly. The drinks created mild euphoria and a loss of inhibition. It also provided a temporary escape from the pain he felt inside. He would have preferred wine or brandy, but the grain alcohol did its job and the orange juice made it taste better. The more he drank, the more his thoughts filled with anger at Stern and took him to new pathways in his brain, places where he could plan his revenge and decide how to kill Stern.

He was glad he had said nothing to Stern when their eyes met earlier that day. Anything he might have said would've been premature and it would have spoiled everything. Now that it was time for justice, Michael was in control and no longer powerless. He would play a role totally foreign to his basic nature—executioner.

Chapter 4

Michael spent the next week thinking of Stern. Rage filled every cell of his body, but it soon gave way to contemplation and planning. He hadn't seen Stern since their previous encounter at the store, but he knew Stern and Hilda had long lists of prescription drugs on their medication charts, so they would be back often.

Michael was at work in the pharmacy, thinking that the next time he and Stern met, it would be different. He wasn't sure how, but he knew that once he engaged Stern in conversation, it would lead to him making contact with Stern outside of the pharmacy. Michael was still exhilarated and excited to know that he would be the one to kill Stern and avenge the deaths of his family and others killed under Stern's direction. He was evil and had to be punished.

Before punishing him, Michael wanted to know what was in his mind. How could Sterns inflict such cruelty on innocent people? Michael had to take him under his control, question him about the war, and humiliate him the way he did the Jews and others before putting Stern to death.

Michael remembered a few things about Stern that were common knowledge at the camp. He was a heavy smoker, loved to kill Jews at random, used women for violent sex, and played cards with the guards and chess with certain prisoners. He considered himself a master chess player, and when he found someone who challenged him, even a Jew, he made sure to keep him alive, rewarding him with an occasional loaf of bread. To others, Stern appeared mean and cruel, but Michael knew he was more than that. Hans Stern exhibited a depraved indifference to human suffering. He should never have been born.

Chess was my game too.

It was near closing time. Dan had already gone home and Michael sat in his office, reviewing literature related to drug interactions. He heard the front door open and the sound of rapid footsteps. An out-of-breath Hans Stern appeared at the pharmacy counter. He spoke to a technician and asked to speak to Dr. Ross. Michael recognized his voice. His hands trembled as he walked to the counter.

"Mr. Sanders, it's nice to see you again," he said calmly. "I'm Michael Ross."

"How do you do? Yes, yes, I know your name," Stern said in a heavy German accent. "Please, I come to your pharmacy because it reminds me of the apothecaries we had in Europe. The chemists were always very helpful."

"Thank you for telling me that. What can I help you with?"

"I am sleeping well, but I am tired during the day. The sleeping capsule helps me, and I am happy for that, but it is not possible for me to be so tired in the daytime. I used to play chess with a friend and it stimulated my mind to stay awake, but he has moved to Albany and now I have no one. If you have something that would help me stay awake during the day until bedtime, I would be grateful."

Michael couldn't believe this conversation was taking place. It was like a dream out of the past, only now Michael held the cards, or maybe the chess pieces, and Stern needed *him*. Michael remained calm and unstressed. It was easy for him to do that now. His plan was beginning to unfold.

"Okay, a couple of things, Mr. Sanders," he said casually. "First, eat a balanced diet with plenty of fresh fruits and vegetables. Substitute fish for meat, and no heavy meals or sugar drinks before bedtime. Drink a lot of water, and make sure you exercise. I'll give you vitamin B-complex capsules. Take one twice a day after breakfast and lunch and let me know if it helps."

Stern nodded and said, "Thank you."

"We're closing soon, but I'll check your medications in the morning, and I'll let you know if any of them may be contributing to your fatigue. Maybe lowering the dose of your sleeping medication would make a difference, but we'll talk next time."

"Yes, I will let you know. Thank you." Hans Stern studied Michael's face. "Have we met outside the pharmacy? Do I detect an accent? Are you from here?"

"I was born and grew up right here in Oneonta. Never left the States, except for my stint in the army. I lost my parents early in my life in an auto accident. My grandparents were from Europe, and they raised me. It's *their* accent you hear. Nice seeing you again."

"Yes, and you too."

"One more thing, Mr. Sanders. I'm sorry you lost your chess partner. I know what it is like not having someone to challenge you and stimulate your mind. I don't know how well you know the game, but I want to let you know that I was state champion three years in a row when I was in college."

"Really? We must play."

"I'm a little busy for chess these days, but I'll keep it in mind. Have a good night."

The Nazi left and Michael heaved a huge sigh. He'd just made his first move. A smile swept across his face.

This is only the beginning. The best is yet to come.

Chapter 5

It was Thursday, a day Michael reserved to stay home and use his time alone to meditate and listen to music. The horrible images of Stern shooting Jews in the back of their heads at random streamed through his mind. Stern would walk up behind them, shoot, and laugh. Now Michael would have the last laugh. He was in no rush and he relished each moment as he refined his plan for revenge.

The slower, the better.

Michael stuffed a scrambled egg inside a warm croissant and sipped strong black coffee as he listened to the strains of Liszt's *Hungarian Rhapsody* wafting through the air. He thought about the first moment he and Ilona met. It was in 1922. They were both twelve and too shy to say very much to each other.

***

I went with my parents to visit the wine shop owned by Ilona's father, Istvan Kovacs. He was not only the proprietor of the shop, but was the winemaker as well and owned the vineyard. He made the sweet Tokoi dessert wine, which was famous in Hungary and all of Europe.

I remember looking at the rows of grapevines growing on the sunny hillside. At the end of each row was a rosebush that added spots of color to the landscape. The grapevines usually received just the right amount of rain to make a wonderful wine. Some years were better than others, but that's the way it was in general with crops. Grapes were no different.

Ilona was at the shop, a young, sweet girl with black braids and a fresh country look. Mr. Kovacs introduced us and remarked with a smile, "Ilona helps with the harvest, but I always see her eating a few grapes off the vine as she placed them in her wooden basket."

My father, Ferenc Rosen, had become friendly with Istvan and often chatted with him about the intricacies of winemaking and The Great War, which had ended in 1918 with an armistice a few years earlier.

I watched Ilona as she placed bottles of her father's deep amber, syrupy sweet wine on the shelves. She wore a typical Hungarian peasant dress, embroidered with flowers showing the vibrant colors of our Hungarian flag—red, white, and green.

I looked at Ilona as she filled the shelves. She turned toward me for a moment, our gazes locked, and I caught her slim, shy smile before she looked down at the floor. It was a vision I carried with me *for life. We didn't speak, but we knew in our hearts we had found someone special.*

Chapter 6

As Michael drove to work the next day, he added bits and pieces to his plan to kill Stern.

Will killing him make me like him?

There was no time for ethics. Only action could make things right. Stern had not only killed Michael's family, but thousands of other innocent victims too.

Someone has to speak for them.

He arrived at work, and it wasn't long before he saw Hilda and Hans Stern walking through the front door. Hilda went to the cosmetic section and chatted with Briana, a pretty girl with long, flowing brown hair, hazel eyes, and a winning smile. She was a twenty-year-old college student who worked part-time at the pharmacy. She knew whatever there was to know about face creams, makeup, and hair coloring products, and she had built up quite a following of women who trusted her advice.

Stern walked through the store, puffing on a cigarette. He picked up items, looked at them, and then placed them back on the shelves as if he were just biding time. Michael watched Stern's hand tremble as he held a match to light a new cigarette, his furtive eyes scanning the store. Stern glanced toward Michael and, before he knew it, the German was standing in front of him. Stern spoke in a low voice as he inhaled the fumes of the cigarette deep into his lungs.

"Mr. Ross, it was a pleasure talking to you the other day. It was very helpful."

"I'm glad. We're rather informal here. Please call me Michael."

"Thank you, I am Harry."

"So, what can I do for you?"

"Well, my wife came to pick up a few things. I saw you were not busy and I thought we might chat for a moment."

"Of course," Michael answered.

"You told me you play chess and won several championships."

"I did, but I haven't played since I was in college."

"Is that where you studied pharmacy?"

"Yes. I studied at the university in Albany, and then went on to earn my PhD. I felt I had something to offer in the world of academia and, ultimately, became a professor and taught pharmacy and pharmacology at various universities until I retired and opened The Chemist's Shop."

"So, you grew up here?"

"I did. Went to school here and now have my own business. I always liked this part of New York."

"And your family? They live here too?" Stern

questioned.

Michael excused himself to talk to a customer and, after a few minutes, returned to Stern. Michael heaved a deep breath and paused.

"You asked about my family." Michael paused again. "When I lost my parents, my grandparents were kind enough to raise me, and I realized that family meant everything to me. They were wonderful, caring people who taught me that you can only have a fulfilling life when you help others and be kind to them."

Stern turned away. "I see."

"Is there anything special I can help you with? I already checked your medication records and didn't find anything that would make you feel so fatigued."

"I was going to ask you, uh…"

Michael waited.

Stern snuffed out his cigarette in a nearby canister topped with sand.

"I would be honored if you would play chess with me sometime. It would be important. I have played chess all my life and now I have no one. I know I may be asking a great deal, and if your wife would feel I am imposing…"

"My wife died a number of years ago."

Stern shrugged. "Please consider a friendly chess match. I know you are busy and I won't keep you any longer."

"Okay. Harry, maybe you're right. It might help me get out of my rut. You are fortunate to have a wife. I have no children. I'm alone too. So, yes, it might be a good thing."

"Chess may not be a replacement for your wife, Professor Ross. Nothing is, but it can help," Stern said in a matter-of fact way without emotion.

"Okay, you've got me interested. I'm sure I can still play a good game. Harry, I have to go. We'll talk another time."

"Please, please. *Bitte,* wait one moment," Stern said as he quickly lit another cigarette. "Do you think we can play one game soon? Maybe this week? If you need help refreshing your knowledge and strategies, I will be happy to provide it."

"Not this week, but I am free next Thursday. It's my day off, and we can definitely play that evening. Give me a call Thursday morning. My home number is listed. I really have to go."

"Yes, thank you. Yes, I will call you Thursday morning and see you that night, yes?"

"That would be fine," Michael answered as he turned to help other customers.

Stern walked away and pulled on his wife's arm as she was talking to Briana. They both left without purchasing anything.

Two days later, Michael received a note in the mail, signed by Harry Sanders. The note thanked Michael for giving him the opportunity to play chess with him and stated that he was looking forward to the game.

Chapter 7

It was Thursday, another day for Michael to cherish his time at home. The ominous opening strains of Tchaikovsky's *Pathetique* wafted through the air and soon gave way to the sweet, melodic love theme. The music reminded him of the time the Rosen and Kovacs families went to the concert hall to listen to it. He'd sat next to Ilona and was tempted to hold her hand, but he was only twelve and not that brave.

As the love theme played throughout the house, Michael's thoughts took him back to the time when he and Ilona were children. He put his head back on the sofa and closed his eyes.

Dear Ilona,

I will always remember our first meeting and all the times after that. We didn't talk very much at twelve or thirteen and we shared only shy grins as we walked in the countryside. Our families were bound by music, mostly classical, and our favorite event was when they took us to the Liszt Academy of

Music in Budapest to listen to the concerts.

I constantly encouraged my parents, Ferenc and Michla Rosen, to visit the Kovacs' winery often. I told them I loved the sweet Tokoi dessert wine that we drank at home during Passover and wanted to see more of the winery. My father looked at me and smiled as if he knew my special secret was that I wanted to see you. During one visit to the winery, I remember when you taught me about winemaking as we picked grapes together, sometimes feeding them to each other along the way. Time went by and we soon became close friends, but our closeness was more than we admitted. We each knew we had found someone for life.

The brash sound of the phone pulled him out of his daydream.

"Michael, it is Harry. I hope you are not consumed with any activity."

"No, Harry, it's fine." The German accent on the other end of the phone stirred unpleasant memories, but Michael kept his tone even, making sure there was not a trace of anguish.

"I am happy we will have a game of chess tonight. I insist that you come here. Hilda will prepare a special dinner and..."

"I appreciate the offer. I'll play, but I would prefer that we play at my home."

"All right, as you wish. Do you have a chess set?"

"I do, but it hasn't been used for years. I'll check it to make sure I have all the pieces."

"Yes, that is good. I will bring my set as well. It

is complete. What time?"

"Eight o'clock."

"Can we make it earlier?"

"No," Michael answered. "Eight o'clock works best for me."

"I will see you then. I have your address from the telephone book."

***

It was a good beginning, Michael thought. He put another LP record on his new Garrard record player, sat back, and smiled.

Later that night, Michael put on a long sleeved shirt to hide the tattooed numbers. At exactly eight, the doorbell rang. Michael greeted Stern and showed him into his study. Books, hundreds of them, including a leather-bound set of the *Encyclopedia Britannica,* lined the walls. In the background, a corner speaker connected to his High Fidelity system played the music from the opera *Turandot.*

There was a table in the center of the room with two chairs facing each other. Stern set up the chess pieces as Michael brought out a bottle of Stolichnaya.

"Oh, I see you like vodka," Stern said. "I like it very much."

"I do too, Harry, and Russian vodka is the best! They know how to do things in Russia. So, let me know more about yourself. There is so little time to talk at the pharmacy. Where did you grow up?"

"I was born in the capital of Bavaria. Then my

family moved to the countryside, where they owned a large dairy farm."

"I see. So, did you serve in the military during the war?"

"No. I was not in the army, and I was never a Nazi. I did not have to serve because our farm was nationalized to provide food for the German army, so I was exempt from service."

"You were lucky. I was drafted into the army and ended up in the Army Air Corps."

"You were a pilot?"

"No, I was a mechanic in the ground crew in the Pacific, Fifth Air Force, Thirty-Fifth Fighter Squadron and spent a good part of my time in New Guinea, near Port Moresby, working on Lockheed P-38s."

"And you were not hurt in the war?"

"No, though I did have a bout with malaria and dengue fever and spent some time in foxholes, but the happiest day of my life was when the war was over. My troopship docked in Seattle, and from there, a long but happy train ride back home to Oneonta. So, let's play!"

How can I be sitting with this monster?

"Yes, please. We should do it," Stern answered with a slim grin. "Michael, I am sure you are a good player, but are you familiar with the traditional opening strategies, like the Sicilian Defense?"

"Yes, of course. I've used it in my college matches."

"Do you remember any others?"

"I do. I remember The French Defense, the Nimzo Indian Defense, and my favorite, The Ruy

Lopez. I still remember the opening move—pawn to e4, knight to f3."

"I think we will have some wonderful games," Stern said, moving his chair closer to the table.

The Nazi held the two kings behind his back, white in one hand, black in the other, then he put his hands in front of him for Michael to choose. The hand he picked showed the white king, meaning that Michael would play first, which generally was a distinct advantage.

Each man played slowly and deliberately between sips of the Stoli. Michael controlled the game from the beginning and knew, at once, that Stern was an amateur. Michael allowed him to get ahead until he saw the game would soon end. He saw an opening and planned his next three moves. Stern missed his chance to keep the game in play, and Michael won.

Stern clenched his lips and blinked incessantly. "You got me with your knight. I see I have a worthy opponent," he said, surprised.

Stern wanted to play another game and kept pushing for it, almost begging, but Michael refused and said, "I'm sure we will face more challenges in the future."

"I will be looking forward to them, my friend. Thank you."

"And I thank you, Harry, for giving me this opportunity."

Chapter 8

Michael left work early the following day so he could enjoy the afternoon on his porch and catch up with the latest news in the *Oneonta Daily Star*. There was an article in the paper about demonstrators taunting President Nixon and throwing objects at him while he was at a campaign rally in California. Michael didn't approve of throwing things at the president, but it was an angry time in America and people wanted an unnecessary war to end.

Millions of people killed...for what?

He put the newspaper down and closed his eyes. The sun was about to set, and a golden glow surrounded him. He needed to think about Ilona.

***

It was 1933. We were both twenty-three and engaged to be married. I was in my last year at the university in Budapest, a two-hour train ride from our country house, where our families lived and where Ilona's father had his winery. I was studying the sciences in Budapest and would soon have my doctorate while Ilona managed the wine shop.

Ilona and I shared sugar-coated weekends. On Saturday, a morning when I was home from school, we went to the synagogue with our families. Most Sundays were special because that was when we had family picnics in the countryside. Every moment was filled with excitement, revelry, and dancing. The delicious Hungarian food, topped with colorful paprika, was love at first sight. The goulash was always a highlight, richly seasoned and served over homemade noodles. Another popular dish was Toltott Kaposzta, a cabbage stuffed with chopped kosher meat mixed with rice and covered with a sweet paprikash sauce. It was our favorite.

After the main courses, Ilona's two younger sisters, Zsa Zsa, eighteen, and Szilvia, sixteen, placed platters of freshly baked strudel, bottles of wine, and hot coffee on the picnic table for all to enjoy. Even after a full meal, everyone still had the energy to dance the czardas as my father played the accordion. He always wore his favorite green hat, which had a long red feather tucked in its sideband, and Ilona's girlfriends looked so fresh and beautiful in their colorful peasant dresses. The boys wore black shorts with green vests covering their white shirts.

At the last picnic, Ilona and I danced with love in our eyes and I couldn't take my eyes off her. Later, before the day faded into night, we walked into the woods and stopped to kiss.

Michael lingered on the sweet moment of his

reverie and, without thinking, touched his lips to feel the warmth of her kiss.

***

His thoughts turned to the man who called himself Harry Sanders. To Michael, he would always be Hans Stern and he could never think of him by any other name.

Michael's jaw dropped when he remembered that Stern claimed he wasn't a Nazi and never served in the army. He'd presented a picture of himself as a hardworking farmer while the war raged around him and dead bodies piled up, waiting to go up in black smoke, all, of course, unbeknownst to him. Michael knew better.

He believed Stern bought his story about being in the Army Air Corps. Michael had learned the details about what it was like from a friend who really had served in the South Pacific.

The fact was, Michael and Stern shared no truths about each other on the previous night, except for the chess game itself. They shared their lies and only the game had its own truth. With chess, you either win or lose. Playing chess is a war between two opponents, a raging battle where there can only be one winner. The loser lies his king down on the chessboard. Last night, Michael won. His king stood and that was the ending he chose.

Stern played well for an amateur, but Michael was, by far, the better player, and why shouldn't he be? He learned to play chess from his father, who would be a grandmaster by present day standards.

When Stern squirmed and begged for another game, Michael let him suffer, knowing it would keep him up all night, contemplating each move of their game, reliving his blunders and feeling the frustration of how he *might* have won. Stern never saw the loss coming. Michael saw it as a sign that he was vulnerable, driven by his own ego. He would be an easy mark when they played chess, and later, when Michael killed him.

Chapter 9

Michael knew it would be easy to kill Stern, but killing him was not as important as creating the ultimate fear in him before he died. Michael had to torment and crush Stern slowly. He had to be humiliated and unaware of what was coming next, just as the Jews were. But in Stern's case, he had to know *why* he was going to die a painful death and *why* he had to suffer before it was *his* turn to be murdered.

Poisoning him would be uncomplicated but, unfortunately, painless. Michael was a master of drugs and knew all there was to know about the sinister, exotic, untraceable poisons known only to a special few, but poisoning Stern would be out of the question. He had something else in mind.

There were times, in order to keep his sanity, Michael had to let go of his obsessive thoughts about Stern. He had a life outside of him. A real life, in which he indulged himself in music, theater, literature, and the visual arts. He loved movies. They took him out of the present into a different time and another world, many times, a more peaceful place, but not always.

The film he had watched at the local theater one night took him back to the past. It was anything but peaceful.

The movie was *Judgment at Nuremberg*. It dealt with the Holocaust and the trial of four German judges who served before and during the Nazi regime. Michael missed the original showing in the early sixties, but now he sat, mesmerized, as the Nazi judges pleaded for their lives. Later, in bed, he stared at the ceiling for hours, unable to get the film out of his mind. He fell asleep as dawn arrived.

***

Stern called Michael the next morning and asked if he would be up for another game. Michael was available, but declined. It was too soon after he had seen the movie. The judges lied, claiming that they didn't make the laws and judges were obliged to follow the laws of their country. Michael told Stern he would have time for a game the following week, on July 30.

***

On that evening, Stern arrived at Michael's home bearing a platter of freshly baked Linzer tortes.

"My wife made these for you," Stern said with a tight-lipped grin.

"Thank you, that was nice of her. It's a good

thing to be married and living with a woman you care about."

"Michael, do you have many female friends or a girlfriend? You never mention anything about having someone. Don't you miss a woman in your life?"

Michael didn't reply right away. His eyes became watery. "I do. I'm sorry. I lost my wife many years ago. We loved each other so much and I still miss her."

Stern raised his eyebrows. "Well, Hilda cooks and cleans for me. I would miss that, but I am sorry to say she smells like a swine. Still, she knows what her wifely duties are and I have her whenever I want. You know how it is. Women are only good for one thing."

Stern had a far-away look in his eyes and he gulped the wine Michael had poured for him.

What an animal. I'm grateful I'm not like him.

Stern set up the chess pieces. He was lucky enough to play white this time. Michael let him stay well ahead at the opening, until the end game, when he baited his opponent into checkmate in a lightning surprise move. Stern never saw it coming. How could he? He was a true amateur, but didn't know it. He placed his king face down on the chessboard, defeated.

Michael looked into Stern's unsmiling face. He slumped down in his chair, looking at his feet and shaking his head.

"Harry, don't look so sad. You played well, and I compliment you," Michael said, leaning toward him. "You took most of my pieces."

"Yes, but your *en passant* move was unexpected. I didn't know what to make of it, until I realized it contributed to my demise."

His demise? It will come.

"You're a very good player, Michael. I played against many men in Bavaria and won almost all the games and I have never lost two games in a row to anyone. Never!"

"Where did you play in Bavaria?" Michael asked.

"In the countryside with the other farmers."

"I see. I'm sure they were tough to beat. You were fortunate to sit out the war."

"I had no choice. It was either work on the farm and provide the necessary food for the army, or I would have been taken into service. I would never be a Nazi!"

"No, I'm sure. I saw a movie about what happened after the war a few nights ago. It was *Judgment at Nuremberg*. Have you seen it?"

"Yes, I did when it first came out about eight or nine years ago. Would you like to play another game?"

"Uh, sure. So, what did you think of the movie?"

Stern hesitated. "Do you want me to be honest?"

"Yes, of course. We're friends."

"I think it was slanted against the prisoners. The German judges were only doing their job."

"Including Ernst Janning?"

"Yes, of course. He was supposed to be Schlegelburger, who was a fair judge and was the man who wrote the constitution for the Weimer Republic."

44

"Yes, but he sent a lot of people he knew were innocent to their death and many others for anti-Semitic reasons."

"Yes, it is true. There were laws that related to Jews, laws of the land, Michael. A judge does not make the laws. He only upholds them, just as judges do here in America. It's no different."

"You don't think what the judges did were crimes against humanity?"

"No," Stern said adamantly.

"Are there no unjust laws?" Michael asked.

"It's not for a judge to say. In every country, a judge must follow the laws of his land, and for him not to do so would mean he was not fulfilling his obligations."

"So, sending people to their deaths or to concentration camps based on cruel laws against humanity was acceptable?"

Stern started sweating. He squirmed and spoke in a low voice, barely audible.

"A judge must do what he feels is just," he uttered. "We live in a civilized society, and I had no knowledge of the existence of concentration camps when I lived on the farm in Bavaria."

"I see, but you saw pictures of them."

"I did, after the war. I could not believe it. I'm still not sure if it ever..."

Michael looked at Stern. Sweat glistened on his cheeks and forehead, where it filled the lines of his furrowed brow. Michael stopped talking. He felt he might have gone too far in this discussion and may risk losing Stern's friendship if Stern felt he was being baited. It was still too early for Michael to

45

make his next move. He backed away from further conversation.

"We're being too serious," Michael said with a smile. "Let's have another drink, Harry."

"Something cold, please."

Michael brought out two Bock beers. Stern looked more relaxed.

"Ahh, a nice German beer. Now all we need is some schnitzel." Stern smiled.

"Come on, Harry, we don't have the schnitzel, but we'll have some of Hilda's Linzer tortes. I'm not sure they go well with beer."

"Everything goes with beer, even Linzer tortes," Stern said with a slight snicker.

"Mmm, these are good." Michael bit into a torte filled with raspberry jam and rolled his eyes with delight. "Let's play another game!"

Michael saw the excitement in Stern's eyes. He wiped his brow, made the first move, and took the lead by capturing many of Michael's pieces, including his queen. Michael kept the game where he wanted it to be. Only *he* would decide who would win and who would lose. It reminded him of the concentration camp. When the prisoners arrived, one Nazi would decide who would live and who would die. Some were sent to the left and others to the right. The ones who went to the left, the children and elderly, went straight to the gas chambers.

Michael and Hans were into the endgame in the chess match until Michael intentionally made a move that would cost him the game.

"Finally, a victory!" Stern exclaimed, raising his arms. "I was beginning to think I had met my match."

"You played well, Harry. I tried to checkmate you earlier, but without my queen, rooks, and bishops, you made it impossible. Then you got me with your knights and queen. I didn't see it coming. You are a remarkable player."

"Well, it is two to one. We must play again."

"Yes, of course. I'm sorry that I brought up the war. It might be a sore spot for you."

"Not at all, my friend. Feel free to always ask me anything you want to know."

"Thank you for saying that. I will. I don't know anyone who lived in Germany during the war."

"I'm from Bavaria."

"Isn't that part of Germany?"

"Yes, it is a state in Germany, but I like to think of it as disconnected because of its historical borders as a kingdom. So, I usually say I'm from Bavaria."

They shook hands and said goodnight.

Chapter 10

The Chemist's Shop was operating at a significant profit due to the professionalism of the staff. Michael had also accumulated quite a bit of money from his teaching pension and from sales of textbooks he had written.

He had his breakfast, read the Saturday newspaper, and thought about a few things that were on his mind. He wanted the pharmacy to continue helping people in the unlikely event that something would go wrong between him and Stern. Michael made an arrangement with Dan to transfer ownership of the pharmacy to him if Michael was unable to continue working. Anything could happen, Michael thought.

The next day, August 2, was a Sunday, and the pharmacy was closed. Michael showered and let the hot water run over his back to ease the chronic pain he felt as the result of the hard kick by a Nazi's boot. Walking helped his discomfort, so he took a short drive to Neahwa Park. He walked with his shoulders back and stomach tucked in, breathing the sweet country air.

The park was filled with activity on this sunny, summer day. Young children tumbled on the grass under the watchful eyes of their mothers. One group of teenagers passed a Frisbee among them as the breeze rustled the leaves on the tall trees

A woman sat on a bench in the distance. He didn't see who she was at first, but when he got closer, he recognized Hilda Sanders. She lifted her hand from her lap, offered a thin smile, and gave him a brief wave.

She was slim, about sixty, with short, graying brown hair that peeked over her forehead. She had dark circles under her sorrowful eyes.

"Mrs. Sanders, it's a beautiful day. I am glad to see you out enjoying it."

"Professor Ross, it is nice to see you here too."

"May I sit beside you?"

"Yes, yes, of course. I do not know if you remember me. I mean, it was a large auditorium with so many people, but I attended your lecture class, Introduction to Biology, at the Adult Education Center."

"Wonderful. I hope you found it to be a good learning opportunity. I didn't know you were interested in biology."

"Actually, I was not, but you taught my friend's two sons at the university. They told me that they looked forward to your classes in pharmacology and said you were the best teacher they ever had. I had to see for myself. The only available class you taught for adults was biology. I thought it might be interesting and signed up for it. After your first lecture, I, too, looked forward to attending more of them."

"Thank you for your kind comments. What did your husband think of you going?"

"He never knew. It would upset him. He liked me to stay at home and cook his meals. We eat together but never talk. I'm glad your lecture took place at a time when Harry played chess with a friend who now lives in Albany."

Michael smiled.

"Teaching is always a learning experience for me as well as the students. What did you think about the lectures? Did it arouse your interest in plants and animals?

"I cannot say I understood everything, but I enjoyed your talks on evolution."

"I'm glad you did. Darwin presented our civilization with a wonderful gift. And how is Mr. Sanders?"

"He is well. I know he plays chess with you. He is a very good player. I mean, that is what he has told me. I do not know this game. I know it is very complicated."

"Yes, it is, but your husband won the last match. Thank you for those wonderful Linzer tortes. I had one this morning with my coffee."

"You are welcome. Baking is one of my few pleasures. I am usually alone and have few interests. I know that we've only known each other for a short time, but I am from Europe, and I have high regard for anyone who is a professor. Dr. Ross, my husband is not the person you think he is."

Michael's ears perked up. Was she going to tell

him the truth about her husband? That he was a Nazi officer at Auschwitz? That he killed people? He didn't want to hear *anything* about that. Michael wasn't supposed to know and didn't want her to tell him, fearing that it might interfere with his plan for revenge. He thought of excusing himself, telling her he had to continue his walk, but leaving now would be too abrupt, too unnatural, and she might sense that she already knew the truth, that her husband was a Nazi SS officer.

"Well, Mrs. Sanders, that's the way it is with people. We're not always what we appear to be. Many of us have inner lives that we don't talk about, but let's discuss you."

"Yes, that is what I wanted to talk about, me. You are a professor and a learned man. I don't mean to take up your time, but…"

"Please, Mrs. Sanders, you can talk to me about anything."

"Thank you for telling me that. My marriage is not a good one. It never was. My husband has been cruel to me in many ways. I have to express my feelings to someone I respect. I knew it was all wrong even before we were married, but I was young and came from a poor family."

"I'm so sorry. Where did you grow up?"

"In Hamburg, Germany."

"I see. So you married him because you thought he could give you a better life?"

"Yes. Maybe I shouldn't be telling you these things, but I trust you and I know what I say will stay between us."

"Yes, of course," Michael said sympathetically.

"What you say is up to you, Mrs. Sanders. I know that sometimes I need someone to talk to and express some of my deeper feelings with. For me, getting things out to a person who is understanding makes me feel better."

"Ahh, so it would be a good thing then," Hilda replied. "From our wedding night, and all our years together, he was brutal. He hit me and did other things that I cannot say. I was going to leave him, run away, and go anywhere I could hide. Life with Hans is unbearable."

"Hans?" Michael asked

"Yes. That is his real first name. Many Germans changed their names because of the war."

"I can understand that. So, I take it you didn't run away."

"No, I didn't run. I had my six-year-old daughter, Marlena, to think of. Then one day, just before the end of the war, Hans brought Erika to me. She was less than a month old and such a pretty baby. She needed my care because Hans told me her mother died in childbirth and her father had been killed in battle. I was happy to be a mother to this little orphan and it was a good feeling." Mrs. Sanders wiped away her tears.

"So, things were better for you?"

"Better? No." She looked down at her knees. "Well, I thought things would be better, but Hans was distant and we didn't talk much, and after a while he didn't bother me anymore. You know what I mean?" Hilda looked at Michael and then whispered, "For sex." She hung her head again and continued her story.

"I was grateful for that because he was such a cruel man. We never had a loving relationship. There was never any affection of any kind. I just went about my household duties, took care of my girls, and pretended we were a normal family.

"What I learned...and I'm sorry to have to tell you this, professor. Never, never have I told anyone, but the pain I feel is ripping my heart apart, and I will not carry his secrets to my grave." Hilda sighed, took a deep breath, and spoke slowly with her eyes closed and her head bowed.

"Hans had been raping little Erika since she was twelve. Many times. I knew nothing of this and she said nothing until she cried out her words to me when she was eighteen and left home." Michael felt pity for this grieving woman.

"I'm so sorry. You don't have to go on. I would never have guessed your husband was so cruel. He didn't give me that impression. But where is Erika now?"

"She never returned home and lives alone in New York City and talks to none of us, not even her sister, but she has a gift. She is a ballerina and dances with the New York City Ballet. I am glad her life is filled with music, the classics, things Hans had little interest in. I feel so much guilt for not knowing what he was doing to her. She is so beautiful with her dark hair and fair skin, unlike Marlena, who is blonde and blue-eyed. I'm sad that Erika never smiles." Hilda wiped away more tears.

"That is a tragic story. No mother should have to live with that pain. I never would have guessed that about Harry."

"No one does. He has lived a double life in ways I cannot tell you. If I did ever say *anything* about certain things, he would kill me for sure. I would be dead. Maybe it would be a good thing." She sighed. "I would be at peace. Erika will not see me, and Marlena is married to a Jew. They have two sons, our grandchildren, who my husband does not allow me to see because they are Jew babies. There are times I want to swallow all my sleeping pills."

"That would be terrible. You'd have to take at least thirty at once, and that's not easy to do. But it would take that many, or you might just end up in a coma. Mrs. Sanders, you've said enough. You don't have to go on. I am so sorry you had these tragedies in your life."

"Sometimes, I just want to die," Hilda said with tears flowing down her cheeks. "Is that wrong? Is it really a sin? To take your own life? If it is, I won't do it. What do you think about this?"

"It's not a sin. Sometimes we have to do whatever is necessary to take us out of a bitter life that is so bad that it's not worth living. I'm a very religious man and, under the circumstances, I don't think, in your case, it would be a sin. A person may truly find a better life after death. I believe in Heaven."

"I know you're a learned man, Professor Ross. I did not know you were religious too. Thank you."

"It was my pleasure to talk to you today. I am so sorry your husband took your life away. I feel your pain. Whatever we talked about will stay with me. Please take care of yourself."

If she attempts to take her life, I hope she

succeeds. Ilona had to take hers because of Stern.

Michael continued walking, then began to sprint until he came to a wooded area, where he sat with his back against a tree and looked up at the cloudless sky. Thoughts of Ilona and his little girls filled his mind and heart. They were alive within him. He reflected on his wedding day, a fairytale come true.

***

It was 1934. Europe was restless and so was I. This was to be a happy day in my life, but I couldn't control my thoughts. I heard rumors that a concentration camp was constructed at a place called Dachau, where political prisoners, mostly Catholic, were exposed to cruelty and torture. I was worried. Rumors of German troops marching into the Rhineland in violation of the Treaty of Versailles were everywhere, but it was our wedding day and love filled our hearts.

We waited so long to marry and have each other for life. Now that my education was complete, there were no further obstacles. I had my doctorate and was offered a wonderful position at the local university. Ilona looked beautiful and radiant as a bride. She wore her mother's white satin wedding dress, which had a string of colorful country flowers embroidered on the top. We were finally bride and groom and the center of attention.

After the ceremony at the synagogue, our families, friends, and everyone in the entire village danced around us in the countryside to the sound of violins and cimbalom. Ilona and I gazed deep into each other's eyes as we danced and shared our look of love. I was filled with joy knowing our hearts beat as one and that Ilona was mine forever.

Chapter 11

Michael awoke drenched in sweat, shaking and gasping for breath, as he recovered from a horrible nightmare.

In his dream, Magda and Roza were already twenty and dancers for the Hungarian National Ballet Company. As the sad but beautiful ballet *Romeo and Juliet* was about to begin, every seat was filled with people dressed in black uniforms and brown leather straps across their chests. Ilona, Michael, and Eva sat spellbound by Magda and Roza's performance and clapped along with the audience as they watched them and the other dancers pirouette their way through the music.

When the ballet ended, the dancers bowed and, with darkened faces, accepted bouquets of black roses. Then the entire audience disappeared in a flash. Only Michael, Ilona, and Eva lingered. They stood on their feet, clapping and yelling, "Bravo," as the twins stood in front of the stage, gave their final bows, and then danced off toward spirals of black smoke. Eva jumped out of her seat and, with a tattered rose in her hand, dashed to join them. Michael turned toward Ilona, but she was gone too. Only he remained in the theater. The lights dimmed, leaving him alone in the darkness.

Michael didn't know what to make of it, but he felt guilty that they'd died and he'd lived.

***

Stern hadn't called for a week and Michael didn't see him or Hilda in the pharmacy.

Something must have happened. Does he still have Nazi connections? Did he learn the truth about me being in Auschwitz?

Michael wanted to call him, but it would be against his rules. He had to be in control of every detail. He continued to wait.

Time played out to his advantage. Stern called.

"Michael, I am sorry I have not been in touch. We have missed many games."

"Yes, we have. Are you all right? Were you sick? I was worried about you. I miss our games too."

There was a long pause.

"Harry, are you still there?" Michael asked.

"It's about Hilda," Stern whispered into the phone.

"Hilda?"

"Michael, is it possible for me to come to see you. Are you busy with something? It is very important."

"If it's important to you, then it's important to me."

Stern arrived a half hour later. They sat in the kitchen.

Stern took a deep breath. "Michael, Hilda is dead."

"Oh my God! That's terrible. What happened? When?" Michael asked, trying to feign shock.

"Ten days ago. I'm alone now."

"I am so sorry." Michael walked to where he was sitting and squeezed his shoulder. "You should have called me sooner, Harry. I know she had a cardiovascular condition."

"Yes, she did and I do too. She was always there for me whenever I needed her. Now I have no one."

"My heart goes out to you, Harry. It's a terrible thing to lose your wife, especially since the two of you had been so close and shared so much love. Be thankful for the time you had."

"I am, and I know you understand. You mentioned losses in your life."

"Yes, they were painful, so I know how you feel." Michael clenched his jaw and looked down at the floor. "Can I get you something to drink, some schnapps?"

"It has been awhile since I had schnapps. That would be nice, thank you."

Michael put two shot glasses on the table. "It's from Europe. You will like it." Each man gulped their drinks and sat silently.

"I'm sure you were in contact with your family, Harry."

"I did get word to them, but my relationship with my daughters was severed years ago, and you are my only friend," Stern said. "Only my daughter,

Erika, came to the funeral. She stood in the background, said nothing to me, and left soon after. We did not speak. It only made the funeral sadder. I loved Erika. She was very special to me. When she was young, we were very close."

"Harry, you should have let me know. I would have..."

"I didn't want to bother you. I know you are very busy."

"Was she in pain at the end? Was it a heart attack?"

Stern lowered his eyes and spoke in a low voice. He looked away for a moment, then turned toward Michael.

"She took her life. Maybe it was an accident. I don't know, but they said she took a large amount of sleeping pills."

Michael closed his eyes. He had an inner feeling of satisfaction witnessing Stern's anguish, but felt sadness for Hilda too. He said nothing and poured two more glasses of the strong schnapps.

Chapter 12

During Michael's most recent chess game with Stern, he had picked up pieces of information from him about his family, especially his daughters. He told Michael that he and Hilda had adopted Erika as an infant after the war. He added that she was a ballerina and lived alone in Manhattan to be near the art world. He said he wasn't close to either of his daughters. Michael surmised that Erika must have had serious hard feelings against Stern because she didn't even speak to him at Hilda's funeral.

Hilda already told Michael that Marlena was married to a Jew. Michael thought that would be reason enough for Hans to break relations with her.

Michael believed Stern's daughters had to pay a price too. He had to kill them, but needed to know their last names in order to find them. He could extract that information in a surreptitious manner from Stern during one of their chess games. If that failed, he had a close friend, Avner, who had worked for the Mossad, Israel's master intelligence agency and the world's most efficient killing machine. Avner lived in Albany. He was retired, but he still maintained contact with present Israeli agents. It would be easy for him to get the last names of Stern's daughters and their addresses. For the Mossad, it would only take a matter of hours, if that long. Erika might be easier to find. She lived in Manhattan, was connected to the ballet, and probably kept her last name—Sanders, or even Stern.

Michael believed his plan to kill them was well thought out. It wasn't perfect, but he knew the enemy of a good plan was the search for a perfect one. Michael would have his vengeance on them and honor his family, along with the families of tens of thousands murdered by Stern. Erika would be gassed. He would hide a canister of deadly nerve gas in her apartment, trigger it remotely, and kill her as she slept. He learned a lot from his discussions with his good friend, Avner.

How can I be thinking these things? I have become like him.

A different scheme would be in place for Marlena. She lived with her husband in Vernon, New Jersey, and had two young sons. Michael would never kill any young children or family members not connected directly to Stern, but Marlena was Stern's daughter, an adult. She would be drugged, kidnapped, taken to a motel room, and gassed. They had to be gassed. Michael wouldn't have it any other way. Both women would never anticipate *why* they would ever be killed. They did no wrong. Magda, Roza, and little Eva were innocent too.

***

The next afternoon, Michael checked Hilda's list of medications at the pharmacy and found that she had refilled her prescription for sleeping pills one day before she took her life. Did she plan it so she would have the full thirty capsules?

Later that night, Stern called. "Michael, I am sorry if I am bothering you. Can we talk for a moment?"

"It's not a problem. What's on your mind?"

"Now that my Hilda is gone, I really feel alone. I have to be honest and tell you we did not have a very good marriage in many ways, but she always did what I asked. Now that she passed away, I miss her. I wake up alone."

"I can understand that, Harry. It is devastating to lose your wife. I know how you feel. Are you aware of why she did it?"

"No, I could never imagine. I let her buy anything she wanted and she could see our daughters and the grandchildren whenever she pleased, but she did not see them because they lived so far away, Erika in Manhattan and Marlena in New Jersey."

Stern is delusional. He has created a fantasy world in his mind in which he twists events and rearranges them so that no bit of truth remains.

"She must have been depressed and hurt for reasons only she knew," Michael said. "Did she leave a note?"

"Yes, a brief one. I do not remember exactly, but it said something like, 'Tell our girls I love them, and we will meet again.'"

"I see. Was she a religious person?"

"She was when I met her, but after we were married for several years, she stopped going to church and never went back."

"So, do you have any plans for yourself? You still have your family, your daughters."

"To be honest, we were never close. Why did Hilda do it?" Stern asked. "Why?"

"We'll never know," Michael replied. "She felt hurt and damaged for some reason, but you said you were good to her. So, what are your plans now?"

"Now that Hilda is gone, this house is too big for one person. I have to sell it and move somewhere else. I will miss our chess games."

Michael's heart sank.

Will I lose him? This is unexpected. Stern could soon be gone. Then what?

Michael had to act quickly, but he wasn't sure what to do. Stern could just disappear or stop at the pharmacy, say a simple goodbye, and take off. Michael would never be able to find him.

***

Every conversation Michael had with Stern was based on lies. No truth ever passed between them during their chess games, but Michael knew the most important truth. Stern was a monster concealed in the outer trappings of Mr. Normal.

Stern's superego fueled his exaggerated sense of importance, and killing innocent people had filled him with an extraordinary sense of power, which gave him the sick life he craved, a life where he could have absolute power over others.

I could get a gun, shoot him, and it would be over. Period!

But it wouldn't be over. Michael's revenge to honor his family had to come only after Hans Stern knew *why* he was being tortured.

Maybe I am fighting windmills. It might not matter to Stern if he knows the reasons or not. He doesn't know the madman he is, but I do.

Michael called Stern the next day and invited him over.

"Would you like some tea, coffee, or something else?" Michael asked.

"Strong tea would be fine."

Michael returned to the kitchen, brewed some tea and placed a small platter of Linzer tortes in front of Stern.

He sipped his tea and pointed to the plate. "Are these the cookies that Hilda..."

"Yes, they are." Michael nodded. "Probably the last thing she baked in her oven. Where would you move, Harry? Would you stay in New York State?"

"No, I don't think so. There is no one to cook and clean for me now and I have to change my surroundings. I have friends in South America. They live in Paraguay."

"I see. How soon will you be moving? It will take time to find a buyer for your house."

"Actually, I have a buyer and he will give me a deposit if I make the house available in one week."

Michael was out of time. He had to act. The moment for justice was here.

Stern had to be put on trial at once, here in Michael's garage! That would be his courtroom, only the two of them, with Michael acting as judge and executioner. It wouldn't be a sham like the trial at Nuremburg, where the rules of international law were abandoned and the Nazi murderers who were sentenced to prison terms were freed within a few years. Stern would die in his court, Michael's garage, where Michael's rule of law and justice would prevail. Like the judges did at Nuremberg, Stern's verdict would be determined in advance.

Chapter 13

It was time for the endgame. Michael called Stern.

"Harry, I'm leaving on vacation tomorrow and the thought occurred to me that I might not return before you move from Oneonta. I'd like you to come over tonight for some goodbye drinks and maybe a game of chess."

Stern arrived later that evening.

"Schnapps, Harry?"

"*Ja*, sure. Thank you."

Michael brought out a bottle of fine European schnapps and poured a shot glass for each of them. Michael sipped his drink slowly as Stern swallowed his all at once. He poured Stern another, then another.

"Enjoy the schnapps. Not all the stores carry good European liquor. It's much stronger than the others. I bought mine in New York City last year. Help yourself whenever you want more."

A few minutes later, Stern reached out and poured himself another glass. His eyes began to droop.

"Harry, I am sorry you're leaving Oneonta. I will miss you and our games. As I told you on the phone, I have some vacation plans myself and might leave tomorrow or the next day."

"Oh, it is good, then, that I am here tonight."

"Yes, it's fortunate."

"Please, one more game, if you have the time," Stern said.

"I'd like that. We were evenly matched. But first, when I heard you were moving, I wanted to give you something as a remembrance of our chess games together."

"I'm feeling the effect of our drinks already. I am very relaxed. Yes, we were evenly matched, but a gift is not necessary."

"It would be my pleasure to present you with something unusual. I've had it for many years, since I was in college, and it has special meaning for me. I'd like it to be yours."

"Can you tell me what it is?"

"It's a beautiful chess set, Harry, with genuine marble pieces. We can play a match with it later tonight. I have enjoyed our games, but I don't play chess anymore, and now, you will be moving away. I would feel honored to know my prized chess set is in your hands and that you will think of me during one of your chess matches. You're a very good player."

"Thank you, Michael. You are a kind man." Stern smiled. He seemed pleased.

"It's in the garage. We have to walk outside to get it."

Michael didn't waste time. He took a key from his pocket to open the garage door. His Chevy Bel Air was at its usual spot on the left side. Michael pointed the way, remembering how the Nazis led the Jews to slaughter with promises of taking a warm shower. He thought of his little girls, who were told they would be given toys as they skipped and danced their way to the gas chamber.

Now it was Michael's turn to entice Stern with the promise of a wonderful gift. Stern walked toward the garage, convinced he would receive a genuine marble chess set.

After they were halfway into the garage, Stern stopped and turned to let Michael walk in front of him. Fear filled Stern's eyes as he saw Michael with a small wooden bat, held high, ready to strike.

"Was machst du?" Stern yelled. He angled away from Michael, but it was too late.

Michael struck a strong blow on Stern's head and knocked him unconscious. He dragged him to a wall and handcuffed Stern's left arm to a sturdy pipe about ten feet from Michael's parked car.

He closed the garage door, sat on the dull, gray, paint-stained floor with chips of cement missing from dropped tools, and leaned his back against the front fender of his Chevy. Michael was out of breath, his heart racing. He swallowed gulps of air as his hands trembled. Stern was unconscious, but breathing.

Stern is mine. He will never know what is coming next, just as my family didn't know their fate as they suffered in dark, crowded cattle cars with no food or water and the smell of urine and feces on the floor and in the air. His demise will be slow and painful, but first I have to know what thoughts were in the evil mind of this SS officer while he was on his rampage of death and destruction of innocent human beings. I have to get into the mind of a Nazi killer.

Michael gazed at Stern. He was slumped on the garage floor, his head down, his right arm limp in front of him and his left arm handcuffed to a pipe behind him. He took Stern's car keys out of his pocket, drove Stern's car about a mile to Stern's house, and left it in the driveway with the keys under the mat. As he walked back to his house, he thought of Ilona.

***

It's been a long journey, dearest, but we're almost there. I couldn't help you at the camp, when you needed me, and I've borne the burden of that guilt since our fingertips slipped apart.

I love you so much and always will. That will never end. What a gift we had been given. My life was filled with your love and the love of our wonderful, sweet, and innocent daughters. Thank you so much.

What I'm doing now is to honor you and our girls in the only way I can. You know me to be a peaceful, caring person, but when I thought of a punishment for Hans Stern that would fit the crime of killing our family, a different part of me emerged, a part I never knew existed. I need to punish him for killing our family and thousands of others but I can never match Stern's cruelty. I'm too unlike him.

I had the good fortune to cross paths with Hans Stern again and, when I looked into his evil face, a storm raged within me, but soon I was the one in control. I am now his master, so don't worry, my love. He will die and never be near you. He will go to a place where the heat of the flames will constantly burn his flesh, and he will rot in agony in the fires of hell for all eternity.

***

Michael walked back to the house and entered the garage. Stern groaned as he regained consciousness. He opened his red and swollen eyes and pressed his lips together. Stern pulled on the handcuffs and screamed, "*Was haben sie getan?* What are you doing?" Michael's house was isolated from the others in the countryside. Only he heard Stern's cries.

Michael remained silent. He fixed his eyes on Stern and smiled. *Who would have thought this day would ever come?*

"Why are you doing this?" Stern yelled. "Are you crazy? We are friends. What has come over you? Is it a trick you are playing? My wife just died, for God's sake! Release me. My wrist is hurting. Take these things off. Do it now! I insist!" Stern said, making a fist with his free hand.

Michael observed Stern's behavior. He appeared as if he didn't have any idea why *anyone* would do this to him. Although Michael knew the truth, he questioned himself again. *Is it him? Is he Stern?*

He looked into Stern's eyes. They were old, sorrowful, and pleading, a sharp contrast to his younger days at Auschwitz, when his stares at Jews could mean only one thing...their deaths. He remembered Stern's voice in the camp, shrill and piercing. There was no doubt. The man handcuffed to the pipe *was* Hans Stern. Harry Sanders and Hans Stern were one and the same!

Stern's screams continued. His labored, high-pitched voice rang through the garage, echoing off the walls.

"Was haben sie getan?"

Michael remained silent. He watched Stern squirm and beg to be freed as Stern held his head in his hands and repeatedly whispered, *"Was haben sie getan."*

This is just the beginning.

Michael rose to leave, turning his back on Stern.

"Don't go," Stern yelled. "Is it because Hilda took her life, Michael? Are you blaming me? I do not know what you are thinking. Just tell me."

Michael left the bright lights on, closed the garage door, and walked to his house. He sat on his sofa, put his head back, and savored every sweet moment, knowing that Hans Stern was *his* prisoner in *his* court, where his sentence would be death.

Michael was relaxed. He snacked on some cheese, English biscuits, and a glass of full-bodied red and listened to *La Boehme*. He had Stern exactly where he wanted him.

There is no rush.

Michael returned to the garage the next morning and sat on the floor, his back against the front fender of his Chevy Bel Air. Stern appeared drained after spending the night handcuffed under the intense garage lights.

"Get me some schnapps, some water," Stern demanded in a hoarse voice. "What are you doing, Michael? I have never hurt you. If you don't let me go, I'll call the police"

Michael didn't answer. He felt no anxiety, only peace, as he listened to the faint strains of the opera coming from the house.

Calling the police would be the last thing Stern would do. They might discover who he really was. Besides, how could he call them?

Michael thought of the few times their eyes had met. He remembered one occasion when Stern stood in the doorway of the barracks as Ilona laid outside. His laugh and insults were as penetrating as the rocks piercing into Ilona's naked body. There, Stern was in his tailored, gray-green SS uniform with a bottle of beer in his hand, laughing and pointing at Michael's wife. Now Stern was here, a prisoner in Michael's garage.

This is an unexpected gift.

Stern closed his eyes, covered them with his hand, and hung his head. Michael went back to the house, showered, and had breakfast.

Chapter 14

As Michael sipped his first cup of bold, black coffee, he listened to the Carpenters sing "Close To You." The lyrics told of a girl's longing to be close to someone she admired and loved. The song brought memories of Ilona and he tried to remember the last time he kissed her but couldn't. It might have been on the train to Auschwitz, when all that was in front of them were miles of cold, steel tracks leading to gas chambers and crematoria.

Why didn't the allies bomb these tracks? They knew where the tracks were.

When the train had arrived at Auschwitz, Michael stared into Ilona's gaunt, unsmiling face, a stark contrast from her usual clear, bright eyes, sweet smile, and the look of love for her family. He'd looked into her watery eyes and felt her pain.

***

Now, in the year 1970, Stern was his, a prisoner. Michael got dressed, putting on a long sleeved shirt, and brought a piece of dark bread, a container of milk, and Stern's heart medication to the garage. The stench in the small space was nauseating.

Stern was asleep. His head was slumped over his chest and his right arm by his side, lifeless. His pants were soaked with urine and the stench of his feces permeated the air. Michael shook him, gave him the bread and milk, and sat against the side of his car's front fender with his knees up and his arms folded around them.

Stern gulped the milk and ate the bread, following it with the heart medication. Some of the bread and milk dribbled onto his shirt.

"Have we met before?" Stern asked, squinting. "Were you ever in Argentina?"

Michael didn't answer. "Did we meet in Argentina?" Stern cried out.

"Are you a friend of Fernando? Did he put you up to this? Was it one of his friends?" Stern looked at Michael with a clenched fist and fire in his eyes.

"Why are you treating me like this? I'm an innocent human being. I have never done any harm to you or anyone. You must let me know if you know Fernando."

Michael remained silent for a moment. Instead, he asked Stern if he ever used another name.

"No," Stern was quick to respond, "I am Harry Sanders. That is my name and I have never used another."

"Okay. Harry, you sit here until you're ready to tell the truth. I'll be back after lunch. If you're still not ready, I will come back tomorrow."

He ignored Stern's pathetic screams of, "*Gehen*

nicht. Gehen nicht. Don't go!" Michael closed the garage door and left Stern under the glaring, bright lights.

***

Michael returned the next morning with a gallon of tap water and gave Stern a glassful. Stern's hand trembled as he drank, dribbling the water onto his sweat-stained shirt.

"Hans?"

"Yes," Stern answered in a hoarse voice.

"You are Hans Stern?" Michael questioned.

"Yes, but..."

"Are you Hans Stern, yes or no?"

Stern was silent.

"I will come back later."

"No wait! *Gehen nicht*," he said weakly. "I am Hans Stern." His glazed eyes searched Michael's. "How do you know me?"

"That will come later. I will say one thing. From now on, if anything comes out of your mouth that is not the truth, *anything*, I will leave you here to die and rot in hell. Otherwise, you will have a chance to live. Do you understand that?"

Hans drew a labored breath. "I understand. You will only hear the truth. I promise."

"Were you a Nazi officer during the war?"

"Yes," Stern answered with a downward gaze. "I was a major."

"Were you at any concentration camps?"

"Yes, I was at Buchenwald and Auschwitz."

"Is that the truth?" Michael asked as he moved

76

his face closer to Stern and looked into his inflamed, half-closed eyes.

"Yes, yes, I swear," he said, staring back.

"Are you sure? I think you're lying."

"No, it is the truth," Stern said, banging his hand on the garage floor. "Please do not leave me here. What I said was the truth. I don't know why you are doing this crazy thing. I have never done anything to hurt you. Please, a cigarette."

"What were the names of people you knew or were friendly with at the camps?" Michael asked, his finger pointing at Stern like a dagger.

"At Buchenwald, I knew Ilse Koch, but she was crazy. She would walk around the camp naked with a whip and..."

"Okay, I don't know anything about her. Who was commandant at Auschwitz when you were there?"

"It was Rudolf Hoess."

"Were you friendly with him?"

"I was his *only* friend. Michael, why are you doing this? Let me go and I will tell you anything you want to know. I will not wait any longer," he said firmly.

"What is the name of another Nazi officer that you knew well?"

Stern muttered, "I was in Treblinka and became friendly with Franz Stangl."

"But you said you were only at Buchenwald and Auschwitz. That's it, Hans! I only wanted the truth. You could have gone free, but..." Michael threw up his hands.

"Stop, please don't say those things!" Stern

pleaded. "I am so sorry. I *was* at Treblinka for so short a time that I forgot. It was maybe a week."

Michael walked back to the house.

Let him wait. Millions of innocent Jews and others waited in agony, not knowing their fate, before they were murdered. Now it's Stern's turn to wait. Besides, he lied by not mentioning Treblinka. That was a small point. He will be more careful next time because he knows there will be consequences. It doesn't matter, and he's not aware I'm not quite ready to kill him.

What must he be thinking? What is he feeling? Many Jews had to wait and wonder, just as Stern must be doing now. They knew nothing of their destiny before they were killed. Let that monster drive himself crazy and live in fear in the little time he has left. I'll decide when he will die.

Michael returned to the garage courtroom.

"Hans, you lied, and I thought about letting you die. You had that one chance to be truthful, and you lied. Maybe that worked at Auschwitz, but it doesn't work in my courtroom. You even lied about being a good chess player, but you're only an amateur. I'm going to do something different. Maybe it will give you a chance to live."

"Yes, anything. I want to live. I was not lying before. I—"

"Stop, Hans! You lied. If it happens again, you're dead! Did you lie? Yes or no?"

"Yes, I did," Stern answered meekly.

"Say it again, louder."

"I lied," Stern said, increasing the sound of his voice.

"I can't hear you!" Michael demanded.

"I lied, I lied, Michael," Stern yelled.

"I'm going to put you on trial, right here. Look around you. This is my courtroom. I'll be the judge, *your* judge. If you have a winning case for any one of your actions, just *one,* I will set you free, and that is a promise. Think of it as a chess game, Hans. If you play things right, you will win."

"Thank you for giving me that chance. I know that you will let me go. I have always known you to be fair. I had that feeling about you when we played chess."

"Who else did you know well at Auschwitz? Maybe you were never there?"

"Oh, Michael, I *was* there. I knew SS-Sturmbannführer, Richard Baer, Karl Hocker, Mengele and..."

"Okay, Hans, I believe you. Here's a reward." He filled Stern's glass with water and watched him gulp it down.

He saw Stern eyeing some rolls of toilet paper on a shelf, but Michael said nothing to him. Michael endured the smell, knowing that it humiliated Stern.

"Let's talk, Hans. You have only shared your lies with me. I thought you would be smarter than that. I know you are familiar with the term, *Arbeit macht frei."*

Stern shrugged. "Yes, it means work will make you free. It was in bold iron letters on top of the gate at the entrance to Auschwitz."

"Listen to me, Hans. In your case, right now, *die wahrheit wird euch frei machen.* Do you understand?"

"Yes, the truth will make *me* free. I didn't know you spoke German so well. I tell you the truth and I go free."

"Yes, I give you my word."

"Thank you. I know you are an honorable man."

"Maybe you can help me understand a few things, Hans, from your viewpoint. Why do you think Germany was so anti-Semitic?"

"It was Hitler's way. He saw history as a racial struggle in which the Jews sought world domination and opposed Aryan beliefs. Nazi's believed that only the superior German Aryan Race would persevere and dominate the world. Besides, Michael, Hitler saw Jews as corrupt and inferior. Also, Christian Semitic beliefs, which painted a picture of Jews as Christ killers and worshippers of the devil, helped support Hitler's views."

"Okay, I'm the devil now, and you're my only customer. As the devil, what would Hitler and the rest of you think of me?"

"Please, give me something to eat."

"Later. Answer the question."

Stern took a deep breath. "We would think you are an evil person causing harm to others. When Hitler was sentenced to prison for five years, it was because he led the Beer Hall Putsch in Bavaria. While he was there, he dictated his book, *Mein Kampf,* to Rudolf Hess. In it, he said 'the personification of the devil as the symbol of all evil assumes the living shape of the Jew.' It doesn't mean you, Michael. I know you are not an evil person. Hitler knew the Jews were hated everywhere in the world. You are not like them. I still don't know why Jews are so hated. I have never thought about it. I just knew they were bad people and Hitler said they would hurt Germany. He didn't invent racism or anti-Semitism. There was a long history of suspicion and dehumanization against Jews for thousands of years. Hitler embraced the notion that Jews were evil and established laws to hurt the Jews and bring Germans to his side in a common belief. Besides, anti-Semitic laws were in effect in other European countries."

"Really? Where?" Michael questioned.

"Eastern Europe. They had discriminatory laws against Jews in effect starting in 1938."

"I see. Did you order the killing of large numbers of people? Remember, only the truth will set you free, Hans."

Stern hesitated, touched his parched lips, and answered, "Yes. It is true, but I have never done anything on my own initiative. I was loyal to the Third Reich, just doing my job. I was a soldier following orders. A soldier doesn't question if the laws are right or wrong. In *every* military force in the world, it is imperative to follow the orders of your superiors!"

"Even unjust laws? Illegal orders? Killing innocent people too?"

"Yes, if those were my orders. But what I did was *not* just about *following* orders, it was more than that. If I did not do it, I would be killed. It was about my *survival*, a basic instinct in all human beings. Maybe you would do the same."

Michael asked himself if he would do it. Stern says it wasn't only about following orders for him.

It was about his survival. *What would I do?*

I could never kill an innocent human being, never! I would go down fighting and take as many Nazis down with me as I could.

Michael crossed his legs and sat against his Chevy, facing Stern. He put on a pair of sunglasses because the glaring lights were too much for him.

Stern quietly sat in his squalor. He cupped his hand over his eyes, but did not complain.

"Hans, do you think there are evil people in this world?"

Stern took has hand away from his eyes and squinted. "Yes, there are many evil people. They hurt others for no reason."

"Aren't *you* one of them? Come on, be honest, you've killed thousands of people. That makes you evil, doesn't it?" Michael snapped.

"No, I killed for the flag of my country. I was a soldier and did what I was told. Sometimes it is necessary for civilians to die in wars. You may say killing is wrong, but in a war, it is right."

Stern paused. "There are rules of war that must be followed just as in the game of chess. We make the rules, then follow them as we play the game. Many died in Vietnam while Americans ravaged their country. Countless innocent people are being killed by your bombs, right now as we speak, and American soldiers are following their superior's orders to go into villages and kill all the men, women, and children. Is it right for you and wrong for us? That is what war is all about, Michael. It is a dirty business.

"In Germany, we had stored a supply of

smallpox bacteria and planned to inject Jews with it and then send them across the channel in small boats in the hope they would infect the British with the deadly bacteria, but we followed the rules and didn't do it. We also had a large supply of poison gas, but we never used it. Gassing people to death would also be against the rules. It is a terrible death."

"Yes, it is."

"But we didn't do it."

Michael shook his head in disbelief. "That's a lot of crap, and you know it. You didn't do your killing only on the battlefield. Your workplace was in the concentration camps, and you specialized in killing the elderly and children immediately and putting the others to work at hard labor 'til they dropped. Maybe you find some sick justification in your clogged brain to believe that everything your country did was right. Hans, think concentration camp, the gas, the crematoria. Think, Mengele." Michael was breathing rapidly and leaned against his car, trying to calm himself.

Stern said nothing until Michael asked, "Why do you think the Jews didn't resist? Was it hopelessness? Were they worn down and humiliated to the point that they didn't want to live? And don't give me that bullshit about orders and survival. You always try to squeeze that in."

Stern perked up.

"Oh, but they did resist. We suppressed all information about the uprisings and revolts. We never wanted word of it to spread. They resisted in the Warsaw Ghetto and many fought back in

Sobibor and Treblinka. In one camp, hundreds of German soldiers were killed. Also, many Jews escaped from the trains on their way to Auschwitz. They contrived different ways to get the railway cars open enough for them to jump to safety. They always did it when the train was on a curve so the guards watching the entire length of the train would not see them. They escaped and many joined the resistance and fought against us."

Michael shed a tear and wiped his eyes.

Those poor people on the trains were in the wrong place and born in the wrong time. If only...

Stern continued to talk, but Michael retreated into his own world for a moment before he spoke.

"I didn't know there were so many Jews who resisted. It wasn't easy for them. They were so weak, without food or drink. Were there any uprisings in Auschwitz?"

"There were. One day, a group of Sonderkommandos attacked the SS guards at the gas chambers and crematoria. They killed our soldiers with knives and pieces of wood with nails in them. They took the soldiers' weapons and shoved many of them alive into the ovens. Those Jews were strong and effective, maybe because they were so well-fed as a reward for the horrible jobs they had to do. They opened fire and killed almost one hundred of us. Then they threw a satchel containing gunpowder into a crematorium and blew it up. After they were captured, I personally had them killed. But, for Jews, any kind of significant resistance was impossible."

"Why do you say that?"

"Because the Jewish leaders contributed to the destruction of the Jewish people. They did nothing to protect them."

"So, the Jewish leaders were to blame for the plight of the Jews? Come on, Hans."

"Yes, it's true. Jewish leaders feared that loud protests from them might provoke anti-Semitism and hurt the Jews even more, so the leaders did nothing. Believe me, anti-Semitism was already widespread, and the leaders felt that more protests would make it worse. The truth is that they were wrong. If the Jewish leaders encouraged demonstrations and outcries, it might have helped."

"I'm not sure. There were major protests by Jews and others in America at Madison Square Garden before the war, but they accomplished nothing. Maybe it was because the Jew's 'savior,' President Roosevelt, was an anti-Semite too. But what was *your* reason for killing tens of thousands of innocent people *just because they were Jews?"*

"I told you. Orders! Survival! Sometimes, logical reasons cease to exist. Racism was the reason for hanging black people in the south. When Nazis burned the Jews in the crematoria, it was no different. Hate is everywhere. It is part of life. It is normal.

"For me, I could no longer think. I was just driven to defend the ideals of my country. Eichmann felt the same way. Americans quickly forget about the concentration camps that were set up in the United States during World War II to imprison Japanese American citizens. You say that the concentration camps in Europe confined people only because they were Jews? That is true, but the Nazis sent many others to concentration camps because they were gypsies, homosexuals, and other venom of our society.

"In the United States, Japanese American citizens were taken from their homes in the middle of the night and put in concentration camps. Why? They were citizens, like other Americans. Your country believed it was the right thing to do, just as Germany believed that rounding up the Jews and putting them into *our* concentration camps was the right thing.

"The strange part is that the Japanese never killed or imprisoned Jews, even when they were part of the Axis powers. They were different from us and not anti-Semitic. Actually, there were a significant number of Jews brought to safety from Lithuania in the early forties by a Japanese diplomatic official named Sugihara. He issued them transit visas."

"What about Italy, your other Axis power. What did they do to hurt the Jews?"

"Italy? They did nothing to hurt them. The Jews were treated like all the other Italians." Stern shrugged.

"So, it was only the German bastards that killed Jews, right?"

Stern was silent.

"I don't get it, Hans. It's too terrible to be believable. Why didn't ordinary soldiers question their superiors?"

Stern said, "There were a few German soldiers who refused to shoot some of the prisoners when they were ordered to do it, and they were not punished. Their superiors looked away, but the nature of soldiering is to be obedient. Discipline depends upon strict compliance, to obey without questioning."

"I don't know about that. There are such things as illegal orders. American soldiers would not act that way. If an American captain asked a corporal to do something as simple as pick up the captain's laundry, it would be an illegal order."

"But he might do it to stay in the good graces of the captain," Stern replied.

"Maybe, but if he would be asked by a superior to kill another soldier or a civilian in front of others, the American would refuse."

"Then he would have to be punished," Stern said.

"Only in your army, and you would probably be the man to kill him. Your men live in fear. The only fear American soldiers have are for drill sergeants." Michael smiled.

***

Michael thought of Stern as a blind zealot, but he was right about what had happened to Japanese Americans. When the US government interned Japanese American citizens against their will, Japanese Americans lost their property and their rights as Americans. They also suffered from psychological disorders, and many died as a result of poor medical care. *It was wrong*. The Supreme Court held that what the American government did was legal.

But they were wrong too. Imprisoning people because of their race or religion is wrong under any circumstances. After the attack on Pearl Harbor, we lived in fear and succumbed to insane acts, such as imprisoning Japanese Americans. A sad time in our history.

Michael walked back to his house and had lunch as he listened to The Beatles. For dessert, he had a cup of bold, hot coffee with an éclair and sat on the living room sofa. He sunk his teeth into the creamy custard. It reminded him of the mocha kremes he enjoyed with his family in Budapest.

***

It was a happy day for me. We'd visited our favorite pastry shop on Kossuth Lajos Street, on the bank of the Danube in Budapest. Ilona asked for a platter of pastries, which included a variety of fruit strudels and small, Tokoi cream cakes. Ilona and I had coffee with an added dollop of rich vanilla ice cream and the girls had milk.

I couldn't take my eyes off my daughters. They were all prettied up in their fancy city dresses and busy chatting with each other as we sat around the table, enjoying our cakes. I imagined them as young ladies.

I looked at my young girls, their faces bearing milk moustaches.

"Tell me, what you would you like to be doing when you're grown up?"

"Can I go first? Can I go first, Papa?" Roza

pleaded. "I want to write things, books maybe, even poetry. I wrote a poem when I was only five called, 'The Peek-A-Boo Kid.' It was about a boy who tapped other boys and girls on their shoulders and said 'Peek-A-Boo.' Most of them were annoyed, until one day, he tapped a girl on the shoulder and when she turned around, she greeted him with a big smile. They became friends forever and it all started with a smile. Magda read it and told me she loved it. When I was sick and Dr. Hershkowitz came to the house to make me better, he read a poem I wrote about our family and how much we loved each other. He told me I should be a writer. Can I be a writer, Papa?"

"Roza, you're a lovely girl. You can be anything you want, and I'm sure your poems will bring pleasure to everyone who reads them. What about you, Magda? What would you like to be?"

"I only want to be a singer, Papa," she said as she bit off a piece of flaky apple strudel and washed it down with milk. "I sing more than I talk. I tried to think of something else I wanted to be. A nurse, maybe, or a singing nurse so I could make sick people happy. First, I feel the music, then it comes out of me like magic and I can't believe how beautiful it sounds." She opened her mouth and cupped her hands around her lips as if in song.

Ilona reached across the table, held Magda's little hands, and said, "Magda, you would make a wonderful singer. You may not notice me listening when I'm busy cooking or cleaning the house, but I hear every note and it makes me smile."

Then, it was little Eva's turn. "I want to be a

dancer, Papa. I know it."

"You dance beautifully, little Eva, like a ballerina with so much emotion, but what if you couldn't be a dancer? What else would you be?"

"Nothing. I only want to be a dancer, nothing else."

Ilona's face lit up and she turned to me.

"It looks like our girls will be a gift to the world of the arts, Miklos. I can already see them doing what they love. Do you think it's strange that none of them said they wanted to be a mother?"

"I guess they're just being who they are, Ilona. It seems our work is cut out for us—ballet lessons for little Eva, a voice coach for our songbird, and for Roza, she just has to keep doing what she's doing and she will change the world with her words."

I ate the delicious pastries with my family until we were stuffed. There was no better life I could ever ask for and no better gift than my family. My girls would change the world. I was sure of it.

Chapter 15

As usual, the day began with music for Michael. The Violetta aria of *La Traviata* filled the air while he prepared his breakfast. He tended to his flower garden most of the day, and later in the afternoon, he sang along with "Love Me Do" by the Beatles.

Michael called Dan at the pharmacy to see how things were going. He reminded him of the arrangement they had agreed to, which gave Dan total ownership of the pharmacy in the event that Michael retired or was no longer available.

He returned to the garage with a cheese sandwich and a large glass of apple juice for Stern, who was asleep with his chin pressed against his chest. The stench in the garage was overpowering, forcing Michael to wear a surgical mask, which helped him ignore the smell.

Stern awakened and rubbed his red eyes, a result of the harsh, bright lights that surrounded him twenty-four hours a day. Michael shook Stern to get his attention and the interrogation continued.

"Hans, your explanation of why the Nazis

singled out the Jews left me thinking. Why was it so easy for you to torture and kill them? How could human beings be so cruel?"

"I cannot answer that," Stern said, still half asleep.

"Answer it, and I want the truth. I will know if you're lying. "

"I will tell you, but I know it will make you angry."

"I'm already angry for the atrocities you've inflicted on the human race by following the orders of a madman. How could you have been so stupid? Just tell me," Michael insisted.

Stern hesitated for a full minute, shaking his head before he spoke, his voice hoarse and scratchy, his body and mind worn thin.

"All of us believed the Jews were subhuman. They weren't people. They were insects. That's what made them easy to kill. They had no real feelings about life, love, or music. They never laughed and were ugly with big noses. They weren't human and had to be destroyed, like vermin." Stern shrugged, his mouth turned downward as he rubbed his eyes "The world should be thankful to us for getting rid of them."

Michael was stunned to hear it first-hand. It was the one truth Stern believed. *How delusional.*

Many Nazis felt the same and viewed Jews as slime and subhuman, which made them as easy to kill as stepping on cockroaches. Michael had wondered why so many human beings could commit such atrocities against other humans. Now he had some idea. The Nazis leveled their hatred on

92

the Jews, gypsies, and homosexuals in the belief they were ridding the world of vermin and had created reasons in their minds to support it.

It was mass insanity.

The odor of Stern's body and the air in the garage intensified, so Michael increased the speed of the exhaust system and sat with his eyes closed until Stern began to speak.

"And yet..." Stern said.

"What?" Michael asked.

"There were many Jews who served in the German army. Some were generals."

"I don't believe that. Let's get on to something else."

"It's true, Michael, I swear. I met Helmut Wilberg. He was a Jewish general in the Luftwaffe."

"A general? How did he get to that rank if he was Jewish?"

"He was a Mischling."

"What's that?"

"It is someone of mixed blood, half-Jewish, or had some Jewish blood. There were different degrees. I am not exactly sure of the percentages."

"Was it a well-known fact that Wilberg was Jewish?"

"Some Jewish officers kept their backgrounds secret, others did not. I spoke to Helmut on several social occasions and he told me he was half-Jewish."

"So, again, how did he achieve this high rank?"

"He told me that Germany was his homeland and that came first."

"But he was still a Jew."

"Hitler declared him an Aryan."

"I see. When you're a dictator, you can change the rules. Was Wilberg smart?"

"Very smart. You have to understand that there were many Jews in the German army. I don't think many of them were religious, but the few that I spoke to claimed they were not fighting as Jews but were in the army to fight for the fatherland. In my mind, I excused them for being Jewish and I didn't see them as Jews."

"You excused them…" Michael shook his head.

"I can tell you something that most people don't know," Stern said as he sat back against the concrete wall with a half-smile on his face.

"I learned from a friend that there was a Nazi soldier named Werner Goldberg. He looked pure Aryan with his blue eyes and blonde hair." Stern continued smiling and shook his head. "His picture was on the front page of a Nazi magazine with a caption, *The Ideal German Soldier*. That was a laugh. He was Jewish."

Michael didn't smile, but turned away. Stern was becoming too chummy and he wasn't sure if it was a good thing. Although, when Stern was at ease, he spoke of events known to a very few, which interested Michael, but he had to end the camaraderie. This man killed his family. Maybe not all of them directly, but he was responsible.

He went back to the house, had some wine, and took a short nap before he returned to his court. Stern was usually compliant with everything Michael asked of him. In true Nazi spirit, Michael assumed he wanted to survive and being agreeable was his strategy. But when Michael stepped into the garage, Stern was angry.

"Why am I here, Michael? I still do not know. Why do you leave me alone for so long? I answered all your questions. I have been honest in every way. Can I go home now?" Stern begged.

"Not yet. I gave you my word that I will release you, and you know I'm an honorable man."

"Yes, yes, I do." A thin smile crossed Stern's lips. "I understand you just want to learn what the war was like from a German officer's perspective. You are curious, a professor, a learned man, and who can give you better information than an SS-officer?"

"Yes, you're right. I do want to hear about the war from your view."

"Ahh, I *knew* it was about your curiosity. That is the reason for all this. Now, I understand."

Michael looked Stern squarely in the eye and asked, "Who is Fernando?"

"Him?" Stern scowled. "That bastard! He helped Hilda, me, and my daughters get into Argentina, for a price, of course. A huge price. I paid him the agreed amount in pesos, but he kept asking for more and threatened to report me for being a war criminal. I couldn't take that chance, so I paid him in the way he wanted, with unflawed cut diamonds, the swine."

Michael paced back and forth in front of Stern.

"*Are* you a war criminal?"

Stern squirmed. "I am not sure if I am listed. Perhaps I am and I'm afraid to find out, but I knew I would never be put on trial for something that happened so long ago. Many of the witnesses are already dead and because I've been free for so many years, no one is looking for me anymore. I knew I would always live out my life as a free man."

He's right, except for one thing. He will never live out his life at all. It's only a matter of hours before I bring the scum the justice he deserves.

"I'm interested. How did you get to Argentina?"

"It was not easy. Thousands of Nazis fled to South America by using the ratlines. I was one of them."

"So, those were well-established escape routes?"

Stern nodded. "I couldn't do it alone. None of us could. I got help from the Vatican and the Red Cross."

"The Vatican? The Red Cross? Educate me. How did *that* happen? I want to know the details."

Stern took a deep breath. "It was all so long ago. The Red Cross issued travel documents to thousands of Nazis during the post-war turmoil. I was one of them, along with Hilda and my girls, but there were complications. I could not use them to get to South America. However, they helped us get to Italy, where we spent six months in Rome."

"I assume that this is where the Vatican came in."

Stern hesitated. "It is. I still had a fortune in diamonds, beautifully cut stones, and gold jewelry. It was better than money because it always kept its value. The gems I had could support my family for our lifetimes. One small, perfectly cut diamond would buy us rent in an exclusive neighborhood in Rome for a year. I wanted to work, I had to keep busy, but I couldn't take a chance on getting a job because I felt I might be discovered."

"You sound like you were proud of how you escaped, but remember, you said you couldn't do it without help."

"It wasn't about pride, damn it! It was about survival. I wanted to live. That was the most important thing to me, life!"

"Yeah, life is important to most people. Everyone wants to survive. No one would want their life taken from them, but you know about those things. How did you *get* this fortune? I want to know more about how you got the diamonds and gold."

Stern appeared drained and tired. "Many Jews in concentration camps hid valuable gems and used them as bribes to get food. I took many cut diamonds, sapphires, rubies, and jewelry from them, only small bags sometimes, but put together, it was a fortune, enough to live ten lives. Some prisoners swallowed the diamonds if they knew they would be searched and retrieved them later."

"And the gold?" Michael asked, pulling up a chair.

"Gold teeth were taken from the corpses after they were gassed and before they went into the crematoria. Their bodies were stacked in piles, and many of the officers helped themselves. I melted the gold I took while still at Auschwitz and made them into coins and small bars so I could easily use them to pay my expenses after the war. When I reached

Italy and later Argentina, my fortune gave me a better life."

"So, you paid your costs with the gold teeth of dead Jews." Michael shook his head. "Okay, now, you're stuck in Rome. You're afraid to get a job because it might put you in the open. Then what?"

Stern looked down at his feet and spoke in a low voice.

"I met a fellow Nazi officer, Gunther, who was actually working in Rome, picking up rubbish at the Coliseum. He told me there were several priests and a few bishops who helped Nazis escape to South America. They knew where all the established ratlines were. Some of the clergymen didn't accept money for their services. I don't know why. They just helped the Nazis. Many of us believed Pope Pius wanted the Nazis to win the war. Others of the cloth demanded artworks, cut diamonds, and gold."

"So, who was the one who actually helped you?" Michael asked, soaking up the first-hand story.

"It was a pro-Nazi bishop in the Vatican who had connections in Germany. Through him, Nazis escaped to South America from Italy or France and he helped me get to Argentina. The cost was high, but he delivered."

"You mean Gunther just told you about this source? Why didn't he contact the bishop himself and escape?"

"He told me he liked Rome. He had a young, sexy Italian girlfriend and felt safe. He gave me a secret phone number, and I contacted the bishop in Rome, who arranged for new identities and passports for my family. Before I met him, I thought of staying in Rome too, even without working. My diamonds would pay my expenses and I would not have to work, but that would be no life. I was young and needed to keep busy. I was offered a job as a mechanic, and I almost took it because I liked Europe and spoke enough Italian to get by."

"*Almost* took it?" Michael asked. "Why didn't you take it? You were safe?"

"Not really. The problem was that Gunther disappeared. I went to the Coliseum, but he was gone. A week went by and no Gunther. I thought the worst, and that is what brought me to the bishop. I was scared."

"Really? A scared Nazi SS officer? Come now." Michael laughed.

Stern paused for a moment, then said, "I successfully made it to a private ratline created by the bishop himself and used only for his special customers. The velvet bag I gave him was more than he expected."

"The bishop? Did he also hate Jews?"

A smirk crossed Stern's lips. "Oh, absolutely. He was pro-Nazi and a man of religion...both. His weakness was diamonds. He derived great pleasure from pouring them from one hand to the other to watch them sparkle.

"He was famous for writing a book when he lived in Austria, which showed his support for Hitler. His book made it clear that he hated Jews and provided his reason. He told me the Nazis were not guilty of anything, and they were treated as scapegoats by an evil system. The bishop thought of the Nazis as anti-communists and because of that he felt the National Socialist Party deserved his support. This bishop was no different from me and other Nazis. We believed that what we did was right for our country and the world. We wanted to stop communism, just like America." Stern paused. "When the Nazis heard of his book, they flocked to him for help."

"And the bishop, the 'altruist' that he was, did what he thought was right for *him*? I mean, helping the Nazis did make him rich."

"That's true, it did, but he earned every lire," Stern replied. "He arranged for forged Italian passports for us, and soon we were on a ship bound for Argentina, a country that has always been receptive to the Axis powers and a place where my forged passport would be accepted. It is important for you to know that the Nazi escape operation involved many countries. Juan Domingo Peron, himself, created a plan to bring high ranking Nazis to fascist Argentina, including Adolf Eichmann and Josef Mengele. You may not know it, Michael, but Peron was as fascist as they come."

"I always knew it. So, it was Peron who initiated the plan and created the network of ratlines?"

"Not just Peron. It was a group conspiracy, which included the Swiss government, a few bishops in the Vatican, Croatian priests, and the Argentine Catholic church. South America became a Nazi paradise!"

Michael shook his head. "I'm not sure I believe that. The truth, Hans, remember? The truth. How did Switzerland become involved? I always thought of them as neutral."

"Michael, I know you are a learned man, but perhaps there are things beyond your understanding. The Swiss are neutral only militarily. You would have to be crazy to invade Switzerland with all those mountains and every Swiss man a trained soldier with guns in his house. But they were business people, and they made money on secret bank accounts and on commissions for storing wealth. Switzerland became a sanctuary for Nazi gold and art."

"I didn't know everything was so well thought out. Leave it to the Nazis, the cowards. When they had to escape, they figured out a plan so that they could run like rats...ratlines, how apropos. What happened after you got into Argentina?"

"Someone had to help me further. I needed a place to live and some sort of job so I could keep my sanity. Another friend introduced me to Fernando, who grew up in Buenos Aires. He was smart, spoke Spanish, English, and German, and his specialty was lining up assassins for people who needed his services. He arranged the right man for the right job. Fernando was able to do anything for a price. Always a high price, but he delivered first-class work."

Stern stopped, his eyes darting about. He took a deep breath, his hands trembling as if the mere mention of Fernando's name put him in a state of panic.

"Go on," Michael said, waiting.

"Okay, he found us an apartment and got me a job fixing Fiats and other European cars in a small repair shop on a quiet street in Buenos Aires, not far from Garibaldi Street, where Eichmann lived and where I would be unnoticed. I had to work. I did not want to live my life in the shadows, looking at the world from an inconspicuous window on a side street. I felt safe in fascist Argentina. It was a country similar to Germany. The soldiers even did the goose step, but I had to keep busy or I couldn't live," Stern said proudly. "Fixing cars helped me keep my sanity."

"Come on, stop bullshitting me. You have no sanity. You're *here,* in America. I don't get it. You had a place to live and a good job. You could have stayed put, like most of the other Nazis who ran to Argentina with the other scared rats. They were happy to be free and safe. Don't bullshit me, Hans. Why didn't you stay in Argentina where you *knew* you were safe? There has to be another reason. Let's have the truth," Michael said, stabbing his finger at him.

Stern took a deep breath.

"Yes, I *would* be safe if it weren't for Fernando. After a while, he thought I was holding out on him and asked for more money and diamonds. He, basically, did not like me. He sneered when he talked to me in spite of the enormous amount of gems I placed in his hands. I couldn't stay in Argentina, Michael, not with Fernando constantly breathing down my neck for more diamonds. I knew, in the end, one of his assassins would kill me. I would have to hide out like an animal unless I gave him *everything* I owned.

"I don't know why he hated me. I was not a Jew. I was a well-known, high ranking SS officer, and I paid him with enough cash and diamonds for him to live a luxurious life. If I gave him everything, I would be living on the street and I could not let that happen. He was a crazy man who didn't care about other people, the bastard." Stern's handcuffs rattled as he pulled on them. "I had to stop him or I would be dead."

Michael looked at Stern. His red, swollen eyes and cracked lips had taken a toll on him. He kept breathing rapidly in short breaths with anger contorting his pale face. Then he hung his head and was silent. He appeared to be worn out. Michael turned away when he heard the trickling sound of Stern peeing in his pants while he held his only free hand in front of his eyes to avoid the penetrating glare of the lights.

Michael didn't give him a chance to rest. He liked it when Stern rambled on. He was weak enough to tell the truth

"Skip to the end game. You know, like the end game in chess," Michael said. "Obviously, you weren't interested in dying. How did you get Fernando off your back?"

"It wasn't easy. I phoned him and told him I had an original artwork. It was a Van Gogh called *Painter on the Way to Tarascon*. I told him it was worth a fortune and I would give it to him if he left us alone. He agreed and said that if I gave him such a precious artwork, he would never bother me again."

"I hope you went along with that. Your life was worth more than a painting. How did you know he would keep his end of the deal? You only had his word."

"I already knew his word meant nothing. He was a liar and I had to stop him in the only way I knew how. I arranged to meet him the next day at the Alvear Palace Hotel, a short distance from Buenos Aires, where I booked a luxurious room for a week. I placed the colorful painting against a small table facing the door.

"When Fernando entered, his eyes widened and they were all over the Van Gogh. It was as if he saw nothing else. He went closer to get a better look. He examined it, fingering the brush strokes, and as he was looking at it, I snuck up behind him. I had to do what I had done to so many others before him, but my hand trembled as I held my silenced luger to the back of his head. I fired twice, then a third time until he fell to the floor. His blood splattered all over the Van Gogh and onto the plush white carpet. I put my jacket over my bloodied shirt, hung a 'Do Not Disturb' sign on the doorknob, and left."

"And the painting with the blood? Did you take it?"

"No, it was only a copy worth a few Argentine pesos."

"So, it was over between you and Fernando?" Michael said with an inner smile, knowing that Stern would not see the humor. Michael was surprised by his answer.

"Not quite," Stern said, shaking his head. "Not nearly. I knew that after Fernando's body was found, his friends would come looking for me. But even before I conceived the idea of killing him, I had already planned to get out of Argentina and into

Paraguay, which also provided a safe haven for Nazi officers. Hilda, the girls, and me were ready to leave until a friend approached me and said that five Americans were killed in Buenos Aires for their passports. Four of the passports were brand new, with not one stamp on them. They were worth a fortune. I was amazed that the man gave them to me as a gift and thanked me for connecting him to the bishop when I was in Rome. I had the passports altered and now had another new identity. I used them to come to America and we settled in Oneonta."

Michael stared in disbelief as his mind raced.

There was no way he could get into the States that easily. There were no ratlines to America.

"Is that the truth, Hans? That last part about how you got to the States sounded kind of shaky."

Stern looked down at his knees and closed his eyes.

There must have been a lot of money passed and a few dead bodies along the way for Stern to get here. I'll let it rest. For now.

Chapter 16

The next morning, Michael woke up exhausted. Stern had revealed some truths about what it was like to be a Nazi officer, but he never expressed the way he *felt* about having the power to kill so many people.

There was no remorse for sure. Jews were vermin to him. Did he feel nothing?

Stern was a vicious killing machine, specializing in killing Jews, but now Michael had a taste for blood...Stern's blood. When Stern killed Jews, it was part of his day's entertainment, and he was all business in his role as an executioner. Now the power had shifted. There was a new Jew in his life, *his* executioner.

Michael prepared a cheese sandwich for Stern and returned to his courtroom in the garage.

Stern had his eyes shut. He was still partially covering them with his right hand, always protecting them from the bright lights.

His eyes fluttered open and Michael enjoyed watching him wake up and squirm in his own soggy feces. Michael held his nose and backed away. The real trial had not yet begun.

Stern said nothing, but Michael observed that the handcuffs kept his left shoulder pressed too firmly against the pipe, preventing him from slumping over when he slept. It was important to protect Stern's wrist from leaving handcuff marks. Michael carefully went behind him to pull the handcuff over his shirt sleeve.

Stern was awake but appeared pale and sad. Dark circles framed his eyes. Strands of greasy hair hung to his nose, red and runny from the overnight chill. His unshaven face showed a reddish-blond beard after only four days in captivity. He had little opportunity for movement, but having his right hand free fulfilled a few of his needs. The air inside the garage reeked of a mixture of old urine and something burning. That, combined with Stern's repulsive body odor, made it unbearable.

The smell was too much for Michael, but he felt it was worse for Stern because he had to endure it twenty-four hours a day. One thing Michael did give him was copious amounts of water. Stern was grateful for it, but he had to pay a price. Fresh urine constantly soaked Stern's pants and flowed onto the garage floor. Michael opened the rear door of the garage to let in some fresh air.

"I have told you so much," Stern said. "And you have said nothing about yourself." There was a challenge in his eyes.

"We will get to that when I feel the time is right," Michael said, acting indifferent.

Michael kept up his incessant questioning.

I must know how a Nazi officer thinks. Wear him down. Make him wait like he made the Jews wait, standing body against body on the train to Auschwitz. In the heat of the dark cattle cars, with no food or water, the clickety-clack sounds of the wheels on the tracks pounded into the ears of the doomed passengers.

Forced to step in each other's excrement, they endured the smell of sweat, urine, and feces that permeated the air they tried to breathe. Covering their mouths and noses didn't help. Sometimes they would hold their noses to get a few seconds of relief but only have to pay for it a moment later with deeper breaths.

The Jews didn't know what would come next. Many died in puddles of their excrement.

Stern had to sit in his.

"One thing is bothering me, Hans. What happened to Hoess? He was the commandant. Did he slip through the cracks?"

"No, he never got away, but he tried. I actually know the truth about him told to me by a reliable friend. He got the hell out of Auschwitz as the Red Army approached in 1945 and went into hiding. He was tracked down by a German Jew and eventually fell into the hands of the Polish authorities, who hanged him outside the entrance to the gas chamber. Then my friend told me something interesting that was previously unknown to me." Stern paused.

Michael leaned forward. "I'm listening."

"Before he went to the gallows, Hoess revealed that he had been ashamed of being weak-kneed when he pushed hundreds of children into the gas chambers, until Eichmann explained to him that it was important to kill the Jewish children first so they would never be allowed to reach adulthood and take revenge in the name of their parents."

"I'm sure there are some children still seeking vengeance for their parent's murderers, even today in 1970."

"For them, if they were seeking revenge it would be necessary to do it outside the law, or they could be punished. The law is not always forgiving."

Michael put his head down and whispered to himself, but Stern heard him. "Killing the children first to prevent future vengeance? That's unthinkable." Michael sobbed, and added, "Hoess felt weak-kneed and was ashamed of feeling that way? The bastard! What shame did he feel about gassing children in the gas chambers and stuffing them in the crematoria?"

Hoess was another monster who should have never been born.

Michael took a deep breath. "And Himmler, what happened to him?"

"Himmler, the head of the SS Police, disguised himself in a sergeant's uniform and wore a patch over one eye, but it was his own comrades who turned him in to the British. He found a way to commit suicide to avoid standing trial."

"How do you know all these details? Not everything was in the newspapers. I didn't know about the patch. Are you not telling me everything about yourself?"

"I learned these things from other Nazis who liked to talk. We only had each other and talked only about the war, years after we escaped and were free. It made us bond together. We had no other friends. I don't know, maybe some of the information were rumors. Please let me clean myself up. There is no need for me to sit in my crap. Please," Stern begged.

***

Michael pondered the insanity of the Nazis and their hunger for killing. He imagined the ones who escaped to Argentina, sitting together around a table, drinking German beer, laughing and talking about the old days when they murdered millions of people.

For Hitler, it was not just about power. It was revenge he was after. He had to get even for how bitterly Germany was treated after World War I. They were blamed for the war and had to pay reparations to the victors, which would have taken Germany two hundred years to pay off.

"It was the end of the war," Stern had said. "It was an armistice, which meant the countries should've just stopped fighting. Germany should never have had to pay reparations. Hitler was never able to forget the humiliation that German people had to feel. He would get even for them."

Those were Stern's words.

He always had a reason to side with Hitler. How did he become this angry, evil man? Who created this animal? Was it in his genes? He craved power and maybe learned his evil ways from the corrupt thinking of the National Socialist Party. It was easy for him to become part of the nefarious scheme to destroy Jews and so-called other undesirables, then create the superior Aryan race and conquer the world. That was him, all right. Stern fit in.

Michael believed most of the German people supported Hitler. He didn't *seize* power. He was elected to it. They cheered him on as he created a new Germany full of hate and anger. Mass insanity was everywhere.

Michael was convinced that the German people *knew* what was going on, but closed their eyes to it. They ignored the sound of marching boots and loud banging on the doors of their neighbors who mysteriously disappeared into the night. Didn't they question where their neighbors went? Or did they know and wanted to be part of the new Germany ruled by a madman?

In the late thirties, the German people understood that no German was allowed to purchase anything from Jewish businesses, and Jews were excluded from certain professions and could no longer attend a university. They had to be separated from Aryan life. The Nazis found the Jews, rounded them up, and sent them to concentration camps. The German people followed those rules and most never questioned them. Michael wanted to know more.

"Hans, how the hell did the Germans figure out who was Jewish?"

"The truth is that most of the Jews made no secret of their identity. I could never understand why. I would have run."

"Yeah, I could see *you* doing that. I want to hear more."

"We also depended on informers. People had to prove they were not Jewish by showing church affiliation and baptism certificates. This may surprise you, but even your country's IBM was complicit in helping the Nazis commit systematic genocide of the Jews by allowing them to use their punch card system to find them."

"The Nazis may have had good methods to find Jews, but I don't think an American company like IBM would be involved with the Nazis," Michael said with authority.

"It's true. They were! I don't want to make an issue of it. You are in control, but companies such as Chase Bank and other financial institutions supported the Nazis. And Ford, old man Henry Ford, was the most notorious anti-Semite of all, along with your hero Charles Lindbergh. They were both awarded medals by the German government. Kodak was another company. They did not just make cameras and film. They made detonators and supplied the German military with them."

Michael was silent.

Why wasn't the world crying out against these obscene acts? It was an insane time. When Hitler came to power, those who challenged him were the first ones killed. They were the brave ones, the real heroes that we never knew, who now sleep quietly. Where were the voices?

Damn! Where were the voices?

Michael sat against his Chevy. Stern was a mess. His eyes bulged with red rivers of broken blood vessels, and he appeared drained. Michael pressed his lips together and stared at him. He had to get into Stern's head, a head filled with anger and hatred. He had the blood of thousands of innocent human beings on his hands. But, here in Oneonta, he masqueraded as an average man, living a quiet life in a small town. No one would suspect his secrets. His violent crimes were well hidden. He fit in so well.

If they only knew.

Michael stared at Stern. He was slumped over. His chest heaved with every deep breath as Michael shook him.

"Hans, it's hard for me to believe that a once civilized culture such as Germany, the land of Goethe, Schopenhauer, and Nietzsche, could commit these atrocities against human beings."

Stern shrugged.

"Was Germany an enlightened society gone mad?"

Stern spat out bitterly, "Don't say that! You must—"

"I *must* do what?" Michael said, digging his finger into the tip of Stern's nose.

Stern lowered his voice to a whisper. "It was not the way you think. Times were bad for Germany after The Great War. We were humiliated, forced to pay money, and we were only allowed to have one hundred thousand men in our army. When the Führer came to power, he overcame the chaos, created a strong economy, built roadways, reunited a crushed people, and, of course, rearmed the nation's military to over six hundred thousand men to become the strongest force in the world. Even Hitler was surprised that the formation of his new powerful military was never challenged," Stern said proudly. "Hitler laughed at Chamberlain after he signed a treaty with Britain stating that Germany would not be involved in any war and laughed again when he saw photos of Chamberlain waving the agreement in front of the British people, exclaiming that now we would have 'Peace in our time.'"

Michael shook his head. "Germany did get screwed after World War I. Hitler took advantage of that and hurt the German people even more. Using rhetoric, he made himself the spokesman of German longings and made them feel like victims and they bought it. Millions turned out in droves to cheer him as their savior. After the war ended in 1945, the Allies took a different course than they had taken after the First World War. America helped rebuild Germany and other European nations into thriving economies using the Marshall plan. Think of it, Hans. We won the war. Then we helped Germany get back on its feet. What would have happened if you won?"

Stern jumped in. "If we won, *all* the nations of the world would have thriving economies, like we had in Germany. Dictatorships are the most efficient forms of government. Just think of how long it takes to get anything done in your country. It takes forever to get a bill passed in Congress. When Hitler saw the problem, he made a decision and it was done."

"Interesting, Hans. You see things in a different way. Well, it didn't take the United States long to develop the atomic bomb. We saw the problem, made a decision, and it was done. Maybe we're just smarter than you."

"We almost had an atom bomb. If we had it, we would have won. We could also have won if we didn't invade Russia. It was over for us at Stalingrad. We couldn't beat the Russians and the Allies at the same time, but I believe that if Hitler could have arranged for the Japanese to invade Russia, we might have had a chance. And England, we should have invaded them. They would have fallen easily, and then there would have been no D-Day."

"Those are a lot of what-ifs. The bottom line is that we won and *you* lost."

Stern took a deep breath, clenched his lips, and said nothing. There was silence for a few moments until he uttered a few words.

"You know, the Third Reich's policy on Jews was not all bad. There was an SS officer, Leopold Von Mildenstein, who supported the Zionist movement to send the Jews from Germany to Palestine. They would have their own country and freedom. They didn't have to die and Germany would rid the country of Jews."

"Why?" Michael asked. "Because they were sub-human devils with horns?"

"No!" Hans shouted. "We wanted them out because the Jews had beliefs that were different from German ideas, and because they believed differently, we thought it would be best if the Jews moved to Palestine and shared their common beliefs in their homeland.

"I read a series of articles written by Mildenstein who praised Zionism, saying it would be a great benefit to Jews and the world."

"That's bullshit. They were different from the Nazis all right. The Jews were smarter and found their own homeland after the war, Israel. They built a civilized nation out of the sand. Your understanding of history leaves a lot to be desired. Let's talk about someone you really knew, Adolf Eichmann."

"Yes, I knew him, but not well, and I never spoke to him in Argentina, even though I knew where he lived," Stern replied. "Most people do not know that, before the war, Eichmann was in Palestine with Mildenstein. They negotiated with the Hagana leaders to accept Jews from Germany into Palestine. It didn't work out, but Eichmann was in favor of the Zionist movement."

"Yes, for all the wrong reasons. To get rid of Jews. Well, now the Jewish people have their own homeland, Israel, a country that has contributed so much to our civilization in medicine and technology. They have one of the best armies in the world to protect themselves from threats by neighboring countries. If the surrounding countries lay down their arms, there would be peace. If Israel laid down their arms, there would be no Israel."

Stern was silent.

"Since we're talking about Israel, Hans, what about the Eichmann trial? Did you follow it? I saw him on TV in the bullet-proof glass booth in Israel, chanting the 'we were only following orders' bullshit."

"I have watched him in that box in Israel, too, with great interest in 1961. He should never have been tried there because Israel wasn't even a country when Eichmann was accused of crimes. It was an illegal trial."

Michael shook his head. "I don't think that's an issue. What he did was a crime against humanity. There was nothing that could be done to punish him for his crimes. All Israel could do was hang him."

"Michael, did you read what the famous writer and philosopher, Hannah Arendt, thought? And she was a Jew. She said Eichmann was incapable of thinking when he committed the acts he did and was not aware that the consequence of non-thinking was genocidal. Eichmann was not at fault for any killings. He was not in his right mind."

"That's nonsense and a naïve claim. Pure bullshit. Eichmann knew what he was doing. You're a good follower and you question nothing. You're a sheep, Hans, a sheep. I read her book. She wanted to sell them and counted on sensationalism as a marketing ploy. She made the animal Eichmann into 'Mr. Nice Guy' who she said had no concept of what he was doing. She didn't understand that the real Eichmann was a fanatical anti-Semite."

"Eichmann said that he had to obey the rules of war and his flag. That is what every soldier in the world does," Stern said steadfastly.

"Not if the rules of war relate to unjust and illegal orders!" Michael snapped.

"We never questioned whether our orders were legal or illegal. Soldiers do not do that. We just followed them or we would be killed," Stern replied weakly. "Survival comes first."

"Tell me, Hans. Do you think that if I was ordered to shoot and kill a group of innocent men, women, and children, that I would do it?"

Stern took a deep breath and looked down at his knees. He stroked his chin with his right hand as he pondered. "I have come to know you. I do not think you would do it."

"I wouldn't. It would not only be illegal and a crime against humanity, but my personal sense of decency would stop me from even considering it. No amount of force, *none,* could ever make me do it. You have a family, Hans. What if someone killed them and claimed they were ordered to do it? What would you think?"

"I wouldn't think at all. I would track them down and kill them," he said, lowering his eyes.

"But that would be an illegal act." Michael shrugged.

"I would have to protect the honor of my family. Nazis know the meaning of integrity. *Blut und Ehre* was inscribed on my boyhood knife. Blood and Honor," Stern shouted.

"Calm down. I would understand your need for vengeance." Michael paused. "Trust me, I do. But your action would still be against the law."

"There are some things that are above the law," Stern said, confidently.

Michael couldn't believe what he was hearing.

He has no idea I am going to kill him.

"Like what? Give me an example," Michael insisted.

"It would be a *just* thing for me to kill the people who killed my family," Stern said, opening and closing the fingers of his left hand, which were attached to the pipe behind him.

"What if it was someone of authority who killed them to prove something to himself or was told to do it by a superior?"

"Michael, there are some things that must be taken care of by a person in their own way. Under circumstances like that, it is the right of a human being to act in his own behalf. It is the right thing to do and is above and beyond the law. I know how you think, always following the law, doing what is right. I know you. That is very commendable, but irreversible acts of revenge ensure justice, which cannot be achieved in any other way. Besides, sometimes the courts are wrong and let the guilty get away. How would you feel if your family was killed and the person who did it was never punished?"

"You make a good point. I'll think about what you said."

"If you do, you will see the merit in what I say."

"So, do you still think the Nazi courts did the right thing by sending people to their deaths because of the anti-Semitic laws they had to follow?"

"I cannot say this enough. What else could the judges do? What would you do? They just carried out the laws. They had no responsibility for creating them, and they would be killed if they didn't. Why should judges be punished for following the laws of their country?"

"So, you're saying that the judges *would* be punished if they didn't adhere to reprehensible laws? What kind of justice is that? Why have trials at all? In America, it took a long time for us to see that certain laws were unjust, especially acts against minorities, but we fixed many of them and are still working at it. I take it that you believe that the anti-Semitic laws relating to Jews in Nazi Germany were just?"

"They *were* just because they were created by our Führer for several good reasons."

Michael scowled. "Like what?"

"We know that Germans are an Aryan race. It was proven. We are descended from advanced conquerors and are considered the strongest race in the world, physically and mentally. All blonde hair and blue eyes."

"Your *Führer* didn't quite fit that description. Your point?"

"Nazi laws called for only one leader. He would hold all the power, not like the democracy you have here. Democracies may not work in some countries. Some monarchies do good things for the people. But as I said, dictatorships get things done and are the most efficient form of government. No wasting time voting on bills in Congress and having them go back and forth for years. The laws in Germany were created so that we would have a strong economy, but we realized that our wealth would be threatened by Jews and communists. Jewish Bolshevism saw Soviet Communism as a Jewish conspiracy, which had grown since World War I. We did, too, and couldn't allow it."

"So, your dark-haired, brown eyed Führer had the Jews killed!"

Stern held off a moment. "Michael, since we met, I felt you have suspected me of being a Nazi. You were right. Maybe you took this drastic action against me to prove something to yourself or maybe to learn how a Nazi thinks. I am not sure, but I answered all your questions. I have told you the truth, and you agreed to let me go. You promised you would if I were truthful and I know you are a man of your word. You could have asked me these questions during one of our chess games, and I would have told you who I was. You didn't have to humiliate me like this. Will you please let me go?"

"I will, I promise you, but not quite yet. We need a little more time together."

"All right. When you release me, would you please allow me to shower in your house?" Stern begged.

"Yes, of course, after a few more questions. But first, let me ask if you have any questions for me."

"Questions, no, but I do have a concern. You said you allowed me to win at chess, and that I am an amateur. I have beaten most of the prisoners at Auschwitz. How could that be?"

"Ah yes, chess. Maybe it had something to do with your choice of opponents. They may have been fair players, maybe even amateurs like you, but they were already physically beaten, deprived of food and sleep, exhausted and in pain. Even *I* might have lost to you under those circumstances." Michael paused. "But I doubt it. Or maybe they, too, let you win for their own reasons."

Stern nodded. "I don't understand any of this. I thought we were friends. We were always so nice to each other. You played well. I thought we were a good match."

"You played poorly. You were no match for me. I let you win," Michael said, stabbing his finger at him.

Stern shook his head, "Okay, forget chess for a moment. I am trying to understand this. Did Hilda ever say anything about me?"

Michael took a deep breath and imagined Stern searching for answers to his dilemma, answers he would never find, just as the Jews could never comprehend that the unthinkable was happening to them.

Michael observed Stern tightening his lips and looking downward. His pants were soaked with urine, his shirt disheveled and wet with sweat, as he sat in his soiled underwear. His face was old and worn, a sharp contrast to the elegant, young SS officer dressed in his clean, pressed uniform and shined boots that Michael remembered at Auschwitz.

"I think about death too much, Michael," Stern said in a weak voice. "I do not know why. I don't want to die and I know it is not your intention to kill me."

"I didn't want to die either, Hans, but I died a long time ago, while you've lived."

Michael knew there were only a few moves left in this endgame. Things had to come to an end soon. He returned to the house, leaving Stern sweating under the glaring lights, and listened to *Swan Lake* again. Then he went to bed and fell into a deep sleep.

Chapter 17

It was a cool, sunny August morning. Michael showered, dressed in a short-sleeved shirt, and opened all the windows of the house to air it out before he went to the garage.

Stern's face was drawn and wrinkled. His eyes blinked rapidly and his hand trembled when Michael handed him a glass of water to take with his heart medication.

Stern looked up at him.

"I'm exhausted and can't last much longer like this. How can you allow me to be this way? It's inhuman. It humiliates me. I'm not an animal. It is time you let me go. I have told you everything you wanted to know."

When Michael didn't answer, Stern cried out, "Kill me, damn it, but until I know what this is all about, I'm not saying anymore."

Michael pressed his lips together. He looked at Stern and knew he had to begin the end game.

"Michael, do *you* have a different name? I think you do," Stern said weakly.

"My name is A11328. Take a look." He pushed his arm in front of Stern's eyes.

Stern stared at Michael's left forearm, wide eyed, then turned away and looked down at his knees. His free hand began to shake and he bit his lips. Stern took a deep breath and appeared to be faking composure.

Michael saw fear in his eyes as Stern looked up and spoke in a low voice. "I see you have been to Europe."

"I was born there and my name was Miklos."

"So, you are Hungarian?"

"Yes, I was born in a small town not far from Budapest."

"But you told me you were born here, raised by your European grandparents, and were in the army."

"I lied."

Stern bit his lips, looked down, and squinted at Michael's forearm again. He looked away and said nothing.

Michael sat against his car. He folded his arms in front of himself, breathing deeply. Then he got up and shoved his tattooed arm in front of Stern's eyes.

"Take a good look, Hans!"

Stern turned away. "I understand everything now. You have been to a concentration camp and when we met in the pharmacy, you suspected I was German because of my accent. You grew up in Europe, and it was easy for you to know I was German. It would not be that easy for an American who was born here." Stern shook his head. "I should have known. Now I understand how you felt. Some things trigger memories. You surmised I might have been a Nazi. You were angry and now you know what you guessed was true.

"But to do what you are doing now is extreme. I admitted I was a Nazi and told you the truth. I hope you are satisfied with my answers. So, now the game is over. My king is lying on its side. You have won and you have what you want. When it is the right time and you let me go, I will understand that we will no longer be friends."

"This *is* the right time. I told you my name was Miklos."

"Yes, Miklos Ross, I assume."

"Did you know an Ilona in Auschwitz?"

Stern felt pressured. "Damn it! Michael, enough!" he stammered, slapping his hand on the garage floor. "Stop asking so many questions."

"Did you or didn't you? Answer my question."

"I only knew one Ilona...Ilona Rosen. She had my baby."

"What? Are you crazy? What the hell do you mean *your baby*?"

"She is the mother of my daughter, Erika, born in the camp. What difference does it make to you?"

"What! Fuck you, Hans," Michael cried and slapped Stern across his face. "Stop lying, you pompous ass. *Your* daughter? I don't believe you."

"Why would I lie?" Stern asked, rubbing his stinging cheek.

"I met Ilona when she came to Auschwitz, and Erika was born before the Soviets came. When I first saw Ilona, I knew I had to have her. She was beautiful, but a fighter and would not obey. In the end, she did."

Michael flew into a rage. He began punching Stern in the stomach and slapped him across his face

"You bastard, you never knew any Ilona." Michael was beside himself. He put both his hands on Stern's chest, pushed him closer to the wall, and rammed his knee into his balls.

Hans grabbed his crotch and screamed, *"Was machst du? Bist du verrückt?* What are you doing? Are you crazy?" He held up his fist to Michael.

"All the officers did those things in concentration camp. We took the women we wanted. You would understand if you saw her. I hurt her when we first met, then she submitted to me without fuss. She was a beauty."

Michael held his head in his hands. Tears flowed along his cheeks. He tuned Stern out, letting him ramble on.

"After a month, she told me she thought she was pregnant. I had not done anything to prevent it, and I still had my way with her while she carried our baby. When the baby was born, I even enjoyed watching Ilona nurse her, my little daughter. I called her Erika, after my grandmother. Ilona added a middle name, Eva, but we couldn't keep an infant in the camp and I brought the baby home to Hilda. The next day, Ilona accidentally touched an electrical fence and was killed. When we got to Italy, the bishop arranged the proper papers for all of us. Why does this upset you? Did you know her?"

Michael was numb and drained. He sat on the floor, motionless, and cried, feeling Ilona's shame and humiliation as Stern forced his lust on her.

More tears fell along his cheeks.

***

Oh my God, Ilona! You must have been so terrified, so helpless...your body violated and infected with this animal's sperm. An evil man overpowering you, forcing you into submission. An electrified barbed-wire fence became your friend in that insane place. I'm glad you found your freedom. My heart aches.

I don't know how to be evil, Ilona. You know that. I'm trying so hard to dehumanize Stern but I realize it's not possible. He's already less than an animal. I can't bring him down any lower. It's not in me. I can only do what I can.

I don't know how to do it. Sometimes, I wish I had Stern's evil mind, just for a few moments, so I could know how to be cruel and inflict pain on him.

***

Michael held his hand against his heart and felt the erratic pulsating beats surge through his palm and the rest of his body. He didn't protect her. How could he carry this burden?

It had all happened so fast. The men in marching boots came out of nowhere and took their lives away. His pain would always be with him, but at least now this wild, insane beast was in Michael's power, handcuffed to a pipe and tamed.

Michael felt weak and pushed everything out of

his mind. He went into his car, leaned back on the seat cushion, and passed out.

When he awoke, he looked at Stern in the blazing lights, his chin resting on his chest. He walked back to the house.

In a daze, Michael opened a bottle of Rémy Martin and placed it on a coffee table. The room was dark except for two amber pendant lights that floated down from the ceiling on a thin wire. Its glow swept over him. His hand trembled as he poured the cognac into a snifter glass. Leaning back on the couch, his heart throbbed with pain and his eyes were wet with tears as he sat in the subdued light.

Stern never surmised that Michael was Ilona's husband. *The bastard made my sweet Ilona his whore.*

***

At least Stern will die like my little girls did, gasping for air. The Nazis killed them. I blamed Stern because he was one of them, an officer. My girls were gassed, but I could never kill Stern's daughters now. Ilona's daughter? Never!

Ilona, please don't feel you betrayed me. What you did was not an act of unfaithfulness. Our love was pure. You were a victim of the overpowering insane circumstances surrounding you. Everyone in the camp would understand that you did what you had to do, and they would also know why it was necessary for you to take your life.

Michael couldn't shake the image of Hans' filthy hands all over her body, torturing and raping her, the same hands he'd been looking at in the garage for days. His mind wouldn't allow him to escape his thoughts and run to a quieter place. The terror that Ilona must have felt was unimaginable and it consumed him. It must have been living hell for her, trapped and tortured with no escape. Michael could never know the truth of the horror she was forced to endure.

Everyone in the camp was caught up in the only truth they could see and feel. An abominable, bizarre nightmare. All the prisoners, including the Nazis, lived inside this insulated insane asylum, where torture and death prevailed.

Michael swallowed another glass of the Rémy, then another until he slipped into a deep sleep. He awakened a few hours later, still exhausted. All he could think of was Ilona's agony.

There was one thing Ilona and the other prisoners had in common. They'd lost control of their lives. There was no question that the power was in the hands of the Nazis, who demanded obedience. Ilona was forced to do their bidding just as they'd forced Michael and everyone in the camp to do the same. He thought of Stern's daughters again. His heart pounded.

Could I kill them? Kill Ilona's child? Kill Erika? Never!

***

The next morning, he went back to the garage.

Stern was slumped over, looking at his knees as sweat poured from his brow. Stern looked up at Michael.

"I am sorry to have upset you by telling you about that woman. She meant nothing to me. Had you seen me often at Auschwitz?" Stern asked, staring up at him.

"I only remember your menacing face mocking her as you threw my wife, naked and bleeding, out of the barracks while you stood in the doorway pointing, calling her a *shlampe*. You laughed. Yeah, I remember your cruel laugh."

"*Oh mein Gott*! Ilona was your wife?" Stern shouted, his hands shaking. "She was Ilona *Rosen*?" Stern bit his lip and looked away.

"And I am Miklos Rosen." Michael glared at him. "Do you remember what you did? Do you remember throwing her out, bleeding?"

Stern kept his head down. His hands trembled and his eyes were pressed tight as he spoke in weak, broken sentences. "I don't remember an incident like that." He paused. "Times were different then. It was a crazy world. If I did do it, it was at the beginning, when I first took her out of the women's lineup. I was trying to help her."

"Out of a lineup? You bastard! You chose the women you wanted to make your whores out of a lineup? You sick fuck! You took innocent women and made them subservient to your debauchery. Well, the war is over. You never were a man, only a coward. You ran along the ratlines to South America, like the rat you are."

"Michael, stop! Stop it now! I was only—"

"Don't give me the 'following orders' crap. Were you following orders when you raped my wife and called her a bitch? Was that one of your orders?"

"That was only when I first met her. Were you there? You saw it?" Stern asked, cupping his hand over his eyes.

"Yes!" Michael yelled, pointing his finger between Stern's eyes like a dagger. "I *was* there. I covered her body with my pajama shirt as she lay on the ground. She whispered and asked me why I didn't protect her. I had no answer and I keep that guilt deep inside me to this day. It was you, Hans! You! You destroyed her and made her take her life."

Michael hung his head and cried.

"You're the vermin, Hans Stern, you bastard. You took my life away, my family away, and tens of thousands of others. You are lower than a worm. You lived in America with your diamonds while my wife and three innocent little girls were dead. And thousands others. Damn you! For what? What did they do to you? Did they hurt you in any way, so you had to kill them?

"You didn't even know them. You didn't know their names, except for the fact that they were Jewish children. How sick is that? Why did you do it? To satisfy your ego? You evil scum! The sad part is that you don't even see yourself as a monster. How could you? You lived to satisfy your inflated ego. Killing and raping women was your entertainment."

Stern sat with his lips tight, looking down. He

said nothing and sat quietly as his urine poured onto the garage floor.

Michael breathed heavily. "You're so filled with your sense of self-importance. You thought of yourself as God, deciding who lives and who dies. A big shot SS officer. A major who had to prove that you were a supreme being over all mankind by killing innocent people, including babies," Michael said, shaking his head and sobbing.

"The world revolved around *you*, Hans. *You* had to satisfy *your* lust! Animals kill for a reason—food or protection, but you were lower than an animal. You killed human beings for the fun of it, you bastard.

"I asked you before. Were your orders really to rape my wife? Who told you to do that? Commandant Hoess? Another sick lowlife? Or did you think up those orders all by yourself so you could have your way with her? You lived for lust. I loved that woman. Were you ordered to send my three little girls to the gas chamber? Ilona took her life because she already knew she was dead after you tore her body apart and took her baby away. She just had to finalize it. And your Hilda's suicide? I made that happen."

"You? I don't believe it," Stern said, surprised.

"Trust me, Hans. It's true. She's dead, isn't she? She took her own life to get away from you, and I made it happen—me, Miklos Rosen from Auschwitz. Why do women run away from you and kill themselves? Did you ever wonder about it? I can count two, and how many others were there. Your daughters don't speak to you either. Did you ever wonder why? Did you rape them too, you animal? Maybe it was their only way to escape your clutches because they can't rub your filth off their bodies after you've contaminated them.

"Hilda told me about you when I met her in the park, and I told her it was all right to kill herself! She looked at me as a learned man who understood her pain and trusted my words. It was me, I made it happen. Did you ever beat Hilda? Tell the truth!"

"No, never!"

"You know you're lying. Did you keep raping Erika, your own daughter, sticking it in her until she had to run away from home? Hilda told me she's a dancer. Thank God she has music in her life. Maybe that's what kept her alive. Otherwise, she would be dead too. Do you know where that musical gift came from, Hans? I'll give you a hint. It didn't come from you. Tell me, did you get Erika pregnant too?"

Stern was silent.

"I'll tell you this. I know where your daughters live, and I promise you, I will kill them—gas them. Maybe it will help put Erika at peace the way Hilda is now at rest. Marlena will have to go too. Let her children suffer without a mother. Think of your girls lying dead, their eyes wide open, staring at nothing. They will die for one reason only. Because you're their father. It will happen soon, very soon!"

"But Michael, they are innocent."

Michael approached Stern, spit in his face, and watched his saliva drip down to his lips. "Yeah, they're innocent. You're right. They *are* innocent, but you know something, Hans? My girls were innocent too. They were *really* innocent. They were gentle and never harmed anyone. They were beautiful, sweet girls with everything to live for and so talented that they would have given the world a gift like no other, but you didn't allow the world to have that gift. You stopped it all from happening."

"I am not that evil man you describe. Times were..."

"Shut your mouth. You were a Nazi and Nazism was organized evil. Your girls at least lived until they were adults, but their lives will be over soon. I promise you that and it will give me pleasure to do it. Your girls have been infected with your genes and are probably evil too. Trust me, you know me as a man of my word. I will gas them. Both of them."

Stern took a deep breath. "Stop, just stop. I didn't do anything that..."

"Fuck you, Stern, you stupid bastard. Killing you is too good for you. You deserve to be tortured to death, your head slowly tightening in a vise, and a large knife slammed through your hands so you can watch your blood pouring out. Or I could leave you here to die handcuffed to this pipe and let you starve to death in your pile of shit."

Michael looked down and lowered his voice.

"You see, keeping you in squalor and making you live in your own shit is small-time punishment for the torture you inflicted on others. I'm not a master like you and don't know how to inflict pain the way you do. I tried hard in your case, but I don't know how to be evil. Not even to vermin like you.

"For me, killing is wrong, but I would make an

exception in your case, the way Israel excluded Eichmann from Israeli laws against capital punishment. He was hanged. He was evil and you're no different. You know something, Hans? The animals that roam the forest have a dignity about them, and they are beautiful. You're a member of the lowest life form. You kill for pleasure and you don't belong in their company."

"Michael, I know there is nothing I can do for you to change the past, but I have a great deal of wealth in money, diamonds, and art works. I would give them all to you, and you could start a foundation to help the victims of the..."

Michael stepped up to Stern, grabbed him by the shoulders, and banged his head against the wall. "You don't deserve to live, you scum, but I will allow you to stay alive. Sign this paper. It's an admission that you killed my wife and daughters and others in Auschwitz. I just want to have it and never see you again."

"But it might be used to put me in jail."

"It's up to you. I give you my word that I will not use it against you."

"I will sign it, but I will say it was forced on me."

"Yes, you could say that and it will probably keep you out of jail."

Stern signed the paper, gave it back to Michael, and looked up at him.

"You are not going to kill me, are you? I am sorry about Ilona. Those were different times."

"You called the shots back then, and I agree, times *are* different now. I won't kill you. It's too

135

bad that the death and suffering you caused others doesn't haunt you, but that's understandable. You enjoyed shooting them in the head from behind. That was amusement for you. You don't have a conscience, but I'll let you live."

"So, I can take a shower?"

"Yes, of course. You've said what you had to say and you were honest. You at least deserve a shower. Think about it—warm, clean water flowing over your body. All the excrement, sweat, and filth washed away, but you could never be clean, Hans. You were dirty when you were born and always will be. Yeah, I'll let you bathe, but first let's clean you up so you don't contaminate my shower."

The stench surrounding Stern was unbearable. Michael donned a surgical mask to cover his mouth and nose as he hosed away the urine and feces. He pulled Stern's clothes off, except for his shirt, and washed and dried them in his machines while Stern lay handcuffed and half-naked. Michael gave him his heart medication with some water. Stern showed a confident smile.

"There, doesn't that feel better?" Michael said in a relaxed manner as Stern put on the clean clothing.

"Yes, thank you, Michael. And my shower?"

"In a few minutes."

"I know how you feel about me, and I am glad you are more understanding now. I was too young when I met Ilona. Hitler made us all feel powerful. For Germans, it was about revenge. We got screwed at Versailles, and we had to get even with the countries that made life impossible for us. Hitler showed us the way. We were going to take over the world. The Third Reich was supposed to rule for a thousand years. I promise you I will disappear and we will never see each other again."

"You're right about that. We will *never* see each other again. Lying in squalor was too good for you. I have to speak for my family."

Stern remained quiet and appeared to be relieved. "What about my shower?"

"I always keep my promises, Hans, just not to you."

Michael got into his car and turned on the engine. Gasoline fumes filled the garage. Stern screamed, "*Mein Gott.* What are you doing, Michael? Stop playing these games. What about my shower? *Was machst du?*" Stern yelled, coughing.

Michael kept his mask on.

"Imagine yourself in the shower, looking up and expecting nice, warm water to come out. You waited and waited, and then...well, you know the rest."

Michael coughed, turned off the circulation switch, and closed the garage door behind him.

Chapter 18

It was over. Michael walked into town, dazed and shaken. There was a slight drizzle in the air. Most of the stores were closed. Only the amber glow of the streetlamps remained lit. Everything was peaceful, a glaring contrast to the violence that had taken place earlier.

A few pedestrians passed him with a smile and a nod. They could not be aware of what Michael had done. Within minutes, two police cars, an ambulance, and a fire truck sped by, their sirens screaming into the night air.

Michael's hands trembled. His heart raced. It took him fifteen minutes to walk back to his house. Red lights flashed around him as firemen with Scott air packs on their backs emerged from the open garage door. Michael made his way through the crowd and told the police at the barricade that he lived there. He asked what happened.

"A man was found dead."

"Oh my God," Michael said. "What have I done?"

Michael rushed toward the garage but was stopped by a young officer. He told the policeman, "I killed that man," as he turned to see Stern's bagged body loaded into the ambulance. "He murdered my family in Auschwitz."

The police officer handcuffed him, read him the Miranda rights, and escorted him to the police station.

Michael sat in the cell at the edge of his bed, deep in thought.

It's over. Killing Stern had lifted a heavy burden from Michael's shoulders. All he had to do now was wait and see how things would play out.

***

The next morning, at the arraignment, Michael asked for a conference with a lawyer and the judge provided a public defender to act on his behalf. After the prosecutor presented the case, the judge explained that he was charged with murder in the first degree and bail was denied.

On the advice of the public defender, Michael pleaded not guilty. Afterwards, the lawyer spoke to him privately and said that Michael's case was beyond his level of expertise. He suggested he seek private counsel, adding that the cost of a defense in a matter like this would be extremely expensive.

Michael was given a phone book and researched local attorneys. He made the calls allowed and met with several of them over the next few days. One in particular captured his interest and he asked her for a conference.

When he met Brenda Coleman, he told her why he killed Stern and the circumstances that led to it. She appeared to be a competent attorney and showed a strong willingness to help build a winning defense for him.

"It might be difficult, Michael, but I believe there is always a way."

Ms. Coleman graduated from State University of New York Buffalo Law School with honors in 1948 and entered into private practice, where she'd specialized in criminal law and procedure. She lived in Schenectady, about a one-hour drive from Oneonta, with her engineer husband and their two teenage sons.

Brenda was slim and in her mid-forties with sparkling brown eyes and dark hair. Michael saw an air of confidence about her, which made him feel she had a passion for winning difficult cases. She told Michael that she had been the defense attorney in hundreds of criminal cases, many of which involved negotiated pleas and included a large number of dismissals. Although she was a highly successful lawyer, she had never handled a high profile murder case.

The People vs. Michael Ross would be a new experience for her.

Michael liked her optimism and hired her. She returned the next day with her paralegal, Jeff Hartman, to discuss the case. Hartman was tall with dark hair and in his late twenties. He graduated from Bronx Community College and had worked with Ms. Coleman for four years researching case law.

Michael told Brenda about his family in Hungary and the sad events leading up to his immigration to America. Meanwhile, the *Oneonta Star* ran a screaming headline:

Oneonta Professor Arrested For Killing Hunted Nazi

Michael sat in his cell and spoke to Ilona.

My dearest, it's amazing how my lawyer's face looks so much like yours, with her high cheekbones and brown eyes. I think she will help us. Stern is finally gone. Thank God for that. I can't help but think of what our lives would have been like without him and all the other Nazis.

I think of our girls all grown up with children. Our grandchildren. Imagine that, small children for us again. They would love your cooking. The stuffed cabbage, the goulash, and, of course, your strudel.

Even if our daughters didn't grow up to be ballerinas, we would have a family full of love, maybe even here in America. I know it's only a dream for me, Ilona, but I can't help thinking about what could have been. It makes me so sad, but it's all I have.

The only gift I bring you today is to let you know that Hans Stern's death is behind us. I could not protect you at Auschwitz and I felt guilty about that. But I have killed Stern, the man who took our lives away, a small punishment for what he did to us.

I will be tried for the crime and maybe I will lose my case, but that doesn't matter. Perhaps it does in one way, which I will tell you about another time. I only want my trial to keep the memories of the Holocaust alive by punishing one evil Nazi, who was an example of most of the rest.

The world has to know what we and others have suffered. They could never imagine the horrors. The Holocaust, as we call it now, must not be forgotten. Some may say it never happened, but I doubt it. It was too horrible for the world to forget.

You would never understand it, Ilona, but there is a resurgence of anti-Semitism by a group called skinheads. Believe it or not, they still support the Nazi movement from years ago. Can you imagine that? They burn down synagogues and kill Jews even now, so many years later. Why? What did we do? Jews have contributed so much to our civilization, but that's the way it is. I want my trial to stand out as a beacon against inhumanity. You are always in my heart, my dearest. Our little babies are there too.

Chapter 19

Michael and his lawyer had their first in-depth meeting to plan the strategy for his defense. The trial was scheduled to begin in a few months, on November 2. He was escorted from his cell in Oswego Correctional Facility to a featureless room enclosed by stark concrete walls painted a somber gray. Michael sat across a table from Brenda and her paralegal.

"So, where do we go from here, Ms. Coleman?"

"Call me Brenda. We're going to spend a lot of time together, so let's keep it to first names. We'll just talk about the charges against you and develop a plan to challenge the prosecution and get you out of here."

"Just an overview?" Michael pulled his chair closer.

"Yes, you could call it that. We're allowed all the time we need in here. How do you see things from your point of view? What would you like the outcome to be? I'm sure you would like to go free."

"I would, but if I had to serve a long sentence, it

143

wouldn't be the end of my world. I do have a personal reason to want to go free, but the important thing is that I would like the trial to show the importance of the Holocaust so that it will never be allowed to happen again. I want to bring up Hans Stern and show why we must be vigilant against people like him. I *had* to kill him. He destroyed my family. There was no other way for me. In the name of my family, I had to kill him. So, we have to bring him up."

"I'm afraid we won't be able to bring Hans Stern into this case at all."

Michael leaned forward and hung his head. He paused and looked up, his eyes glazed with tears. He asked, "Why not?"

"Because he is not the one on trial here. You are, so information relating to Stern is inadmissible and irrelevant."

Michael felt shot down. *This is not really happening.*

"Why are you saying that, Brenda? I'm not concerned about what happens to me. I just want the truth told about how an evil man destroyed my family. I want it to be an important issue in my case and let it set an example for others to remember that we must be aware of those who threaten our civilization."

"I know, Michael. It *is* important, but it would be difficult to get him in. The law is the law, but maybe I can figure out how to do it. We can talk about that another time. My job as your attorney is to protect you and achieve the best possible outcome. We have to destroy every aspect of the prosecutor's case, every legal challenge, every medical issue and try to discredit the prosecution's witnesses."

"Does that mean we can't bring Hans Stern into this case at all, for *any* reason?" Michael asked in a low voice.

"We can't do it directly, unless the prosecutor brings him up and establishes a foundation, but that's unlikely. Stern didn't commit a punishable crime. You did. Maybe we can indirectly make him an issue, but my thinking now is to get a jury verdict that will find you not guilty. Juries can be fickle. Some jurors vote with their perception of the defendant rather than the facts relating to the case. If I wanted to convince a jury, I would say A, B, and C, and then give the reasons to support it. It would be natural for me to want to interpret the facts of the case and present them in a way so it would be in your favor. Lawyers do it all the time. In your case, try not to perjure yourself, and I don't want to know about it if you're going to lie. I will be able to put a spin on the facts, in my own way that will help you."

Michael looked down at the floor. "Is there anything we can do to bring my case to light? I mean, the facts about Stern and the Holocaust itself? That's what I'm interested in."

"Look, Michael, maybe because you want it so much it's difficult for you to understand *why* it can't be done. The trial promises to be high profile. It has already made national headlines. If you want to get out of here, you have to be part of the defense team and not try to bring the impossible into this case. Do you want to stay in prison, or do you want to listen to me?" Brenda asked in a cold tone.

Michael whispered, "Stern can't be brought in?"

Brenda shook her head and looked up in disbelief. She smiled and spoke softly, "No, we may not be able to do that. We don't live in a society where a person can decide who lives and who dies. We're a nation of laws. Whether Hans Stern is a good guy or bad guy doesn't matter. What you did was still murder."

"Okay, so what's our case?" Michael asked.

"I'm not sure yet, but I have some ideas. Based on the truth, you could be found guilty and go to prison for life. But our *interpretation* of the truth could make the difference. That's my job! There is a way out of this, and I will put every ounce of my strength and energy into your defense because I believe, for various reasons, you're legally innocent and your story should be told.

"I'll try to bring Stern into your defense, but it will be tough, and honestly, there's only a slim chance. When you told me about the idyllic life you lived with your family and how it was turned into tragedy by one man in Auschwitz, I sat mesmerized, in tears, not believing that Stern or any human being could be so cruel."

"Yes, it was a tragedy. I died along with my family." Michael lowered his eyes.

Brenda looked at him tearfully. "I put myself in your shoes and imagined it happening to *me*, to *my* husband and *our* boys. If I survived, I would have no life, and I might seek justice in my own way. Remember, I lived through the war years and was lucky to have grown up here."

"I'm glad I have you on my side." Michael touched the back of her hand.

"There is one thing we can try, and we may be able to make a strong case for it, although we would be treading on thin ice."

"Go ahead, tell me what you're thinking."

"I will, but hear me out. It's complicated. It might take a while for me to explain, but keep listening and don't be put off about what I'm going to say."

Brenda stood and walked around him, her head down as she stroked her chin, deep in thought. Michael sat quietly.

"We can plead insanity!" she said.

Michael looked straight into Brenda's eyes.

"No pun intended, but are you crazy? Forget it! No way! Everyone who knows me would never believe I'm insane."

"We don't need *everyone* to believe it. We only need to convince the jury. Listen, we plead insanity, which would normally mean that you didn't know right from wrong, but that's not the only ground for an insanity plea. I will make every effort to show that you acted in a manner inconsistent with normal human behavior when you killed Stern. There is a subset of the insanity plea, which is a departure from the notion of knowing right from wrong. It's called irresistible impulse. "

Michael remained silent, attentive to every word.

"Here's the deal. You were not able to control your urge to kill Stern. New York State uses a Model Penal Code test for insanity and, although we may be pushing it a bit, we can still make a case based on irresistible impulse.

"Basically, you were not able to control your impulse to do wrong. It was out of your hands. You were driven to kill Stern. That defense would give us a slim chance, very slim, but it's all we've got. However, this is one time where the burden of proof rests with the defense and proving it will be up to me. Not an easy task but I'm optimistic."

"So, you're going to say I was crazy with an emphasis on the idea that I acted in an uncontrollable way? Do think the jury will buy it?"

"I hope so, and the truth is, Michael, I buy it. I probably would do the same thing you did under the circumstances. Every man and woman on that jury is human. We don't have to win all of them over, just one.

"The *voir dire* is a process used by lawyers to question prospective jurors as to their backgrounds and their ability to make objective judgments. I would choose people who have had losses in their families, sympathetic people, Jews or Italians, perhaps. I would hope for a Holocaust victim or someone who had family or friends who were in a concentration camp. The prosecutor would object strenuously to that last part for sure, but you never know. We might even challenge the victim's cause of death. If we can prove his death was caused by something *other* than the charge against you, and that carbon monoxide asphyxiation was not the cause, we win!"

"And what would the prosecution be looking for in a juror?"

"I know David Weisman. He was the prosecutor many times when I acted as defense counsel. In this case, he will want jurors who are authority figures, CEO's, accountants, maybe even train conductors. More rigid people who follow rules and orders. Remember, Weisman is still a nine-to-five employee of the State and will probably be less emotional and more mechanical. I'm just guessing, but we'll be prepared. Weisman is a good prosecutor."

Michael soaked it all up. "I'm getting an education in the law here. You never know, I may have a new calling." He blinked his eyelids several times in quick succession. "I have to be honest, Brenda. I thought about Weisman and the evidence against me. If I were the prosecutor, I'd relax. It would be an open and shut case for him."

"Michael, don't follow your calling. Winning cases is an art form."

"What *will* the prosecutor look for? Can you figure that out in advance?"

Brenda heaved a deep sigh.

"Each lawyer is going to have some idea of what will be presented during the opening remarks. I know Weisman's style. He will present the facts and evidence of the case, explain why you're responsible, and then ask the jury to find you guilty. He likes to keep things simple."

"I see. So, you'll present your opening statement the same way and ask the jury to find me not guilty?"

Brenda smiled. "Close, but no cigar. Keep your day job. I want the jury to use their imagination and put themselves in the defendant's shoes under similar circumstances. I always add some emotion during my remarks and keep the jury thinking about their own feelings and how they might react as the defendant. I have to tell you something. Being a woman helps."

"I see. By the way, I do have friends who could testify on my behalf, other college professors, people who know me at work, who would say that I'm a person of integrity, honesty, and..."

"Michael, I'm not going to present testimonials. They don't mean anything and will only send a message to the court that we're reaching because we don't have a solid witness list."

"Who will we bring?"

"Our witnesses will include a psychiatrist, someone I know very well, who will present an in-depth evaluation of your state of mind on the night of August sixteenth. I will probably bring a cardiologist and maybe you."

"I see. Who do you think the prosecutor will bring?"

"He will definitely bring in a court psychiatrist, probably Dr. Fisher, and the police officer who was first on the scene, but I'll have to wait until we exchange the list of witnesses. When I examine a witness, I try to plant the seed of reasonable doubt in the minds of the jury. Leave that part to me."

"You're a good lawyer, Brenda."

"Thanks. A lot will depend on what the judge will allow, how well our expert witnesses can convince the jury, and how effective our cross-examination will damage the prosecution's expert witnesses. It's complicated, but I want you to know I'm putting my heart into it."

"Have you ever used this strategy before?"

"Never."

"And you've never tried a case like this one either?"

Brenda shrugged. "Right, never this high profile, and I have to tell you up front, Michael, the judge may not allow any of this, but if he does, we have a shot. Because it's a murder trial, the judge may allow more latitude on both sides.

"Also, because the judge is aware that I have never handled a high-profile murder case like this before, he might ask for a second chair. It means the judge will want an established lawyer to sit with me and help with the defense. It could work well for us and will help the judge too. It will protect him in the event of an appeal claiming you have an inexperienced lawyer."

"What happens if he doesn't allow any of it?"

"I haven't thought about that yet. You want to go over the strategy in more detail?"

"Okay, I'm listening."

"You killed Stern. That's a fact. You admitted it, but entered a plea of not guilty. If you didn't enter that plea, this trial would not be going on. I will prove that you were driven to take Stern's life based on the fact that you acted in an impulsive manner and had no control over what you did. It was not possible for you to resist your impulse to kill him, so you had no opportunity to understand any consequences. We want the court to assign responsibility for your action to mental illness, even though you are able to distinguish right from wrong. I'm speculating, but it may also be a chance to get your Holocaust story told through you or the witnesses. The whole case might explode in the newspapers and it could capture the interest of millions of people. We have television now. News travels fast. That could be good for our side. Gets public sympathy." Brenda smiled and said, "If it doesn't backfire."

"Who is *our* expert witness?"

"We bring in a psychiatrist who will testify on your behalf by giving *reasons* for your action, and if the judge allows, bring out the events about how this evil Nazi officer had destroyed your life by gassing your innocent little girls and torturing and raping your wife until she had no choice but to kill herself. But no promises on getting those things in."

"Yes, I loved my family so much. Now, I have nothing."

"A psychiatrist may view things in a way that could help our case. Even if it's never proven that Sanders is Stern, you *believed* him to be Stern and the psychiatrist may show that this 'delusion' brought on your irresistible impulse to commit murder.

"He may also conclude that you suffered mentally as a result of what happened to your family in Auschwitz, and despite the fact that you've gone on to live normally, you have never married again or had any relationships, proving that your mind is still stuck in the past. We can win our case by a preponderance of evidence. We have to put enough pieces together and create a picture to convince the jury."

Brenda was unsmiling and all business.

"David Weisman is a prosecutor with a creative legal mind," Brenda said. "He's pretty damn good and will take this case seriously. Those who will testify will be on the prosecution's witness list. Our defense team will present our defense witness list as well, and the attorneys will share this information and other things during the discovery.

"Weisman may even have his own reason to bring Stern into the case. You never know, but I doubt it. It would put him on a slippery slope. If he does, then we have the foundation we need to continue testimony about Stern and the Nazis. I don't want to base our case *only* on speculation about how Weisman will proceed in this case. I have to focus on *our* strategy that will get you out of here."

Michael said, "I never planned to plead insanity. The truth is, I think I *did* have an irresistible impulse to kill Stern when I first met him. I started baiting him for a while before I..."

"Stop right there! We will leave that part out. You *never* baited him! You were *never* lying in wait. You *never* planned to kill him. There was *no* premeditation.

"He came to your house to play a friendly game of chess and you knew he was the monster who killed your family. That's it! You felt this uncontrollable impulse to kill him. Your heart was skyrocketing off the wall, and you knew you had to kill him the moment you realized that Sanders was Stern. What you did was uncontrollable, irresistible.

153

You knocked him out, handcuffed him to a pipe in your garage. You turned on your car engine, closed the garage door, and left. You were obsessed. It could have taken only a few minutes."

Michael blurted out, "I intended to report it when I was in town, until I heard the sirens and rushed home."

"Yes, you did. That was the moment we'll say you returned to sanity. So, what do you think?" Brenda asked with a smile.

"It's all so complicated, but are we telling the truth?"

"It's the story I remember you telling me."

Chapter 20

Michael's cellmate was Albert Chisholm, a black man, about seventy, with white hair and a short, cropped beard, yellowed with tobacco stains. Chisholm already owned the bottom bunk. Fair enough, since he was there first.

Michael taught Albert how to play chess and, in return, Albert told him one story after the other about his escapades growing up in Alabama. Most of his stories involved petty crimes, but now he was awaiting trial for something serious—attempted murder. He shot a man who raped his twelve year-old granddaughter. He wanted him dead, but only wounded him.

"My little girl was never the same again." His eyes filled with tears. "She started wetting the bed and sucking her thumb."

"I'm so sorry," Michael said, looking into his cellmate's watery eyes. "You did the right thing. How much time do you think you'll get?"

"I know I'm going to end up with a long sentence. You know how it is in this country. Black is bad if you're in the criminal justice system, and I don't have enough cash to get the best justice money can buy." Albert heaved a deep sigh. "I'd be lucky if I appeared before a judge like 'cut 'em loose Bruce.'"

"'Cut 'em loose Bruce?' You've got to be kidding. Who's he?"

"Oh, just a black judge named Bruce Johnson who hated cops and let a lot of black prisoners go free, even if they were guilty. The police hated him. They worked hard to make arrests, and when black defendants appeared in front of Judge Johnson, Bruce just cut 'em loose."

Michael smiled.

Albert explained that there wasn't any fairness in the judicial system when it came to black people, "especially for poor man's crimes."

"I don't understand. Are there poor man's crimes and rich man's crimes?" Michael asked.

"Oh yeah, there's a big difference. A poor man's crime is something like auto theft. For example, stealing an old three-hundred dollar jalopy would buy him two years in prison.

"For the rich white guy, there is a different kind of justice. He embezzles twenty million dollars using some pyramid scheme or stock swindle. What happens? A lot of people get hurt bad and lose their hard-earned savings that took years to accumulate, while Mr. Rich White Guy hides the money he stole. Rich white guy gets arrested, hires a high-priced legal eagle, and ends up with six months in jail. That's what we call 'easy time.' He comes out, grabs his money, goes back to his mansion or his villa in Europe, and soaks up the good life. To me, Michael, that ain't justice."

Michael shook his head. Albert is right, he thought. Discrimination was everywhere and there was no honor in the justice system. He thought again. Maybe the poor men had the honor but the rich guys had the system. Michael smiled to himself.

Would there be justice for me?

Michael looked at Albert's dark-colored skin. It was only a thin covering on his body. Everything underneath was the same for everyone, yet his dark skin made a difference to society and it could make a huge difference between life and death in court.

"'Liberty and justice for all' doesn't apply to me. It's just a lot of catchy rhetoric and doesn't have any meaning for me. The truth is, some people are just more equal than others, and money can change things for the better for a defendant, sometimes even for a black man. There's something wrong about that."

Michael wondered how his cellmate was able to adapt to such inequity. It was all about hatred because he was the 'wrong color.' His thin covering of black skin showed nothing of the sensitive and caring person he was underneath.

As if Albert could read Michael's mind, he asked, "How did you deal with hatred, Michael? You're a Jew, right?"

Michael hesitated. "Yeah, I always felt sorry for someone who is filled with hate. It's his problem. He has no life, no humility, but when his hatred destroys my life, my feelings about him change and

I become angry.

"I'm in jail because I killed a depraved Nazi. He murdered my family. People like him should have been exposed *before* they committed their crimes, but when it came to Jews, he was not seen as an executioner. Many felt he was doing a job that some viewed as necessary. Anti-Semitism is too widespread. I want to get the horrors of the Holocaust into my trial to let generations that follow know how a few extreme radicals can destroy so many. I know you understand. You've been a victim."

"We've both been victims," Albert said. "Hatred puts fear into people. When I'm alone in an elevator with a young white girl, I can see the fear in her eyes. She looks away. I know what she's thinking. Will I attack her? Rape her? I'm used to seeing that look in the eyes of white people. I mean, the color of my skin is obvious. It isn't like being a Jew." Albert smiled. "So, it's hate at first sight when many people look at me. And for you?" He paused. "It would take a few minutes longer. Jews don't wear their religion on their skin." Albert laughed.

"What about our noses?"

Albert smiled and shook his head. "Yeah, that's a dead giveaway." They both laughed.

"Some people look at my black color and it makes them see things that aren't there. I want to scream out, 'Hey, I'm just like you,' but I got used to the idea from the time I was knee high that I *wasn't* just like them. Michael, you could be in that elevator with the same young girl and everything would be normal for her. You might even end up in conversation. I have never experienced anything like that, never.

"I'm not a jailhouse lawyer, but I can tell you this. Bringing the Holocaust into your trial ain't gonna be easy. Out of a jury of twelve people, at least *one* of them is going to hate you, maybe more than one, not because of the color of your skin—they can see you're white—but because you're a Jew."

"Yeah, Albert, Jews are minorities too, but my gut feeling is they don't commit many crimes. I think young black men commit a disproportionate number of crimes compared to whites."

"That's true," Albert replied. "Did you ever wonder why?"

"Is it something in the black culture?"

"That's partly true. We've been beaten up so much from the time we were slaves that our culture *has* become violent. People who are oppressed rebel. It's natural. More of us have become defiant and end up in jail, but it's about being poor too. Poor people in crowded urban areas are more likely to become criminals regardless of race. I don't have the answers."

"It's sad," Michael said, looking down at his knees. "Hatred is always there, but money can still buy you a rich man's justice."

It was 10:30 p.m., time for lights out. The prison cells were plunged into darkness, but they were lucky to have each other for conversation.

Albert spoke in a quiet tone. "I'm sorry to hear about your family. I feel bad for you." He said he would pray for Michael and quoted a passage from his favorite book, *The Alchemist.*

"There is only one thing that makes a dream impossible to achieve: the fear of failure."

***

The next morning, Michael awakened and remembered a dream he had. He lowered his head to the bottom bunk and saw Albert lying on his back, reading a thick book he held above him: *Criminal Law Procedures.*

Albert peeked above the book. "I can see you're not up yet, boy," Albert said with a casual glance. "Your eyes are half-closed and you look like shit. What's up?"

"I had a dream."

Albert sat up and smiled. "So did Dr. King, Michael. Come on down here, I gotta hear this."

Michael climbed from his bunk and sat next to Albert. "You were in it," Michael said, pointing his finger at Albert.

"Well, that's a plus. I hope I'm the hero in your fantasy. So, come on, tell me. You want to get your mind going first, or do you want to talk about it before the dream drifts out of your head forever?"

"Okay, here goes. We were both in this jail cell, right? The one we're in now. Only the bars were a glossy white instead of black. You sat on a stool, reading as you always do, and I had my hands on the bars of the cell door, looking out." Michael paused, trying to remember what came next.

"My hands rested on the white bars for months as I looked through them. I held on to the bars until, for no reason, I *pushed* my hands against them, and I couldn't believe my eyes. The door sprung open, just a little at first, but as I pushed, they were wide open. I stood, staring. Nobody was there, no guards, no one. Everyone had disappeared. It was just you and me. I walked out and looked behind me. I stared at you as you continued to read a law book. You glanced up at me, then down at your book and remained silent. That's all I remember."

Albert said, "You know, Michael, if I had trouble falling asleep, I'd try to remember what you just told me." Michael laughed and rolled his eyes.

"Come on, let me know what you think," Michael said, leaning forward.

Albert put his hand to his beard and stroked it. "So, what do *you* make of it? What were you *feeling*?"

"You'll never believe this. When I stood on the other side of the bars, a feeling of serenity swept over me, just knowing I was free. I just stood there thinking that it was so easy. Everything went from bad to good. I thought I should have done it months ago. It struck me that the cell door was unlocked the whole time. What do *you* think of that?"

"Hey, you're the dreamer, professor, not me," Albert said with a shrug and a wide smile.

"I don't know." Michael hesitated. "I guess I was free all along but didn't know it."

"That is," Albert said, pointing his finger at Michael, "until what?"

Michael shrugged, not knowing how to answer.

"Damn, Michael! Until you tried something you *never* thought to do. You were finally ready and desperate. That allowed you to push the barred door open. You never expected it to open. What were you feeling? Tell me, professor, what were you *feeling* at the exact moment when the door opened for you?"

"I felt I could do anything, and I felt relieved and peaceful. I felt free."

"Okay, professor. So, before you felt free, you made your own prison."

"Yes, yes!" Michael shouted.

"Stay cool, relax. It wasn't the bars that imprisoned you. It was your *mind*. As far as the bars went, well, you just put them there."

"Why? Why, Albert," Michael pleaded.

"Hey, I'm no shrink. Maybe you felt some deep guilt about something that happened a long time ago. You imprisoned yourself for something you did or didn't do and built a jail for yourself to live in. It was about punishment, Michael. Guilt always has to be punished. I learned that a long time ago from bein' punished for my bad judgments."

Michael reflected on his last moment with Ilona. *What guilt did I bear? Why do I have to be punished?* He searched deeper.

Ilona asked me to protect her, but I couldn't.

"Okay, Albert, I made my own prison. I get it, but there must be more. Just let me know what you think."

Albert took a deep breath and leaned forward. "You *still* don't get it. Think about it. Your dream was giving you some good advice. It told you that whatever it was that made you feel this guilt had to end, or you could never be free. You had to have a change of attitude. I thought I changed mine and didn't end up in to jail for a few years. Then I shot that man and thought I needed another change of attitude, but you know what? I would have done it again and aimed better. So, you see, life is too complicated for us to think we can figure everything out."

"I don't know, Albert. The idea of the bars. I don't know…"

"*You* created the bars. The advice you got was that you finally had to take action and push the bars open. It was telling you to let go, but you had to be receptive to be able to hear it. Only when you were desperate and ready were you able to find the power to open the door. Before then, you were powerless. You felt free because you finally let go of the guilt and realized it wasn't your fault. You no longer had to endure the never-ending pain of what you did, whatever it was."

"I did let go of some of my guilt when I killed Stern. A weight was taken off me." Michael held his head in his hands. "Why am I alive? Why is it only me?"

"Forget the *why*. You did nothing wrong. You were a prisoner in a concentration camp. Evil men with guns surrounded you. You made a choice to survive in the hope that one day you would wreak vengeance on those who killed your family. Stop beating yourself up. You can't change the past. Tell me, what was *I* doing when you opened the cell door and walked out?"

"Nothing. You just sat there and continued reading and you didn't try to follow me."

"And why was that?"

Michael thought for a moment. "You were already free?"

"Bingo, professor. You got it! I carry my freedom with me wherever I am."

Michael smiled and stayed silent for a long time, deep in thought. "Why did I stand there for months before I pushed the door open?"

"Easy. As I said, you made your own prison with strong bars in your mind, and you were a tough warden, hard on yourself. Let's run through it again. The door was always open, but you weren't ready. Your dream told you that you had to wait for the right time to let go, so you stood for months just holding on to the bars, waiting. When you knew you were ready, you pushed on the bars and found your freedom. Your dream was a gift. Freedom is something you feel inside, wherever you are, but it can only happen after you let go of the guilt."

"Albert, fate must have brought us together. The things you said helped me understand that my feelings of guilt are unwarranted, but I still feel them."

"Here's the deal. You were a prisoner at the time. Did you feel you had a choice, a choice to survive? I think the reason for any of your inaction was to buy time until you found a way to help your family. You're human, and in the back of your mind you knew that anything you could do to help your family would most likely end with your death. It's hard to choose your own death."

"I would die for them."

"I know. I was just thinking out loud."

Michael and Albert sat on the bottom bunk, their backs against the wall, and talked. Their conversations were getting a bit deep for both of them, but Michael felt Albert had helped him see things in a new light.

Michael looked at Albert and smiled.

"Tell me, 'Dr. Chisholm,' why were the bars so glossy white in my dream. Did it have anything to do with racism?"

Albert laughed and kept laughing. He couldn't control himself and slapped his hands on his thighs. He pointed at Michael, shook his head, and continued to laugh.

"Racism?" he said as he wiped the tears from his eyes. "You think everything that's either black or white has to do with racism." Albert was hysterical and continued laughing. "Michael, you've..."

"What? What?"

"You've made my day. Racism, that's a laugh. Black and white are only colors, professor, or lack of color."

Tears flowed along his cheeks past a huge smile.

"Why were the bars glossy white, you ask? I have no idea, Michael, none! Maybe your dream painted them white so you wouldn't even think they were bars. Who knows?"

They sat on the edge of Albert's bunk, laughing in the hellhole of a prison, both free at last.

Chapter 21

November 2 was a cold day. A few snow flurries fell on Michael's defense team as they made their way through the crowd, led by two police officers who cleared their way. As they approached the Oswego Supreme Court building, there were shouts of good luck and reporters fought to get within earshot of Michael's lawyers but couldn't get close. Brenda and Jeff walked up the long row of steps, stone faced, toward the courthouse entrance.

There were other cries from the crowd. "You killed a man, take your punishment," along with a few skinheads who yelled curse words at Brenda and held signs saying, "Guilty," but they were soon shouted down.

As Michael awaited trial, he thought about the possible outcomes. All the pre-trial conferences and opportunities to plea out were behind him. The jury would be left with only two choices, guilty or not guilty.

At first, Michael was not concerned about how the case would end. He told Brenda that he could live out his days in jail by reading, listening to music, and maybe even writing a book—an autobiography. That would keep him busy, and besides, he was a people person and he would be surrounded by men who all had a story to tell. But deep down inside, he had a special reason to be free.

He knew now, after talking to Albert, that if he did have to serve time, he wouldn't allow prison bars to take away his freedom. He would always carry his freedom with him.

***

Court was in session. A corrections officer removed Michael's handcuffs and led him into the courtroom from a holding cell at 10 a.m. He was well-dressed in a dark suit and sat next to Brenda at the defense table.

"Thanks for the clothes, Brenda."

"I bought them brand new, wanted you to look good in court. Judge Jordon keeps three suits in his chambers, but they're not one-size-fits-all, so I had no choice. We don't want to lose this case because you wore baggy pants."

Jeff Hartman extended his hand, wished him luck, and said, "Keep the faith."

"Be optimistic, we have a good case," Brenda added.

"I thought you said it would be a tough one?"

"It will be, but the reason I have a good feeling about this case is that there is another bit of news."

"What?" Michael asked.

"Remember the court-appointed psychiatrist who

met with you several times?"

"Dr. Fisher? What about him?"

"He died on Friday in an auto accident. Weisman didn't ask to reschedule the trial for a later date and instead added the name of another psychiatrist to his list of witnesses, Dr. Morgan. The prosecutor could have asked to postpone the trial and have you examined by a new psychiatrist, but he didn't. We'll have to see what unfolds and deal with it then."

"Is that a good thing or bad thing for us?"

"I don't know anything about Dr. Morgan. I'm not sure if the judge would have allowed for a continuance anyway. Morgan may present a powerful case against you, but we can't know that yet. Weisman probably feels the prosecution has a solid case as it stands, and he wants to put this trial behind him. It's in all the newspapers, too high profile and stressful for the lawyers. Besides, Weisman is getting ready to retire. Let's see how things go. If I feel the judge is strongly on our side and the jury might not be, I may make a motion for a directed verdict."

"What does that mean?"

"It means that the judge decides to take the jury out of the picture and make the decision himself."

"Would he want to do that?"

"He probably won't, but you never know. It may not look good for the judge on appeal, even if it's allowed to be appealed. But we shouldn't be talking about those things. Let's stick to the basics. I don't want to make a lawyer out of you."

Michael looked around the courtroom. Every seat was filled. People whispered to each other.

Reporters were everywhere.

Everyone stood when the bailiff commanded, "All rise."

Judge Robert Jordan was about sixty-eight, a little overweight with white hair and a solemn face. He rustled a few pages on his desk and examined each one carefully. The jury walked in, led by the bailiff.

Brenda turned to Michael and whispered, "Stand up and face the jury."

Everyone at the defense table stood and looked at the jury as Mr. Weisman sat with his head buried in a folder. The courtroom was now silent. Michael watched the prosecutor rub his eyes as he approached the jury box to give his opening statement. He looked tired.

David Weisman was a tall man, average weight, about sixty with graying black hair and a serious demeanor. He graduated from Columbia Law School and became a felony trial attorney. He had conducted over one hundred jury trials to verdict and prosecuted twenty-five first degree murder cases.

"Ladies and gentlemen, my name is David Weisman and I will present the people's case against Michael Ross for the premeditated murder of Harry Sanders, who was found dead in Mr. Ross's garage on the night of August sixteenth, this year. The State's case rests on the fact that Harry Sanders died as the result of carbon monoxide asphyxiation brought upon him by Michael Ross.

"The evidence will show that handcuffs, belonging to the defendant, were used to shackle

Mr. Sanders's arm to a pipe in Michael Ross's garage. The defendant then proceeded to turn on the engine of his car, close the garage door, and leave Mr. Sanders to die.

"Every indication leads the prosecution to believe that Michael Ross's intention was to kill Harry Sanders, willfully and with premeditation. There is no question about it. After possibly baiting the deceased for a considerable time and then luring him to his home, Michael Ross caused Mr. Sanders's death with gas fumes from his 1960 Chevrolet in a closed garage. Those are the facts, facts that cannot be denied.

"The defendant, by his own admission, said he killed Harry Sanders in the manner described. He claims that the deceased was the man responsible for killing his family in Auschwitz concentration camp in 1944. We don't know if there is any truth to that, but it's not an issue in this case. The defense may argue that Mr. Ross had many reasons for taking Harry Sanders's life. However, it was all about revenge, ladies and gentlemen, pure and simple. Ross had the motive and the means with which to carry out this heinous act.

"Harry Sanders committed no. crime. The defense will say that his real name was something different. There is no proof of that. If the defendant felt that Harry Sanders truly killed his family, as he alleges, or was a war criminal, Mr. Ross should have reported it to the Justice Department. They have handled many of these cases.

"Instead, Michael Ross took the law into his own hands and he alone made the conscious decision to, unlawfully, take Mr. Sanders's life, a man with no criminal record, someone who has never hurt anyone. Taking the law into one's own hands cannot be tolerated in this country. No one has the right to decide who lives and who dies.

"Ladies and gentlemen, Michael Ross had no right to take a human life!

"Mr. Ross may ask you to believe that he killed Harry Sanders due to circumstances he claims were beyond his control. However, we will bring in witnesses who will prove that Michael Ross is competent and that he followed a well-conceived plan, with intent and premeditation, to kill Harry Sanders, an innocent person, who posed no threat to anyone."

Weisman paused, looked at the jury, and spoke in a softer tone, "Ladies and gentlemen, we have come a long way from vigilante punishments. We are a country of laws, laws that I, as an officer of the court, have the privilege and obligation to defend. Did the defendant have no other choice? Was there no other recourse but to kill Mr. Sanders?

"The motive for his action was revenge, plain and simple, and nothing else. What Michael Ross did was carefully planned, with the intent to kill.

"I will produce evidence, witnesses, and expert testimony that will support the facts and prove that the defendant in this case had the intention and tools to kill Harry Sanders in cold blood. And Mr. Ross killed him with total disregard for the law.

"Ladies and gentlemen of the jury, you are here in this courtroom to serve the law. You will be charged by the court to base your judgments on the facts and the law. I ask you to please put your emotions aside and act in the name of justice. Weigh the evidence and find Michael Ross guilty of first-degree murder.

"Thank you."

Mr. Weisman sat down, placed a legal pad in front of him, and folded his arms.

***

Brenda Coleman approached the jury. She wore a navy blue-tailored suit, black heels, and no jewelry, not even her wedding ring, except for a string of pearls visible under her jacket. Her only makeup was a touch of red lipstick. Brenda did not speak as she paced in front of the jury. She looked into the eyes of each juror, one by one, seven women and five men, and then introduced herself.

"Good morning, ladies and gentlemen. My name is Brenda Coleman. I am the defense counsel for Professor Michael Ross, and I feel privileged to represent him in the case before you today."

Brenda paused and asked, "What would you do if you answered a knock on your front door and saw a man standing in front of you, a man you realized was the person who murdered your family?" She walked past the jury box and stroked her chin. "What would you do?" She paused again. "How would you react? Would you be calm? Angry? Out of control?" She shook her head.

"Wouldn't you want to do something, *anything?* I might reach out and try to strangle him and not even remember that I did it. Some acts are the result of a strong natural impulse that human beings have and I think we can all understand that feeling.

"Imagine, for a moment, that a man deliberately ran over your young daughter and killed her, right in front of your eyes, as you watched her blood pouring out onto the street. What would you do? What would you be feeling? No one could ever imagine your trauma, excruciating pain, and the hatred you felt for the driver. No one could know how someone would react under those agonizing circumstances. Perhaps some impulse, hidden deep inside you, would erupt and *force* you to take action. If it were my child, after I saw my little girl was dead, no one would be able to stop me from dragging the driver out of his car and pummeling him. It would be reasonable for many to believe that I acted out of human emotion because of what I was feeling and why I had to act."

Brenda paced for a few moments, looked at the jury, and, in a voice just above a whisper, said, "And we're *all* human, aren't we?" She walked past the jury box and sighed.

"You heard Mr. Weisman's opening remarks stating what he hopes to prove in this case, but you only heard his side, and we all know every story has two sides.

"The evidence he will present against my client may seem overwhelming, but it's because the prosecutor has grossly misinterpreted the facts, facts that he hopes will lead you into making an unjust decision. Please don't let that happen. We all know that life, as well as facts, cannot simply be painted black or white. Sometimes a more accurate interpretation of the facts presents them in a new light, a light that is closer to the truth. Look deeply into the so-called facts that Mr. Weisman says he can prove. The truth is that Professor Ross took action consistent with his mental state at the time. His behavior resulted from the emotional and volatile circumstances he faced. His mental state drove him to act in the same manner many of us would under the same conditions. What he did was no different from what you might do if you opened your front door and saw the evil man who murdered your family standing in front of you.

"You will have to make a difficult choice, ladies and gentlemen, and in order for you to arrive at a just verdict, you must evaluate the facts and the law in a new light, a light shaped by the circumstances over which the defendant had no control. I will prove by the evidence supported by the testimony of expert witnesses that Michael Ross's action on the night of August sixteenth was consistent with his mental state at that moment and that he acted under compelling circumstances.

"Ladies and gentleman, this is the first murder case of such magnitude in which I have ever participated. I took this case for one reason and one reason only, to show that what happened in Michael Ross's life deserves to be heard."

Brenda took a deep breath.

"As a jury, you have been given a special honor by our society, a society willing to judge others by its peers. You have a major duty to perform in this courtroom, and you must judge a man whose life is at stake. It is your job to act in the name of justice, because from the beginning to the end of this trial, you *are* the law, and as such, I ask you to keep an open mind and find Michael Ross not guilty.

"Thank you."

Chapter 22

The prosecution called Officer Jack Baker to the stand, and he was sworn.

"Good afternoon, Officer Baker," David Weisman said as he thumbed through his papers. "Were you the first officer on the scene at 1824 Woodland Lane on the evening of August sixteenth?"

"I was," Baker said, leaning forward.

"What were the circumstances that brought you there?"

"It was in response to a call to the station. A man walking his dog passed the house in question. He was concerned because he heard the sound of a car engine running inside the closed garage and he went back to his house to call the police."

"What time did the station receive the call, and what time did you arrive at the scene?"

Baker opened his notebook. "The station received the call at 7:20 p.m. I arrived at 7:29."

"When you got to the address, what were your observations?"

"Flashing red and white lights were everywhere. Two fire trucks were there and an ambulance. I watched the firemen smash the lock out of the garage door with a sledgehammer, then they strapped on Scott air packs and entered the garage. I saw them turn off the car engine."

"Were you able to identify the maker of the car?"

"Yes, sir. It was a Chevy Bel Air. The registration showed that it was a 1960 model."

The prosecutor turned from the witness.

"Let the record show that a 1960 Chevrolet Bel Air belonging to Michael Ross was found in the garage."

Weisman asked Baker, "Then what did you do?"

"I was careful not to touch anything and I secured the scene to make sure no evidence was destroyed or tampered with. At 7:45 p.m., Dr. Warther appeared. He was the medical examiner. A few minutes later, crime scene investigators and a photographer arrived. After the fire chief pronounced the garage safe to enter, Dr. Warther examined the victim and declared him dead. The photographer took pictures of the victim and the garage. The investigators proceeded to collect evidence from the surrounding area."

"Then what?" Weisman asked.

"The medical examiner handed me a pair of surgical gloves and asked me to remove the handcuffs from the victim's left hand and secure the cuffs as evidence."

"Officer Baker, tell the jury how you were able to remove the handcuffs."

"I used my key to unlock the cuffs to release

him."

"You had a key that fit?"

"Yes, sir. Almost all police handcuffs have a standard key."

"I see. So, these were basic police handcuffs?"

"Yes, sir. They were handcuffs that police normally carry."

"Would you say it's possible for an average person to buy official police handcuffs?"

"Yes, police handcuffs and other restraints are readily available." Officer Baker paused, then added, "But in most cases, you have to prove you are in some branch of law enforcement in order to buy them."

A subtle flash of annoyance crossed the prosecutor's face before he asked his next question.

"What did you do with the handcuffs after you removed them from the deceased?"

"I put them in an evidence bag, sealed it, and marked it."

"Would you tell the court how the handcuffs you placed in the bag were protected from tampering?"

"I followed the chain of custody procedures. I gave the sealed evidence bag to the detective who arrived at the scene, and he signed the label on the bag, adding the date and time. Subsequently, the chain of custody records showed that the handcuffs were stored in a secure location in substantially the same condition from the moment they were bagged and labeled. The bag was given to Detective Jack Forrest, who signed for the bagged evidence and brought it to the court."

David Weisman held the handcuffs in his hands

and addressed the judge.

"Your honor, I would like to present the handcuffs in question that were on the deceased's wrists and placed in an evidence bag by Officer Baker." The handcuffs were shown to the judge and defense counsel and placed in evidence.

"Officer Baker, were any other people at the scene who were not first responders?"

Officer Baker looked down at his notes. "No, not until a man arrived on the scene, a few minutes later on foot. He was a man I knew as Michael Ross, a pharmacist at a local pharmacy in town. He approached the ambulance and briefly spoke to the medical examiner. Then he came over to me, identified himself, and said, 'I killed that man. He murdered my family in Auschwitz.'"

"He admitted that he killed him?"

"Yes, sir."

"Then what did you do?"

"Mr. Ross appeared dazed. I handcuffed him, read him his rights, and a patrol car escorted him to the police station for questioning."

"What happened next?"

"A police photographer took photos. Then I sealed off the scene and put up barriers."

"Were there any observations or thoughts that you had relating to this crime scene?"

"Just one. I was surprised to see Mr. Ross at the scene. Something didn't belong. He was well-known and held in high regard in the community."

Weisman clenched his lips and appeared disappointed in his response.

"Thank you, Officer Baker. Your witness,

counselor."

***

Brenda Coleman approached the witness and asked, "Officer Baker, how long have you been a police officer?"

"About six months, ma'am."

"So, you're relatively new to the job."

"I am."

"Is this your first murder investigation?"

"No, ma'am, but this is the first time I'm testifying."

Brenda Coleman smiled at Weisman, who gave her a resigned shake of his head.

"Thank you for your candidness, officer. Were there any designations or serial numbers on the handcuffs you removed from the victim?"

"Yes, there were. The handcuffs were imprinted with the name Smith and Wesson along with a number, and I noted that information on the evidence bag."

Brenda took a few steps away from the witness stand, walked toward the jury, then turned and asked the witness, "Officer Baker, did you make any other arrests that day, other than Michael Ross?"

"Yes, ma'am, one other arrest."

"And what were the circumstances involved?"

"I arrested a prostitute on Chestnut Street and brought her to the station house."

"Did you handcuff her?"

"Yes, it's a requirement when you take anyone

into custody."

"Officer Baker, were the handcuffs used in this arrest different in any way from those used on the deceased?"

"No, they were also Smith and Wesson."

"They were exactly the same brand, I see. And were you able to use your standard key to open the handcuffs you used to arrest this woman?"

"Yes, I was," Baker answered.

"And these handcuffs were also secured in the same manner as the handcuffs you described that were worn by Harry Sanders."

"Yes, ma'am."

"Were both evidence bags kept together at any time?"

"No, the evidence bag containing the handcuffs worn by Mr. Sanders were already transferred earlier."

"Thank you, officer. The defense accepts the handcuffs submitted by Mr. Weisman in evidence."

***

After a break for lunch, the prosecution called the medical examiner, Dr. William Warther, to the stand. He was sworn.

Weisman began the questioning. "Good morning, Dr. Warther. Were you the medical examiner in this case involving the death of Harry Sanders?"

"I was," Warther replied.

"Doctor, could you briefly update the court with respect to your background and credentials?"

"Absolutely. I received my medical degree at Yale School of Medicine and I'm licensed to practice in the states of New York and Connecticut."

"Thank you. When did you arrive at the scene?"

"I believe it was about 7:45 p.m., fifteen minutes after the first responders. I examined the body after the firemen left. I don't remember the time."

"Can you describe the state of the body?"

"The deceased sat slouched on the garage floor."

"I see, and after you examined him, what were your preliminary findings?"

"Harry Sanders had been dead approximately a half hour to forty five minutes and died as a result of carbon monoxide asphyxiation."

"Was your finding consistent with the events that occurred at the crime scene the night of August sixteenth?"

"Yes. I concluded it was a reasonable assessment that Mr. Sanders died when he inhaled copious amounts of carbon monoxide which filled the closed garage from a running car. Nothing else could have caused his death."

"Your witness, Ms. Coleman

***

"Good afternoon, Dr. Warther. Your report states that you were the medical examiner on the night of August 16, 1970, that you are a licensed physician in the state of New York, and you examined one, Harry Sanders. Is that correct?"

"It is," Warther replied.

"And you are the coroner as well?

"Yes, I am."

"Dr. Warther, what was your primary purpose for being at Professor Ross's home the night of August sixteenth?"

"It was to examine the victim and determine his cause of death."

"And what was your conclusion with respect to the deceased's cause of death?"

"It was carbon monoxide asphyxiation."

"I see. Did you check to determine if your diagnosis was conclusive and no other condition might have caused the victim's death, such as a severe heart condition?"

Weisman stood up and objected.

"Your Honor, The People called this expert witness to determine the cause of death and nothing else. He has already stated that Harry Sanders died as a result of carbon monoxide asphyxiation."

"Overruled, Mr. Weisman," the judge said. "The witness may answer the question."

"Mr. Sanders's death *was* caused by carbon monoxide asphyxiation. It's in the report I submitted to the court and there were no other medical issues that could have contributed to his demise. After my evaluation as to the cause of death, the body was placed on a stretcher and taken to the morgue."

"I understand, Dr. Warther, that you *are* here as an expert witness and a medical authority. Because of your expertise, did you at *least* examine the victim for other factors that may have caused his death, such as a heart attack, stroke, congestive heart failure, or a condition related to heart disease?"

"I did not. My diagnosis coincided with the circumstances, and it was obvious the deceased was exposed to high levels of carbon monoxide."

"Would you tell the jury how you came to your specific conclusion?"

"As I said, Mr. Sanders had been exposed to large quantities of carbon monoxide gas. I cannot express it in a different way. I examined his body, which showed he inhaled the noxious fumes to the degree that it caused his death."

"What physical signs led you to that conclusion?"

"Physical? His skin showed a slight redness, but it had no significance."

"Have you ever been a witness in a criminal case involving carbon monoxide poisoning?"

"No, ma'am, I have not."

"Doctor, were you asked to come to your conclusions about the cause of death so it would help the prosecution and not the defense?"

Mr. Weisman stood and objected. "Question is argumentative. Counsel for the Defense is trying to impugn the integrity of the prosecution's case."

Judge Jordon looked at Brenda. "Ms. Coleman, you know that question is inappropriate."

"Your Honor, I withdraw the question and apologize. My intention was in no way to call into question the integrity of the prosecution but merely to ascertain that the witnesses' testimony was free of any influence."

Judge Jordon nodded. "The jury will disregard

the question. Go on, Ms. Coleman."

"Doctor, what were the symptoms and signs that led you to find that Mr. Sanders died *only* as a result of carbon monoxide asphyxiation, exclusive of any other diagnosis?"

Dr. Warther leaned forward.

"Symptoms are sometimes variable and nonspecific. However, I took a sample of his blood and sent it to the lab. The results showed that his red blood cells contained thirty-two percent carbon monoxide as carboxyhemoglobin and that caused his death."

"Do you have scientific evidence to support your claim that carbon monoxide asphyxiation alone was the singular cause of death?"

Warther catched Weisman's eye before answering. "No, but in my opinion, it could be nothing else. He was in a closed garage with a car engine running. What else could it be?"

"So, you ruled out other possible causes for Mr. Sanders's death and stated that no other cause contributed toward it?"

"Yes, no other cause was possible."

"Why do you say that?"

"The circumstances surrounding Harry Sanders's death and the lab results strongly suggest that he died as a result of carbon monoxide asphyxiation. It was obvious."

Brenda walked closer to the witness stand and looked Warther straight in the eye.

"A man is on trial for his life, Dr. Warther, and you are relying on circumstances that *suggest* his death was caused only by carbon monoxide without scientific facts to support your conclusion? You have already told the jury that your diagnosis was made exclusively by what the circumstances suggested—being in a garage with a car running. You have produced no scientific proof to support your diagnosis except for the questionable value of a lab test. Would you say that is a true statement?"

"Yes, well..."

"Dr. Warther, let's get to that lab report. You stated that Sanders's blood levels showed thirty-two percent carbon monoxide. Do you agree that if the deceased suffered cardiac arrest, the amount of carbon monoxide in his blood would be irrelevant?"

Warther remained silent and turned away.

"Answer the question," the judge said.

Warther shrugged. "There is no way I could make that evaluation."

"Let me make this clear for the jury. Based on your testimony, Mr. Sanders's lab test showed that his blood contained thirty-two percent carbon monoxide, an amount you say was the singular cause of his death. You alluded to the fact that the circumstances surrounding the victim's death was central to your decision, specifically that Mr. Sanders was found in a closed garage with a car engine running. That *one* aspect alone led you to conclude it was the singular cause of death. In other words, doctor, your final determination on cause of death is based on circumstances rather than scientific evidence. Is that true?"

"Yes, but the overwhelming circumstances were strong enough to substantiate my diagnosis, to establish the cause of death." Warther shifted in his seat, tapping his fingertips together.

"Even though his blood showed carbon monoxide levels that would not necessarily support your assumption?"

"Ms. Coleman, it's true that the percentages of carbon monoxide in Mr. Sanders's blood does not conclusively prove that it was the cause of his death, but from my experience as a physician combined with the obvious circumstances, carbon monoxide was the singular cause of his death."

"Dr. Warther, are you a board certified pathologist?"

"No, I'm not."

"Do you have training in pathology?"

"Yes, of course."

"But, you are *not* a board certified pathologist. Is that correct?"

"It is, but it's not a New York State requirement. I have accreditation in pathology."

"Does accreditation require extensive training?"

"You just have to substantiate that you know the basics of pathology."

"So, you do not have a degree in pathology, *per se*, just a certificate of accreditation?"

"That is correct." Sweat beaded on Warther's face.

"I understand you are a coroner as well. Is that accurate?"

"It is," Warther replied.

"Doctor, educate me. What special training *does* a coroner have?"

"Sometimes, very little. I'm not sure of the qualifications required in the various states."

"To the best of your knowledge, is it true that many funeral directors act as coroners?"

"Yes."

"Are there cases where coroners are elected or appointed based on who they know?"

"Yes, that's true."

"Were you appointed to your position as coroner?"

"Yes, I was."

"Were there *any* qualifications required?"

"Well, the only requirement is citizenship and residence."

"And, in some instances, no medical training is required?"

"That is correct, but a coroner who is not a licensed physician will not be the primary examiner of a body. His role would be to determine a cause of death from information collected from the physician, law enforcement agencies, and laboratory tests."

"I see. It appears that a coroner has several roles. Dr. Warther, are you qualified to examine corpses for unusual causes of death using forensic methods? Can you act as a pathologist and do autopsies?"

"No. I'm just a regular medical doctor. If I find it necessary, I request a pathologist to examine the deceased, and I can order an autopsy to show cause of death, along with other factors relating to the deceased's physical and medical condition while alive."

Brenda paced in front of the witness stand. "Did you bring in a pathologist to verify Harry Sanders cause of death?"

"No, I did not."

"Why not, doctor? I'm interested."

"It was apparent, under the circumstances, that the cause of death was carbon monoxide asphyxiation and nothing else. I am convinced of it. There's evidence that enough of the gas was found in his red blood cells to confirm that diagnosis."

"Didn't previous testimony call the lab test into question as the definitive cause of death?"

"It called it into question, but I'm here as an expert witness and, as such, can express my opinion relating to cause of death."

"Did you review all aspects of your report that was handed into evidence?"

"Not all aspects. I only looked at the lab results, which supported my suspicion that Mr. Sanders died from carbon monoxide inhalation."

"Your *suspicion*? I see, and nothing else?"

"No. The lab tests, in my opinion, were reasonably conclusive."

"Would someone who solely specializes in pathology—in other words, someone using forensics, with more training—possibly arrive at a different conclusion with respect to the cause of death in this case?"

"Objection! Argumentative," Weisman cried out. Judge Jordan looked at the court reporter, shook his head, and disallowed the question.

"Please rephrase your question, counselor."

"That's all right, Your Honor. I'll ask something else. Was an autopsy performed in the case of Harry Sanders?"

"No, it wasn't."

"Was there a reason no autopsy was performed?"

"Medical examiners and coroners commonly determine cause and manner of death without an autopsy."

"Would you normally call in a pathologist to determine the cause of death?

"Not necessarily. I felt my observations were accurate in this case, and there was no need for an autopsy."

"You *felt* they were. Is that what you said? You *felt* they were?"

"Yes," Dr. Warther said weakly.

"Is it possible that a death certificate, without an autopsy, may show an incorrect cause of death?"

"Of course it's possible. Pathology is not an exact science."

"And, as a result, some people may be convicted of crimes they didn't commit as a result of incorrect information on a death certificate. Is that an accurate statement?"

"Yes, it is. It's highly unlikely, but possible."

"I see, possible. Dr. Warther, I ask you one last time. Did you rule out heart disease as a possible cause of death?"

"Yes, even though his record showed he was being treated for heart disease and his labs showed the presence of Digoxin, a heart medication. I still say inhalation of toxic amounts of carbon monoxide gas was the accepted cause of his death."

"Accepted? By who? *You?*" Brenda said, pointing at him. "You say Mr. Sanders's labs showed that he *was* actively taking his heart medication. Doesn't that conclusively show that he was concerned about his heart condition to the degree that he was diligent in taking his medications up until his death, and isn't it possible that his heart issues, combined with the depression caused by his wife's death, could have caused his death?"

"No, it could not," Warther replied adamantly.

Brenda didn't give up. "Why not?" she demanded. "Was it because you *felt* you arrived at the correct conclusion and refused to look at other possibilities?"

Weisman cried out his objection. "Badgering the witness."

"Sustained," the judge said. "Ms. Coleman, you should know better."

"I'm sorry, Your Honor. Dr. Warther, I understand that the evidence is compelling for you. Was your presumed cause of death indicated on the death certificate?"

"Yes, it was."

"Dr. Warther, based on the deceased's medical history, documented medical records, and laboratory findings related to his severe heart condition, which was diagnosed by cardiologists, is there any way that information could be connected to a different cause of death?"

"Actually, I have not been apprised of the deceased medical history. I only had his labs."

Brenda's eyes widened. "Oh, that's difficult for me to believe. So, you did not review the deceased's complete medical records before you came to your decision?"

"No, I came to what I believed was a reasonable conclusion."

"Did you ask for a medical history?"

"No, I examined his lab report and was aware he was taking heart medications but did not know about the specific diagnosis. I did not review any other records. Perhaps I should have looked further, but I had to make a decision with respect to his cause of death only, and carbon monoxide was the immediate cause, overriding any alternative finding. Breathing in carbon monoxide in this case was too obvious. I didn't have to search the medical records."

Brenda persevered. "Maybe it was obvious to *you,* sir, but it may not be true. If you had known the deceased's medical history, would you have examined him for other issues relating to his cause of death?"

"Possibly, but I stand by my original decision. If I were convinced that his heart was an issue, I would have called in a pathologist and requested an autopsy."

"But you didn't do that."

"No. I had no medical history of Mr. Sanders, other than his labs. My decision, based on his drug history alone, without a diagnosis would be limited."

"If you had read Sanders's complete medical records, is it possible you would come to a different finding, after you read the victim's complete diagnosis, which indicated severe heart disease?"

"Anything is possible, but I don't think so."

"But it *is* possible?"

"I suppose it is."

"Thank you, Dr. Warther."

Mr. Weisman offered a rebuttal.

"Dr. Warther, you are a licensed physician, coroner, and an accredited pathologist. Are those the general requirements to act as a medical examiner in the state of New York?"

"Yes."

Weisman paused and thought for a moment. It appeared that he wanted to pose a question for Warther, but wasn't sure if he should. He took a chance and asked anyway.

"Dr. Warther, how would the effect of stress on Harry Sanders, as a result of being shackled to a pipe, be determined as a contributing factor in his death? In other words, could the defendant have caused the death of Sanders by subjecting him to undue stress?"

"There would be no way of knowing how stress contributed to his demise and it would not be verifiable by observation or any testing that I know of."

Weisman clenched his lips. "I see. How convinced are you that the deceased's death was caused only by inhalation of large quantities of carbon monoxide to the exclusion of any other cause?"

"Almost one hundred percent."

"Thank you, Dr. Warther."

***

At lunch, Brenda and Jeff talked about the case after Michael returned to his holding cell for his meal.

"Can you believe what Warther said?" Brenda asked. 'Almost one hundred percent.' I liked the 'almost' part. It was hard to squeeze anything else out of him. He was a tough cookie, but I think we were able to cast some doubt on his testimony."

"Why didn't Weisman object more often when you were questioning Warther?" Jeff asked. "I noticed you rephrasing your questions many times to ask the same thing."

"Yeah, I wondered about it too. I just wanted Warther to say that Sanders death could have been caused by something other than carbon monoxide. Warther didn't knuckle under. I think Weisman let me go on asking the same question in different ways because he thought the jury would see through my plan on their own and objecting was unnecessary. Weisman is a smart guy."

"I have to hand it to you," Jeff said. "You were a rock. Your persistence paid off. Warther was in real trouble."

"Yeah, but he stuck to his guns. Never give up. As I said, always try to plant one seed of reasonable doubt in the minds of the jury with every witness for the prosecution. Remember, if we can show that Sanders died in a way other than the way stated in the original charge, we win."

"You did a great job. What do we know about Stanley Morgan, the prosecutor's replacement for Dr. Fisher?" Jeff asked.

"Not much. I inquired about him after Dr. Fisher died. So far, I have not received a response to my correspondence. He only has time for a few sessions with Michael."

"I get the feeling," Jeff said, "that the judge feels that it's a free ride for the prosecution and neither Judge Jordan nor Weisman want to do anything to slow things down."

"Maybe. You never know. Morgan is no youngster. He is seventy years old and has been practicing medicine for over thirty years."

"I think we have a good case. It's been a real learning experience for me."

"It's nice to be optimistic about winning, Jeff. I think it helps, but the reality is, you never know." She sighed. "Let's get back in there."

***

Dr. Stanley Morgan was sworn in and David Weisman began his direct examination.

"Dr. Morgan, would you tell the court something about your educational background and training?"

"Yes, of course. I graduated from Johns Hopkins University and did my residency there as well. Afterward, I did a three-year stint in the army as a medical officer and was honorably discharged. I am a board certified licensed psychiatrist in the states of New York and Maryland and was in private practice for more than thirty years before I retired five years ago."

Mr. Weisman turned toward Ms. Coleman, who rose and said, "We concede to this witness's credentials, Your Honor. The defense accepts him as an expert in the field."

"Johns Hopkins, I'm impressed. Have you been published?" Weisman asked.

Brenda almost objected to his personal comment about being "impressed," but let it go.

"Yes, I have written a paper on hyperkinetic disorder, which was published last year in several medical journals."

"Dr. Morgan, what is hyperkinetic disorder?"

"It's a disorder displayed in children, marked by excessive muscular movement, hyperactivity, and an inability to concentrate. My paper was based on original research and addresses the reasons some students do not do well in school."

"And have you appeared as an expert witness in court cases before?"

"I have."

"In your opinion, is Michael Ross competent to stand trial?"

"Yes, he is. There is no evidence of mental illness or any reason that I can determine why he would be incapable of standing trial. He is sane and he knows right from wrong."

"Did I hear you correctly when you said that the defendant *does* know right from wrong? Is that your expert opinion?"

"It is."

"He is not insane?"

"No, sir."

"In any way?"

"No."

"Dr. Morgan, the defendant, who in your expert opinion, knows right from wrong, has admitted to killing Harry Sanders. Let me ask you something else. In your professional opinion, was Michael Ross capable of acting in a way consistent with an irresistible impulse to commit murder?"

"It's not easy to tell if someone acted uncontrollably and whether or not he could appreciate the consequences of his actions. But in this case, in my professional opinion, Michael Ross was a thinking person, and it would be out of character for him not to contemplate the outcome before he acted."

"So, are you saying that Michael Ross's basic nature would not allow him to act in an uncontrollable fashion because it would be out of character for him?"

"Yes, absolutely."

"And would you also say that he is incapable of an irresistible impulse to take another person's life?"

"Yes. Mr. Ross is a well-educated, thoughtful man, and if he chose to wreak his vengeance on someone, he would have planned it in advance."

Jeff Hartman whispered to Brenda, "Why aren't you objecting? Weisman is leading, putting words in his mouth."

"Relax, Jeff. I'll do my best on the cross where I'm allowed to lead the witness. Let him say what he wants, within reason."

Weisman continued. "In effect, Dr. Morgan, if the defendant intended to kill Harry Sanders, it would have to be well-planned, and that would be an act of premeditation. Would it not?"

"Objection, Your Honor," Ms. Coleman interjected. "The prosecution is leading the witness. Premeditation is a legal term. This expert witness is not qualified to make legal judgments."

"Objection sustained. Counsel is admonished to refrain from leading the witness. Rephrase your question."

"That's all right, Your Honor. No further questions at this time."

Ms. Coleman approached the witness stand.

"Dr. Morgan, you said you participated in other criminal cases as an expert witness. Would you tell the jury the number of criminal cases you have appeared in during the past five years?"

"About forty," Morgan replied.

"Forty criminal cases? That's quite a bit, and before that time? I mean, before you retired, in how many cases have you provided expert testimony?"

Morgan leaned forward. "None."

"None, you say? Would you explain why all this expert testimony has been given only after your retirement and not earlier?"

"I had a full-time private practice before I retired five years ago and now have the time to testify in court cases. I was called for this case on very short notice."

"I see. Are you well paid for your court appearances?"

"It's satisfactory."

"Would you say you received more money testifying than you did in private practice?"

"Usually, yes."

"So, when you first retired from private practice, you no longer had income from your practice."

"Yes, that's true."

"And was that the reason you started testifying as an expert witness in court cases?"

"It was one reason. I wanted to stay active to some degree in my profession. I didn't find anything wrong with that. It's not illegal."

"No, it's not. You said, 'it was one reason.' What were some of the other reasons?"

"I thought I could be of help to the justice system."

"Would that include the *criminal* justice system?"

"Yes, of course."

"Have you ever testified as an expert witness in a murder trial such as this one?"

"Never, but my training in psychiatry would..."

"Please, doctor, just answer the question. So, you have never appeared as an expert witness in any murder case?"

"Never."

"This is your first one?"

"Yes."

"I understand. Please let the court know the nature of your practice."

"My practice mostly involved children."

"Children? I see. I'm sure you were able to help many of them. And you never appeared in a murder case?"

Weisman jumped in. "Objection, Your Honor. The witness has already answered that question."

"Objection sustained. The witness does not have to answer."

"Your practice was basically focused on treating psychiatric issues relating to children?"

"Yes," Morgan answered, squirming in his chair.

"And now your practice is limited to being an

expert witness in court trials, and in this case, a murder trial?"

Dr. Morgan looked at the judge.

"Answer the question, doctor."

"Yes, that is what I do. Many other doctors do the same."

"I'm sure they do, but would you say that testifying is a new type of practice for you?"

"You can call it that. It's not illegal," he repeated. Morgan frowned, clenched his lips, and glanced at the jury.

"No, it's not illegal. Some professionals find it quite a rewarding experience. When you were asked to act as an expert witness in cases for the prosecution or the defense, were you asked to take a particular side on a specific diagnosis or question?"

"Based on my training and credentials in psychiatry, I *was* asked to give testimony to support a particular point of view."

"When you say, 'a particular point of view,' does that mean there could be different expert opinions about the same matter?"

"Yes, of course."

"Help me to understand, doctor. If ten psychiatrists were asked to make a judgment about a patient's mental health, would they generally be in agreement?"

"Generally, yes, of course."

"But it's possible that some would not agree?"

"Yes, it's possible."

"So, you're saying, Dr. Morgan, that these ten psychiatrists might not be in agreement with respect to a particular diagnosis or issue involving mental health?"

"Yes."

"Psychiatry itself is not an exact science, is it doctor?"

"It's not an *exact* science. You can't assess the human mind with one hundred percent reliability."

"Thank you. Let's get back to your medical practice *before* you were involved in being an expert witness in so many court cases. What specific areas of child psychiatric services did you provide? Give the court an example."

"I prescribed medication and provided talk therapy. I also treated many cases of child abuse, anxiety, depression, and eating disorders."

"I see, eating disorders. Give the court an example of a specific mental disorder you treated."

"The ones I mentioned *are* mental issues. I also treated hyperkinesia. Some students did poorly in school because they were energized and stimulated to the degree where they were not able to concentrate. Medically, most of them often suffered from muscle spasms. I treated them and most of my patients found that their concentration improved considerably."

"How did you treat them, doctor? With medication? Psychoanalysis?"

"I did do some talk therapy with most of them, but medication provided the best results, if the patients were compliant."

"Would you tell the court what medication you prescribed?"

"Mostly, Dexedrine."

"Excuse me, doctor, but I know about this drug.

Isn't it used for weight loss?"

"It is."

"How does Dexedrine work to do that?"

"The drug decreases the firing rate in the heart, which reduces the blood flow to the abdomen. It's basically a stimulant. As a result, it slows peristalsis so food stays in the stomach longer and people don't get hungry so quickly, so it helps them lose weight. In my practice, I used it to control hyperactivity."

"Help me out here. I'm not a medical person, but you said that Dexedrine is a stimulant. Is that correct?"

"Yes, it is."

"So, you prescribed a stimulant to a child who was *already* energized and *already* stimulated. That doesn't make sense to me, but as I said, I'm not a medical person. Let's get onto something else."

Brenda paced, put on her glasses, and began to read from her notebook.

"You said in your direct testimony, and I quote, 'It's not easy to tell if someone acted uncontrollably and if he could appreciate the consequences of his actions.' Did you make that statement, doctor, and would you explain to the court what you meant by it?"

"Yes, I did say that. The fact that it is not *easy* to determine if someone acted uncontrollably doesn't mean it's impossible for a trained psychiatrist to come to a conclusion about whether he did or did not act uncontrollably."

"Would you say your training was basically in non-criminal matters?"

"For the most part, yes."

"Educate me, Dr. Morgan. As an expert witness, you testified that Michael Ross was not capable of irresistible impulse. Do you say that now?"

"I do. Based on the kind of person Michael Ross is, it would not be possible for him to react impulsively in such a way that he was so out of control, he had to kill Mr. Sanders without thinking. I just don't believe that."

"Oh, so you don't believe that?"

"No, I do not!"

"Dr. Morgan, you're here today to offer your opinion as an expert witness to determine the mental state of Professor Ross. Since all your patients are children, would it be proper for you to make a reasonable diagnosis of an adult to determine his mental state?"

"I'm still a psychiatrist, Ms. Coleman."

"Yes, you are. When was the last time you personally met with Michael Ross professionally?"

"I've never met him."

Murmurs erupted throughout the courtroom. Judge Jordan pounded his gavel to restore order.

"You've never met him?" Brenda glanced at the jury, then back to the witness.

"Dr. Morgan, may I remind you this is a murder case. A man's life is at stake here. If you never even met him, how were you able to arrive at your conclusions?"

"I read his file."

"You read his file?" Brenda took a deep breath, threw up her arms, and paced silently.

"How many minutes did it take for you to read

his file?" Brenda asked sarcastically.

Dr. Morgan looked at the judge and then turned away.

"Answer the counselor's question, doctor."

"How many minutes?" Brenda asked

"I read the file."

"No more questions."

Mr. Weisman approached the witness box.

"Dr. Morgan, is it customary for many physicians to make judgments based on a patient's file?"

"Absolutely. It's done all the time."

"And this applies to psychiatrists as well?"

"It does."

"When you said you read the file, what file are you referring to?"

"The file that Dr. Fisher completed before he died. He spent two thirty-minute sessions with Mr. Ross and documented his findings on two typewritten pages."

"And he was a board certified psychiatrist as well?"

"He was."

"Thank you, Dr. Morgan."

"Your Honor, the prosecution rests."

"Thank you, Mr. Weisman." Judge Jordan struck his gavel. "This case will continue tomorrow morning at 10 a.m."

Brenda turned to Michael, gathered her papers, and whispered in his ear, "I think we did well. Let's see what happens tomorrow. Be optimistic, it's always a good thing."

Chapter 23

Albert sat on the edge of the bed and heard the brash, metallic sound of the jail cell open. His face lit up and he smiled when Michael walked in.

"What's happening, man?" Albert asked. "You doin' all right?"

"I'm not sure. My lawyer tells me we did well, but I know Brenda. She just wants me to feel optimistic for some reason. She keeps pushing that idea."

"That means she's gonna put you on the stand, Michael."

"How do you know that? Is it a good thing?"

"Depends. In the end, the choice is gonna be yours. The prosecutor won't know if you will be on the stand or not, even if she has you on the witness list."

Michael took a deep breath. "Why wouldn't my lawyer put me on the stand? She'll prepare me anyway."

"I dunno. Not much time to prepare you now, unless she comes here later. She definitely won't put you on if she feels the prosecutor's cross examination is gonna rip you apart."

"You sure you're not a lawyer?" Michael smiled.

"I'm no legal lawyer, but I've been around."

"So, I have the right to refuse if Brenda wants to put me on the stand?"

"You do, but you're paying her for her advice. If it were me, and my lawyer wanted me to testify and prepared me, I'd do it in a heartbeat. I'd be convincing as hell on the stand. I think the jury would trust me. I have a kind face and I speak in a soft voice. You know, Michael, when the defendant goes on the stand and the jury is listening hard, it becomes a personality issue. If you come across sincere and come off honest, you can influence the jury to your side, and in court, winning is everything. There's no draw."

"Well, I think I have a good case, but there are some technicalities involved which may not be in my favor. I want to be honest, Albert. I think my lawyer is going to interpret the facts in a way that bends the truth. I don't feel good about that."

Albert leaned back on his bed with his back against the wall and smiled. "Relax. Sounds like your lawyer wants you to win."

* * *

An hour later, Brenda met Michael for a consultation. She looked tired. The harsh lights of the jailhouse brought out the paleness of her face along with the few wrinkles under her eyes, but she had an energy about her that was always present and Michael liked that. She was a fighter. There was no "hello" or "how are they treating you?" She wasn't smiling, and her first words were about the case.

"Michael, we have to get you ready in case we put you on the stand. I'm not sure in what sequence, maybe before or after the psychiatrist, or not at all, but we have to be prepared. Let's talk, just the basics. My job as your lawyer is to guide you on how to answer questions on the witness stand. Answer the questions to the best of your ability. I will interpret the facts of the case and make judgments that I believe will result in a favorable outcome."

"Interpret. You've said that before."

"Look at it this way. Here's what interpretation is all about. Two people can see the same thing in different ways. Both people can look at a map of the United States. One sees a road map, the other a climate map. Each map looks different, but the fact is they are both maps of the United States."

Michael smiled. "Okay, I get it, Brenda. I'm a professor, remember?"

Brenda shook her head and smiled. "Uh, right. Our witnesses can win the case for us, but I want you prepared. Let's practice. Did you have a relationship with Harry Sanders?"

"I did."

"And what was the nature of your association with him?"

"Our pharmacy filled prescriptions for him and I got to know him there."

"What do you mean by 'got to know him'? Did

you become friends?"

"No, we weren't friends. Not even close."

"Did he come to your home?"

"Yes."

"I see. How did that come about if you weren't friends?"

"When we spoke in the pharmacy, he asked questions about his medications. He told me he had trouble staying awake during the day because he had no mental challenges. I gave him some vitamins for his fatigue and we discussed adding activity in his life.

"He implied that he was a very good chess player and had played chess with a friend. That stimulated him, but his friend had moved away. When he said that, I remembered I hadn't played for years. I had learned the game from my father, and I told Mr. Sanders that I liked chess. He begged me for a game and I agreed. I was busy and not available to play right away, but we arranged for him to play a game at my house the following week."

Brenda moved closer. "I see. So, what happened after he came to your house?"

"As we played, I was curious about Sanders's accent. I thought it was German but wasn't sure."

"Don't say you weren't sure. Say, 'I knew it was German.' After all, Michael...Miklos. You're from Europe, you know a German accent when you hear it. Go on."

"We played chess. He may have thought he was a good player, but he was an amateur. We talked about the war and he asked me where I grew up and if I was in the army. I didn't want to tell him too many details. I don't like people to know about my personal life unless they are friends. I avoided his questions. Then I asked him if he was in the service. He said he was an officer in the German army."

Brenda pulled her chair closer. "And you never knew any of this before?"

"No, ma'am. He was very open with me. He said the war was over so long ago, nobody talks about it anymore. I told him I was interested because I never had a conversation with a German officer before. He spoke openly and said he was a major in the army and an SS officer in Auschwitz."

"Tell the court, Professor Ross. Were you a prisoner in Auschwitz?"

Michael looked down at his knees, put his elbows on his thighs, and his hands on his forehead.

"I was, Ms. Coleman."

"Professor Ross, did you recognize this man, Harry Sanders, as Officer Hans Stern from the Auschwitz Concentration Camp?"

"I can't do this, Brenda. I don't feel good." Michael bit into his lip. "We'll do it another time."

Brenda drew closer and spoke in a low tone. "I understand how you feel. Could you take only a few more minutes? I promise, no more than that."

Michael nodded. "Okay. I didn't recognize him at first until I looked into his eyes. I remembered those eyes, ice cold. I said something that he thought was funny, and it made him laugh. The moment I heard his laughter, it was a dead giveaway. I could never forget that diabolical, high-pitched laugh. It was Stern for sure, no question. He killed my family."

"What did you do then? Tell the jury."

Michael didn't answer. He looked down.

"Then? Then what, Michael? What happened then?" Brenda shook him.

"I had no feeling. I was numb. There was a blank space."

"Blank space? What blank space? What did you do?"

"I don't know. I don't know what I did. The next thing I remembered was that I was in town in front of a movie house. I looked at the posters. They were showing a World War II movie."

"And before that?"

"Nothing."

"I don't believe that. You're lying. Damn it, tell me the truth!" She shook him again. "What did you do *immediately* after you knew Sanders was Stern," Brenda yelled.

"Nothing, Brenda. I'm not lying. You have to believe me. Why are you acting so strange? You're not like that. What happened is that I found myself in town in front of a movie house. I saw a poster in front of me, 'Coming soon, *Where Eagles Dare*.' It was a Nazi movie."

Brenda stared into Michael's eyes. "I still don't believe you. Tell me the truth. Did you hit Stern? Did you handcuff him? Tell me. Tell me. Did you gas him? The truth, the truth!"

Michael dropped his head into his hands and sobbed. He looked up at Brenda and whispered, "There was a blank space in my mind where nothing happened, and then I found myself in town."

Brenda's eyes studied her client. Tears rolled down his cheeks and his hands were shaking. "Relax, Michael, everything will work out in the end."

They sat silently for a while until Brenda asked him when he'd realized he had killed Stern.

"Damn! I remembered it when I was in town. Something must have triggered my memory. Is that what you want, Brenda? Damn it, is that what you want?" Michael shouted.

"I've never lied to a judge or jury and I never will. It's the truth as I see it," Brenda replied.

"Are you going to prepare me for the prosecutor?"

"I just did. You're tired, get some sleep."

Chapter 24

After talking to Michael, Brenda realized she had made a big mistake, but felt lucky because she caught it in time. Her original strategy was to put the defense's psychiatrist on the stand and not ask Michael to testify at all because she felt Weisman would tear him to shreds. He was good at that, especially when a defendant testified.

When Brenda looked into Michael's eyes, she saw something in him that was different. He appeared to have a new sense of confidence that helped fortify his resolve. He had to testify.

Brenda prepared to bring two witnesses to the stand. Michael would testify first, followed by the defense's psychiatrist, who would support Michael's testimony. She thought Michael would do well on the direct but was concerned about Weisman's cross. Would Michael be able to stand up to the scathing challenges from the prosecutor?

***

The next morning, Michael took the stand and was sworn. Brenda Coleman began her questioning.

"Good morning, Professor Ross. I'm going to ask you some questions so that the jury will better understand the circumstances in this case."

She paused and walked closer to the witness stand. "Professor, did you kill Harry Sanders?"

"I did."

"Would you tell the court how much time you spent planning your action?"

"None. I never planned anything and had no remembrance of what I had done until I walked into town. When I returned home a little later, I told a police officer that I lived there and that I was the one who killed the deceased. Then I was arrested."

"I see. Would you describe the circumstances of how you met Harry Sanders to the jury?"

"I first met him at my pharmacy when he picked up medication for his wife."

"And at that time, he was familiar to you?"

"Well, I noticed his German accent and he looked like an old, worn out man to me."

"So, when you first met Harry Sanders, you felt no hostility toward him?"

"No, I did not."

"And what was the nature of your relationship?"

"He was a customer. We talked about his medications, and he asked for my advice when he had trouble staying awake and active during the day."

"And did you advise him?"

"Yes, I made suggestions for a diet and vitamin regimen."

"Do you know if it helped?"

"He told me it did, but added that he needed some mental activity to stay alert. Then he told me about his passion for chess, and I told him I was on my college chess team. His face lit up and he asked if we could play sometime, and I agreed since I hadn't played for quite a few years."

"Did you play?"

"Yes, he came to my house the following week for a game."

"And it was a friendly game of chess?"

"Yes, I enjoyed it in the beginning until he began to tell me things I did not want to hear."

"What things?"

"As we played, we both consumed a good deal of liquor, mostly schnapps. We made small talk and discussed events in our lives, things we liked to do and so on. In the course of the conversation, I was startled by the fact that Mr. Sanders opened up more about his life than I could ever have imagined. I was more guarded about *my* feelings and avoided bringing up the tragic events I experienced to anyone. They were times I never wanted to re-live, but Harry Sanders was different. When we talked about the war, he started bragging about the fact that he was in the German army as a major."

"I see. What did he actually say?"

"He told me he was one of the officers in charge of Auschwitz."

"He admitted this?" Brenda asked, surprised.

"Yes, I was shocked, but as I said, we'd had a lot to drink, he more than I."

Brenda paused and paced. "And why is

Auschwitz significant?"

"Because I was a prisoner there with my wife and three young daughters. They were only children. Magda and Roza, the twins, were eight, and little Eva was five."

"What happened to your family in the concentration camp with reference to the deceased, Harry Sanders?"

"Objection, Your Honor!" Mr. Weisman cried out. "The defense counselor is leading the witness, and besides, Mr. Sanders is not on trial here and there is no foundation."

Judge Jordan thought for a moment and said, "Objection sustained. Please rephrase your question, Ms. Coleman."

"Professor Ross, what *did* happen during the chess game? What did you talk about?"

"When he stated that he was a Nazi SS officer, I stared at him with new eyes. I could no longer concentrate on the game. My head was spinning. He took my queen and laughed, mocking me for my failure to protect such a valuable piece. It was a laugh I'd heard before and stood out in my memory. In that instant, there was no doubt in my mind he was the man responsible for gassing my daughters and the reason my wife took her own life. I had no doubt whatsoever that Sanders *was* SS officer Hans Stern. I knew it was him."

"How many times did you see the deceased in Auschwitz?"

"Objection, Your Honor," David Weisman called out. "Again, Harry Sanders is not on trial here, and there is no proof that he and Hans Stern are one and the same."

Judge Jordan looked directly at Brenda. "Ms. Coleman, you're getting into unsafe waters here. Please rephrase your question."

"Professor Ross, when you said you 'knew it was him,' what did you mean?

"I knew Sanders was Hans Stern."

"Michael, what were you feeling when you realized that Harry Sanders, also known to you as Hans Stern, was the man responsible for killing your family and was now sitting across from you?"

"I was boiling over with anger. It was a rage I'd never felt before. Then, there was nothing. My mind went blank."

"You have no recollection of taking his life or causing him any harm?"

"None, until I found myself in town. I feel terrible about it now. I'm not a violent person. Anybody who knows me would tell you that. I would never think of killing anyone. When I reached Main Street my heart was beating erratically and I ran back to my house, hoping what happened was a dream. But when I saw the police and fire trucks, I knew the truth."

"Thank you for your testimony, professor. Your witness, counselor."

***

Weisman rattled some papers in his hand as he approached the witness stand.

"Good morning, Mr. Ross. Did you kill Harry Sanders?"

"Yes, I killed Hans Stern."

"Harry Sanders was the victim, not Hans Stern," Weisman stated.

"I knew him as Hans Stern."

"You perceived him to be Hans Stern?"

"Objection! Perceived. Leading," Brenda shouted.

"Sustained."

Weisman shook his head.

"So, you knew him as Hans Stern?"

"Yes, sir."

"How much time did you spend planning to take his life?"

"None. I didn't plan to kill him."

"Mr. Ross, regardless of the name you call him, isn't it true that you invited the deceased to your home for a game of chess and then, in premeditated cold blood, you lured him to your detached garage, where you bludgeoned him with a bat and shackled him to a pipe. Then you turned on your car, exited the garage, and closed the door, leaving Harry Sanders to die?"

"Yes, but I don't remember doing it."

"You don't remember?" Weisman said with a surprised look and glanced at the jury.

"No."

"Mr. Ross. The handcuffs used to shackle the deceased belonged to you. Isn't that right?"

"Yes."

"Why would a pharmacist need a pair of handcuffs? What was your purpose for owning them?"

"Well, I never bought them, if that's what you

217

mean. I just had them," Michael answered.

"You're saying you never bought them? Did they just come into your possession by some kind of magic? Do you deny having professional handcuffs in your house?"

"No, I don't."

"Come on, Mr. Ross, or professor, or whatever they call you. Handcuffs were found in your home, in your garage. Those same handcuffs were found on Harry Sanders body. How did they get there? Magic?"

"No, sir."

"How did they even get inside your house? More magic?"

"I bought my house from the estate of a former policeman who had died. He didn't have any family and the house was sold as it was, including the officer's furniture, clothing, and other personal belongings, some of which were left in boxes on a shelf in the garage. I believe my lawyer has produced an itemized bill of sale for my house."

"Yes, but it did not itemize every item. So, we only have your word that you didn't purchase the handcuffs yourself."

"Yes, sir, but as you said, why would a pharmacist need a pair of handcuffs?"

Faint laughter rippled through the courtroom. Weisman stood silently for a moment. A hint of red colored his face. He shrugged and said, "Are you saying the handcuffs were already in the garage?"

"Yes. In one of the boxes."

"What else was in those boxes?"

"One had a few pieces of clothing, a gray

sweatshirt with the word 'Police' on the back in large letters, and the insignia of a badge on the front. I think I remember seeing a thin leather wallet with an opening for a badge, but there was no badge in it. Also, there was a pair of handcuffs and a key attached with a rubber band, but I remember the handcuffs being open."

"You noticed the handcuffs were open?"

"Yes," Michael answered, opening his palms and staring at Weisman.

The prosecutor paced in front of the witness, as if in deep in thought. He took a few steps away from the defendant, then quickly turned to face the witness. Each man caught the eyes of the other.

"You did this for revenge, didn't you?" Weisman said. "You had the opportunity, the means, and the place to carry out your vengeful plan."

Michael appeared to be caught off guard and simply replied, "No."

"Mr. Ross, let me ask you again. Think about the truth that lies within you. It was pure and simple revenge, wasn't it?"

"No, it wasn't anything like that. He came to my house for a game of chess. After a while, I knew Harry Sanders *was* Hans Stern, the Nazi officer responsible for murdering my family."

"That was the reason you murdered Harry Sanders? Because you *believed* him to be a man you knew as Hans Stern?"

"Yes, sir. He *was* Hans Stern."

"How did you come to the conclusion that this man, who you thought was Hans Stern, was an SS Nazi officer?"

219

"I looked into his eyes, then heard his laugh. The last time I heard that distinct laugh was when he threw my wife out of the barracks." Michael's jaw tightened and through clenched Michael added, "He called her a bitch."

Weisman shot back. "You just heard him laugh and that was enough for you to come to the conclusion that this was the man who hurt your family?"

"Yes," he answered, choked up. Michael swallowed hard. His eyes filled and a tear ran down his cheek.

"He raped and killed my wife and gassed my daughters. It was his *laugh* that made me look at him again. That's when I realized I was right. He *was* Hans Stern!" Michael yelled.

Weisman took a deep breath. "Mr. Ross, this may surprise you, but there is no record on file that shows that anyone named Hans Stern was an officer in the German army—no pictures, no information about him being a Nazi, and nothing relating to him being an SS officer at Auschwitz."

"That's not unusual. Many Nazis have erased their pasts."

"You admitted to the court earlier, during direct testimony, that you killed the man named Harry Sanders who you *presumed* to be Hans Stern. Please affirm this is correct," Weisman said, pacing again.

"I did, yes. I told you I don't remember killing him," Michael answered, crossing his hands in front of him.

"But you remember being filled with rage."

"Yes, only for a moment."

"Because he laughed like someone you knew twenty-five years ago?"

"No!" Michael spoke directly to the jury. "Because he murdered my family!"

"You know, Mr. Ross, you were mistaken when you killed a man you thought was Hans Stern. The Nazis kept meticulous records. We researched your claim, and the fact is, there was no SS officer at Auschwitz named Stern and no other Nazi officers or non-officers who were named Hans Stern. I don't know what fantasy you were living in, but you killed the wrong man, Mr. Ross. You killed Harry Sanders, a law abiding citizen with no criminal record."

Gasps ran through the courtroom. The jury sat frozen in their seats and appeared to be in a state of shock. Judge Jordon banged his gavel repeatedly to restore order, but the crowd still murmured.

Brenda Coleman stood up and shouted to Weisman, "You know better than that, David. You know that Nazis destroyed incriminating records."

The judge struck the gavel with more force and threatened to clear the courtroom unless everyone quieted down.

Weisman spoke to the court, "Your Honor, the fact that the Nazis destroyed records is irrelevant. The court cannot assume that a record of the deceased's presence in Auschwitz existed and then was destroyed. How can we ever know that is a fact? So there can be no proof of the defendant's claim that Harry Sanders *is* Hans Stern and that this man was even in Auschwitz. The people maintain that an act of calculated revenge for a heinous crime committed by someone else Mr. Ross knew in Auschwitz resulted in the death of Harry Sanders, an innocent man."

Brenda was on her feet. "I object, Your Honor."

"Sustained. Mr. Weisman, save your speeches for closing statements, please. Do you have any other questions for Mr. Ross?"

"Mr. Ross, is it possible that the man you claim was Hans Stern was not a Nazi officer during World War II and you only imagined him to be the person who took the life of your family?"

"No, it is not possible," Michael said, shaking his head. "He was the man."

"I…" Michael started to speak, then stopped. Wide-eyed, he stared ahead, an expression of revelation on his face.

"Yes, Mr. Ross? Are you ready to tell us the truth, that you remember your cold-blooded killing of Harry Sanders?" Weisman scanned the jury.

"No, I…"

"No? Your Honor. I have no further questions for the defendant," the prosecutor said, turning away from Michael.

Before the judge could dismiss him, Michael stood up and yelled, "I have the proof!" He hesitated and screamed out again. "I can *prove* that the deceased *is* Hans Stern and that he *was* an SS officer at Auschwitz."

Appearing stunned, Weisman whirled to face the defendant. "Okay, prove it!"

Brenda immediately addressed the court.

"Your Honor, may we have a short recess so I can confer with my client?"

"Take all the time you want, counselor. I am adjourning this court until after the weekend. The trial will convene on Monday at 10 a.m."

Brenda stood, her lips pressed tight as Michael walked toward her.

"What are you doing? What got into you? You can't just shout out like that in a courtroom. I'm your lawyer. For God's sake, ask for water, tell the court you don't feel well, and talk to me. Don't just yell things out. Now, it's part of the record. Weisman will come to court Monday morning and rip you apart. If Weisman says there was no Hans Stern that means he researched it. He's good at that. It's his specialty, very methodical."

Brenda shook her head and sighed. Jeff patted Michael on the back and told him that they still had a shot at winning and asked him to stay optimistic.

"All right, Michael," Brenda said. "What is this proof you have? Weisman found no one named Hans Stern who was an SS officer in Auschwitz. He's got us. He got us, Michael! He's entitled to full disclosure. What were you thinking? Sorry, I'm all over the place. Let me know what kind of proof you have."

Michael took a deep breath. "You want it short and simple or do you want me to beat around the bush?" Michael asked with a smile.

"Come on, Michael. I'm exhausted. Say something to make me smile."

"I have a document that I took from the records office in Auschwitz shortly before the liberation by the Soviets. It shows Stern's entire history in black and white. His rank service number, his signature, where he was born, everything."

Brenda's jaw dropped and she stared at him, "Michael, uh…"

"Wait, there's more."

"More? What do you mean 'more'?"

"It has his picture on it, in his full dress SS uniform. I see you smiling now. I knew you would. I enjoyed watching you blow off steam, so I waited a bit before telling you. When I first held this document in my hand and looked at it in the barracks, I felt like I was given a precious gift."

"Why didn't you let me know about this before? If we attempt to get this information about Stern into evidence, Weisman is going to kick up a storm and challenge its authenticity. We could get forensics to testify if it is, in fact, authentic, but to validate Stern's signature would be impossible."

"Why?" Michael asked.

Brenda shook her head and looked down. "Because we don't have anything to compare it with. We could have used a legitimate passport, but his was forged and would never be admissible."

"But we *do* have something to compare. I have a signed letter from him using the name Harry Sanders, thanking me in advance for inviting him to my home for an evening of chess."

"Really? Isn't it unusual for him to send a thank you note in advance? It's not generally done. Why would he do that?"

"My impression of Stern was that he was a rigid man who had an exaggerated sense of propriety, or maybe he felt that if he sent it to me in writing, it would be his way of making sure I would keep the date."

"The testimony of a forensic document examiner could show that Hans Stern and Harry Sanders are one and the same man. Where is this document?" Brenda said as she patted Michael on his back and slipped her files into her briefcase.

"It's at the house."

"Is it in good condition, readable?"

"Not mint condition, a little yellowed and creased, but very well-preserved."

"And why didn't you tell me about this before?" Brenda scolded.

"In my wildest dreams, I never thought I would need it. I had forgotten about it. I just kept it as some kind of memento. When I was at Auschwitz, I knew deep inside that I would be the one to avenge my family. Maybe I took it for that reason. I don't know. Weisman was right when he questioned me on the stand. He was right all along. It *was* about revenge."

"And where is the letter from Sanders thanking you for the opportunity to play chess with you?"

"It's in the kitchen drawer to the right of the sink, under a lot of junk. You'd have to dig to find it."

"How do I get into your house? Where will I find a key?"

"It's easy. You'll never believe it."

"Really? You mean?"

"Yep, under the doormat." Michael had a wide grin on his face. "But there is a slight catch."

Brenda rolled her eyes. "What's the catch? Don't be a tease."

"Well, the document is in my house all right. It's there, but I don't know *exactly* where it is. It's been so long since I've seen it, but it has to be there somewhere. I think it's in the study. Somewhere with the animals. It's a little messy, but it's probably in there somewhere."

"You sure?"

"Pretty sure."

"Okay, I'll go over there before it gets dark. If there is any problem, I'll come to the jail. If you don't see me, it means I found it. What's this about animals?"

"I'm not sure," Michael said, scratching his head. "It was just so long ago."

"What does that mean? I have no idea what you're talking about," Brenda said, exasperated

"Oh, I don't know either, but it's there. Could you do me one favor?"

"What?"

"Could you empty the refrigerator? Everything must be moldy and smelly."

"Michael, I'm your lawyer, not your housemaid. I'll make an exception this one time, but I'm adding it to your bill," she said with a wide smile. "Just don't ask me to do the windows." They both laughed.

"Oh, one more thing," Brenda said sheepishly.

"What? Don't tell me you changed your mind about doing windows?"

"No, I just want to let you know that was the first time I saw Weisman flustered in court. It was a beautiful sight."

"But he thought he had me. Why would he be

flustered?"

"I've known David for a long time. We go to conferences together, have coffee. Trust me, I know him. His expression sent a message to me that you really might have proof."

***

Michael returned to his cell. Albert told him his case was set for three weeks down the road.

"That's a long time, Albert. Why?"

"Justice is slow. I got used to that."

"What's your lawyer like?" Michael asked.

"Tom Kennedy is a nice man who knows the law. He's a good lawyer for me. I'm glad to have him on my side. I've always heard from jailhouse lawyers that public defenders are too busy to do a good job." Albert stroked his beard, smiled, and shook his head. "If jailhouse lawyers are so smart, why are they in here in the first place? It doesn't take too much brains to stay out of jail, just follow the law, but maybe that was my problem too. I was so impulsive. After what that man did to my grandbaby, I wanted to kill him. I didn't think twice about it and couldn't give a crap about the consequences. I'd do it again."

"I know how you feel. I really do. Did Kennedy prepare you for your case?" Michael asked as he sat next to Albert.

Albert took a deep breath. "He prepared me all right. At least, the best he could. Except there's one problem."

"Go ahead, what is it," Michael said, focusing on

Albert's face.

"My son's friend, Jamal, actually witnessed the shooting from the side of the road when I shot that scum, Daryl. Jamal saw the bastard pull a gun on me as I was coming at him, but I got him first and Daryl dropped his gun. Jamal looked at me, terrified, picked up his gun, tucked it under his belt, and ran off as Daryl was on the ground."

"And you saw this?" Michael asked.

"I did. Jamal yelled at me, saying, 'I'm getting outta here.'"

"Why would he do that? Pick up the gun and take off?"

"I know why. He was terrified of the police and thought they might show up. He lived in fear of them. There was a warrant out for his arrest for not showing up in court for a minor offense, like sleeping on the street. Why he didn't show up is beyond me. He would have gotten a slap on the wrist and the case would have been dismissed. But he didn't show up and whenever Jamal saw a police car, he'd duck down an alley. Plus, he always wanted to have a gun for protection and this was a good opportunity to get one."

"So, with Jamal's testimony, you would have a good case for self-defense. Did the police turn up?" Michael asked.

"No, but Jamal was gone. If the police showed, we both would have been arrested. I called the police and told them what happened, and they arrested me, but Jamal already left and I don't know what happened with Daryl. I always told Jamal to turn himself in if there was a warrant out for him, pay the price, and get on with his life, especially for something so minor, but he was scared to go to court. He heard too many stories about blacks getting harsh punishments for small stuff. That's the way it is with young black males. They break the law, get arrested, make bail, and hide. They're afraid of appearing in front of a judge. Anything could go wrong."

"Sorry to hear that about Jamal, but I understand what you're saying about black males. Why, Albert, why?"

"I don't know. It's about hatred. All I know is that there is a separate set of laws for black people."

"Where is Jamal now?" Michael asked, shaking his head and biting his lip.

"Nobody knows. He's gone, and Kennedy said there was no funding left for a private investigator to find him. It takes big money for an investigator." Albert looked down, shrugged, and remained silent for a moment. "My lawyer said that finding Jamal could turn the case in my favor. It would mean that he could address Jamal's minor offense in court, get it dismissed, and then have him testify on my behalf. It takes big money for an investigator and Mr. Kennedy's hands are tied."

"I can help you with the money part. I'm not rich but I have enough to get you an investigator. That could be important in your case."

"Thanks, Michael, you're a true friend and someone I never would have met outside of these circumstances, but I'm used to playing the cards I've been dealt. Kennedy is doing a good job so far. He'll find a way, but thanks anyway. You're a good man. I'll be leaving this cell tomorrow, going to new quarters, and will miss you."

"Good luck with your case, but something tells me you will come out of this okay, regardless of the verdict."

"You know I will."

Chapter 25

Brenda drove her '67 Camaro ten miles over the speed limit through the countryside. There was still snow on the ground, but the roads were clear. Her goal was to find the hidden document and find it fast. Taking the documentation with Stern's information was a minor theft for Michael all those years ago. He said he took it for no reason other than just to have it. Maybe, deep down inside, he thought he would use it against Stern if he ever survived the concentration camp, but the reason wasn't important. Now that document had huge relevance and promised to be a major piece of evidence in this case. That is, if there really was a document. Weisman seemed so sure when he claimed that his research showed there was no Hans Stern to be found.

Michael had handled himself well during Weisman's cross examination. Now he had the opportunity to accept Weisman's challenge to "prove it."

His trial had made headlines throughout the

country, but a projected outcome was uncertain. The consensus was that Michael was the good guy, and Stern, the bad guy. That was to be expected. Nazis were never high on people's list of nice people and, maybe because he *was* a Nazi, now Stern's existence in Auschwitz was being called into question.

Although Michael shouldn't have taken the law into his own hands, many people were drawn to his side. Still, Brenda had reminded Michael that nobody has the right to take another person's life, and if Michael was in his right mind, he had options to choose from other than vigilante justice. The law would have to prevail, not popular opinion, but she was his lawyer and wanted him to win. The question of whether he was in his right mind was the basis for the defense's argument.

Was he in his right mind? Brenda pondered the question as she pulled into the driveway. She knew he *did* know right from wrong, but irresistible impulse was all she had. No other argument would result in a verdict of not guilty.

Brenda sat in the driveway of Michael's detached garage. She had visited the crime scene once before, when preparing the case, but now she had a specific purpose. An eerie feeling came over her as she looked straight ahead and imagined what had happened there on that terrible night. The garage door was still taped with yellow strips declaring it a crime scene. Her thoughts were everywhere. How fortuitous it was for him to have a detached garage when Stern was gassed. Otherwise, his house could have gone up in flames. She wondered if the placement of his garage had influenced his decision to kill Stern the way he had.

Brenda flipped the mat at the front door and found the rust-stained key. The door opened into a small foyer and she felt the cooler air as it swept across her face through the open living room windows.

Why were they left wide open? Did Michael have his plan so carefully worked out to avoid the possibility of his house burning down?

The carpet below the windows was wet and dirty. She closed them and noticed the house still had a musty odor despite the fresh air pouring in. She stood in the living room and looked around. To the right was the dining area with two large windows facing a now desolate flower garden bordered by green hemlocks.

A large kitchen with gleaming appliances had a door leading to the outside. Two thick slices of stale brown bread covered with white and green mold sat on the counter. She wrapped a paper towel around them and threw them in the trash. She walked through the rest of the house, closing more windows as she went along. There were two full baths, two bedrooms, and a large study with books taking up most of the wall space. There was an LP recording of *Pictures at an Exhibition* alongside the record player and some Beatles and Bee Gee recordings. Nothing out of the ordinary.

Why didn't the police tape this house off as a crime scene? Maybe they had, but she was so focused on the garage when she visited previously that she hadn't noticed. Maybe they had already removed the tape or never marked it off at all. It was a mistake not to have asked Officer Baker about that, but whether the house was taped off or not wouldn't impact the outcome of the case at this time.

The main question for Brenda was why Michael hadn't told her about this misplaced document when they first met. Was there something he was hiding? If it was so important, why couldn't he remember exactly where it was? He'd uttered something about animals in passing, but that made no sense.

Questions only brought more questions without answers. If this important document existed, how could he have kept it hidden all these years? How was he able to keep it at all? Wasn't he ever searched at Auschwitz? Something within him must have told him to take it. Maybe it was his intuition. Maybe he'd already formulated some kind of plan when he was in Auschwitz and waited for an opportunity to use it for his revenge. It would have been a long wait. If there was no document, there was no Stern, leaving only Harry Sanders.

Brenda's search was methodical. She opened drawers that were filled with thick folders. She opened and examined each one of them. Some contained papers written in Hungarian, others handwritten drafts of his books, written in English. The hours passed into the night. No document. She searched for something to eat and found a can of tuna. That would be safe. She opened it and ate it out of the can.

The thank you note from Harry Sanders *was* in the drawer next to the sink. She had to dig for it, just as Michael had said, and found it under the can openers and other kitchen tools along with a mass of papers. Brenda read it and slipped it into her briefcase.

She returned to his study. One portion of the wall had several framed university degrees and testimonials to his accomplishments in science and teaching. Books were everywhere—novels, biographies, poetry, and books about pharmacology, which showed Michael Ross's name as the author. On some of the books, the author's name was Miklos Rosen. They were probably published internationally years ago, but he must have found them in some of the bookstores. Miklos Rosen...his name sounded as if it was from another time.

Starting at the top shelf, Brenda began the tedious task of opening books to search for the document. Her fingers ran through poems by Emily Dickinson, and she stopped to read one of them she remembered from her high school English class. It was about success. The poem pointed out that only those who have suffered defeat can truly understand success.

Brenda had to move faster. Going through each heavy book of the *Encyclopedia Britannica* took over an hour. She read passages from other books but forced herself not to dwell on the content and stay focused on her search for documents inside them.

She skimmed the pages of Shakespeare, books by Scott Fitzgerald, and novels by Hemingway. Michael's tastes seemed to be endless. One of Brenda's favorite books was there too, a leather-bound copy of *Moby Dick*. She smiled when she read the opening: "Call me Ishmael." She remembered reading those words so many years ago and reminded herself to make time to read the book again.

She continued to search until she read a passage from a book without looking at the title. "All men are enemies. All animals are comrades." She flipped through the pages and, somewhere near the middle, a yellowed sheet of paper fell to the floor. As she reached down to pick it up, she saw a picture of a young man in a Nazi officer's uniform staring up at her. Underneath the picture was the man's name— Major Hans Stern.

The document was written in German. Brenda turned to the cover of the book. *Animal Farm* by George Orwell.

Chapter 26

On Monday morning, Brenda Coleman handed three documents to Mr. Weisman for his perusal prior to asking the judge to admit them. Weisman took about twenty minutes to examine them, made a few notes, and returned them to the defense table.

Michael was recalled to the stand for direct questioning.

"Professor Ross," Brenda began, "The prosecution has stated there was no record of SS officer, Hans Stern, or anyone by that name who had served in a military capacity at Auschwitz concentration camp during 1941-1945, which includes the time in 1944, when you were confined there. During the last court session, you said you had proof to the contrary and that Hans Stern was, in fact, an SS officer at Auschwitz. Is that a correct statement?"

"Yes, Ms. Coleman."

Brenda handed the document to Michael and asked, "Is this the document in question that you say you took from a folder in the office of the SS in

Auschwitz?"

Michael looked at it. "It is, Ms. Coleman."

"Thank you. You may step down, professor."

"Your Honor, at this time we would like to offer into evidence the defense's exhibits, numbers five, six, and seven, which support the defendant's claim that Hans Stern was, in fact, an SS officer at Auschwitz and that Harry Sanders and Hans Stern are one and the same."

David Weisman stood and shouted. "Your Honor, I ask the court to disallow it. I have examined these documents and found no indication to show that they are authentic. They may have been forged or altered and the picture affixed to the document at a later time. In addition, the signature on the document cannot be verified to show that Hans Stern and Harry Sanders are the same person."

Ms. Coleman addressed the court. "Your Honor, with your permission, I would like to explain the significance of these exhibits. The first document, Exhibit Five, was in the defendant's possession and is stamped *Wichtige,* which means 'important' in German. It shows a picture of an SS officer in full uniform and, below it, the name Hans Stern, who held the rank of major. The document, written in German, describes Hans Stern's background, date and place of birth, along with his achievements, medals, and honors as a Nazi officer and is signed by Hans Stern.

"The second document is an English translation of Exhibit Five and is labeled Exhibit Six. It includes a notarized affidavit setting forth the qualifications of the translator and certification that the translation is fair and accurate. The third document, which I labeled Exhibit Seven, is a letter from Harry Sanders sent to Professor Ross's address in Oneonta, New York. It is a note to Professor Ross thanking him in advance for the opportunity to play a scheduled game of chess with him several days later. It is signed Harry Sanders."

Brenda looked at the judge.

"Anything else, Ms. Coleman?"

"Your Honor, the document proves that Hans Stern was, in fact, an SS officer and a member of the Nazi party during World War II. He held the rank of major and *was* stationed in Auschwitz from 1941 until it was liberated by the Soviets in January, 1945.

"Commandant Hoess, Major Stern, and others presumably destroyed these documents since they were not found in the German records at Auschwitz. However, Exhibit Five is an original document in the possession of the defense and represents a challenge to Mr. Weisman's research, in which he claimed there was no information placing Major Hans Stern at Auschwitz."

David Weisman stood and addressed the court, "Your Honor, I request that the defense's exhibits not be placed into evidence because of their questionable authenticity. I am willing to accept the translation from German to English, but that has no relevance to the authenticity of the document."

Judge Jordan looked at the counselors.

"I will accept all the defense's exhibits, subject to authentication. Ms. Coleman, you may continue."

David Weisman took a deep breath and rolled his

eyes.

"Thank you, Your Honor. At this time, I would like to call Ms. Kelsey Albright to the stand, who will testify as to the authenticity of both documents. I contacted her over the weekend and asked her to provide her services relevant to these documents. She was kind enough to oblige."

Ms. Albright, an attractive blonde, about thirty-five, attired in a navy blue pinstriped business suit, approached the witness stand and was sworn.

"Ms. Albright," Brenda began, "would you please state your occupation for the court?"

"I am a forensic document examiner and am associated with a firm called Forensic Dynamics International."

"Thank you. Would you please tell us what a forensic document examiner does and what kind of training is involved?"

"My job is to study documents with respect to handwriting, typewriting, or printing and draw conclusions about a document's authenticity, signature comparison, alterations, or any other issues that arise concerning the document's legitimacy.

"My training consisted of an intensive two-year program under the supervision of an established forensic document examiner. In addition, I have completed a graduate program in forensic science at Oklahoma State University, Class of 1958."

"Ms. Albright, you have before you the original document, labeled Exhibit Five, attesting to Hans Stern's presence in Auschwitz as an SS officer. Will you please render your findings?"

"I have made a complete study of the document and found that the paper it was written on was in use in Europe during the late thirties and mid-forties. The typewriter used also matched the machines used at that time."

"And how were you able to make such a determination?"

"I used backlighting to decipher the manufacturer's watermark on the paper, verifying the time period it was in use and the typeface design of the typewriter keys. They were all consistent with a typewriter capable of typing in the German language."

"Were other parts of Exhibit Five not altered in any way?"

"There was no indication that the document was altered and I can say, with assurance, that the photograph was never removed or replaced."

"With respect to the signature, would you say it was authentic?"

"I can say, with reasonable certainty, that the ink analysis and the type of ink used to sign the document was commonly in use in the forties. In addition, I checked for the authenticity of the ink by examining handwritten notes placed alongside the typical Nazi rubber stamp impression showing an eagle with its wings spread and standing on a globe of the world.

"My conclusion is that the document and typewriter used were authentic for its time, along with the ink, paper, and writing instruments."

"What conclusion did you arrive at with respect to the signature, 'Hans Stern,' on the bottom of the document in question? Was it authentic?"

"At first, I was not able to confirm with certainty that the signature on the document was made by this man. I never knew him and had no connection with this document. However, upon the examination of Exhibit Seven, a letter signed by Harry Sanders, I concluded that the signature on that personal letter was made by the same person who signed the document labeled Exhibit Five, Hans Stern."

"How can you be so sure?"

"I have been specifically trained in United States government forensic laboratories as a handwriting examiner by Dr. Manfred Zeigelman, a noted expert in the field. I have examined the signature and found that it has not been traced. I compared the signatures of Hans Stern on the German document with the signature on the letter addressed to Professor Ross and found strong identifying characteristics. Each signature has several of the same letters in each name and it was easy to conclude that the strong similarity between the 'H' and 'S' in each written signature proves that they were written by one and the same man."

"And you are certain of that?"

"I am."

"Your witness, Mr. Weisman."

David Weisman approached the witness stand, stroking his chin. "Good morning, Ms. Albright. Would you tell the jury if the examination of documents is an exact science?"

"I cannot say it is an *exact* science, but..."

"So, you're saying it is not an exact science? Is it is more of an art."

"No, sir, examiners are trained to make subjective conclusions based on a forensic examination of documents."

"So, these conclusions are *not* scientifically objective, but are merely personal observations?"

"The defense objects. The prosecution is leading the witness. The use of the word 'personal' is his word and implies a judgment outside of forensics."

"Objection sustained. The jury will disregard the question."

Mr. Weisman continued. "While there are some credible aspects to your profession, Ms. Albright, is there a strong correlation between handwriting analysis and astrology?"

"Absolutely not!" she said. "I would not compare the two. They are totally different."

"Ms. Albright, would you please tell the jury the type of certification that is required to be a forensic document examiner."

"There is no certification at the present time."

"Thank you, Ms. Albright."

The judge looked toward Brenda. "Redirect, Ms. Coleman?"

"Yes, Your Honor."

Brenda Coleman approached the witness stand to question the witness following the redirect procedure.

"Ms. Albright, in how many cases have you appeared as a forensic document examiner?"

"About two hundred."

"In how many of those cases were your findings shown to be true and accurate by the court?"

"When it came to detecting alterations,

obliterations, and erasures, I would say all of them."

"And did you find any alterations, obliterations, or erasures with respect to the defense's exhibits five and seven?"

"No, ma'am. None."

"What conclusion did you arrive at with respect to the authenticity of the documents?"

"I did not find any alterations of any kind and concluded that the documents were authentic."

"Thank you, Ms. Albright."

Brenda returned to the defense table, unsmiling.

"How do you think it went with the document examiner?" Michael asked.

"I'm not sure," Brenda replied. "Weisman compared her work to astrology. I hope the jury didn't buy into it. He knows how to turn a jury with just one question. Overall, I think we came out all right. Tomorrow will be our last day in court. You will take the stand again, Michael, and our psychiatrist will follow. Relax, you'll do fine."

Judge Jordan adjourned the case until 10 a.m. the next morning.

Chapter 27

Michael returned to his cell. The events of the day ran through his mind.

This has to end already. The trial should have been a one-day affair, but it's now the center of attention for the entire country. Almost everyone must be on my side because I killed a Nazi. The skinheads aren't, but they are a small minority and have little influence. It's the law that counts, not public opinion, and certainly not the jury's emotions. Why does my case have to be a cause célèbre and make headlines?

Maybe, through me, everyone can identify with why people would want to take revenge on the Nazis. That could be, but there are other legal issues that have even more meaning and have nothing to do with the Nazis.

I read about a case called Roe v. Wade that reached the Supreme Court on appeal. They put it on the back burner for now, but I think it, too, will soon make headlines. It's about abortion, a human issue, and something we should have dealt with a long time ago. A woman should have the right to her own body. I'll never understand human behavior.

Albert was relocated to another cell and Michael claimed the lower bunk as his own. The mattress was so thin he could feel the sharp springs pushing up into his back. For the first time in over two months, Michael was alone. His mind was still consumed with Stern and the night of August 16. He relived Sterns last screams, repeatedly, in his mind. *Was machst du?* In some bizarre way, Stern's cries gave him pleasure. Being alone gave him quiet time with Ilona.

***

Dearest, I'm sorry I wasn't able to be with you for the past few days. The court case consumes me but being in jail doesn't take me away from you. When I lost you and later learned you were in Paradise, I felt cursed by the distance between us, but now I feel blessed that I can enjoy the finer parts of our love that others with the privilege of nearness fail to notice.

Our minds and hearts are joined for all eternity, a gift perhaps few can share. Thank you so much for loving me and being my wife.

When I close my eyes to see you, images flood my mind and I'm taken back to our sweet world before the men in marching boots banged on our door and took our lives away.

Terror, anger, and killing surrounded us—the opposite of our world, which was filled with love for each other and our little babies.

Sit and talk with me for a while. I live in a country so different from Hungary or any place in Europe. There is freedom here in America, real freedom with nobody watching your every move.

You know I am not a violent person, but I'm human, and the visions of you humiliated and in pain will always haunt me. There was nothing I could have done to help you then, and I felt anger toward myself for being so helpless. But when I came across Stern recently, I gave him the justice he deserved. Hans Stern is dead. I killed him, and he knew why he had to die. It was something that I had to do...for us.

I know where you are, in that beautiful place, and the time will come when we will share our lives once more. Don't laugh, but I even think of us getting older together. I know what you're thinking, but don't worry. The beauty I see in you is timeless.

In the scheme of things, the good times we shared with our little dancing girls took place in a brief moment, as fast as the snap of my fingers, and yet, that moment, that snap, was our lifetime, and, for us, it will go on forever.

I think of our sweet daughters and what they would be like if they had achieved their girlhood dreams. What would they be doing now if they were grown up and living in America? Would they remember their Hungarian language? Roza would have been a writer for sure. She couldn't be anything else. I could see her book in the window of Barnes and Noble. "The Collected Poems of Roza Rosen." She was so serene and sensitive.

And Magda, our little singer. She would be a star, Ilona, and we would see her and listen to her voice on Broadway as the lead female singer in Man of La Mancha or Cabaret. What a gift she had, and we were fortunate to have been her first audience.

Then there's the little one, Eva, "Miss Personality." We would drive down from Oneonta to Manhattan, watch her dance the lead in her favorite ballet, "Swan Lake," the one she practiced in our home when she was five. We would send her a bouquet of red roses and watch her holding them on stage, casting a glance toward us as she bowed.

Then it would be dinner at The Plaza with our sweet girls and we would all stay overnight. I thought I needed pictures to remember all of us, but I don't. The memories are right here in my mind. They had so much to give, Ilona.

But I've saved the best for last. I see them older and married with children of their own, their own dancers performing their way up, down, and around the furniture. Maybe they would have boys. Imagine that, Ilona, boys. Either way, our girls would be giving us the best gift of all. We would be grandparents, Ilona!

Chapter 28

"Your Honor, may it please the court, the defense calls Dr. Carl Evans to the stand," Ms. Coleman said.

A tall, medium built man, about fifty with dark hair, took the stand and was sworn.

"Good afternoon, Dr. Evans. Thank you for appearing today. You have been called here to provide expert testimony relating to the mental state of Professor Michael Ross."

Dr. Evans nodded. "Yes, I understand."

"Sir, please state your profession and educational background?"

The witness took a deep breath. "I am a psychiatrist. My undergraduate work was completed at Princeton in 1941. I applied to medical school at Johns Hopkins and was accepted for the class of '42. However, instead of continuing my education at that time, I enlisted in the US Army and was a medical corpsman in the European Theater of Operations until 1945, when I was honorably discharged.

"I started my medical training at Johns Hopkins and received my medical degree in 1953. I did a residency in cardiology at Johns Hopkins and another residency in psychiatry at Massachusetts General Hospital in Boston before I went into private practice as a psychiatrist."

"Are you a licensed psychiatrist in the state of New York?"

"Yes, I am licensed in New York and Massachusetts."

"Thank you, Dr. Evans. What is your psychiatric specialty in your private practice?"

"I specialize in psychoanalysis."

Brenda paced the courtroom floor. "Exactly what kind of therapy *is* psychoanalysis and how do you use it in your practice?"

"The goal of psychoanalysis is to treat mental disorders by investigating the interaction of conscious and unconscious elements in the mind. It emphasizes the influence of the unconscious mind on behavior.

"In my practice, I delve into the unconscious minds of my patients to find their repressed fears and I bring them to the surface. When a fear or conflict is brought to light after being concealed in the unconscious mind, I help the patient see the significance of those fears and how it affects their behavior."

"And then what, doctor?" Brenda asked

"Once these buried events are discussed and analyzed with the patient, it enables me to find the root of his or her neurotic behavior. Once patients learn the root cause of their actions, they have a new understanding of the reasons for their behavior, which helps them make positive changes."

"And what techniques do you use to find the repressed feelings which interfere with healthy behavior?"

"I mostly use free association and dream analysis."

"Did you use these procedures with Professor Ross?"

"I did," Dr. Evans replied.

"How many times did you meet with the defendant, Michael Ross?"

"At the court's request, I met the professor on twelve occasions since he was incarcerated, which constituted eleven hours of analytic therapy. The sessions were held in a medical office at the prison. My goal was to determine the defendant's state of mind at the time of the victim's death. The written record I provided to the court shows the dates, times, and my conclusions after each session."

"Please tell the jury some of your findings, doctor, with respect to Professor Ross."

"During my examination, Professor Ross appeared normal without any abhorrent behavior, but after several therapy sessions, I discovered his unconscious mind was filled with repressed anxiety, phobia, depression, and compulsions. He also was consumed with guilt, which I later discovered was the result of his inability to protect his wife and children from harm.

"My overall impression was that I was dealing with an intelligent, sensitive, and caring man. He told me about his family and what happened in the concentration camp. He was open about his conscious feelings and told me about a recurring dream he had after he was imprisoned here in New York. I was able to find a connecting theme in this particular dream which helped me understand his behavior."

Brenda turned toward the jury, hesitated a moment as she looked at each of them, and returned her attention to the witness.

"Tell us about that dream, doctor, even if it calls for a narrative, if you feel it will help the jury understand Professor Ross's repressed feelings and how they related to his behavior the night of August sixteenth."

Carl Evans rubbed his eyes for a moment and replied in an easy manner.

"I asked Professor Ross for his permission to give him an injection of sodium pentothal, which would reduce the brake effect on his brain and allow him to bring his fears and anxieties from the depths of his unconscious mind into his conscious, the mind we live with every day.

"I told him it would give me the opportunity to examine his buried feelings and interpret their meanings and how they affected his daily behavior. He agreed to the injection.

"As is customary in this type of therapy session, Professor Ross was lying on a couch and I sat behind him with a notepad and tape recorder. I'll include my interpretation as part of the dream as we go along.

"The dream takes place on a dark night. Michael is sitting in the den of his private home, listening to music. The den has a double door leading to the patio. The inner door is made of wood, and the outer door is a wrought iron gate showing indistinguishable words at the top.

"Michael sees a man jump from the roof of his house onto the patio. The man has a dark complexion and black hair. He is wearing a black mask, black hat, and a black cape. Michael immediately begins to tremble. His eyes widened and I had the feeling his heart was beating faster. He is afraid this man will kill him.

"The masked man tears the heavy wrought iron gate off its hinges and bangs his shoulders repeatedly against the inner wooden door, trying to force it open. Michael uses all his strength to hold it closed, but it becomes a back and forth struggle between them. The fight for Michael to keep the door closed reaches new heights when the man's black-gloved hand is partially inside the door. Michael's body is shaking. He's drenched in sweat as he tries to keep the man out, but he's not strong enough.

"The man breaks in, but now he's dressed as a postman and he knocks Michael unconscious. When he revives, he sees the postman dragging Ilona across the floor toward a large room with beds.

"Ilona looks back at Michael. She's screaming with her arms held out to him. Tears fall from Michael's eyes. He remains on the floor, paralyzed with fear, and can't move. Ilona briefly escapes from the clutches of the postman and runs toward a wall held together by pieces of black wire. The postman pulls her off the wall and continues to drag her toward the large room.

"He pulls her so hard that her arms come out of their sockets. Michael sees Ilona with her mouth open, trying to scream, but no sound comes out.

"He, too, tries to scream. His mouth is wide open and his jaw is in pain, but he produces no sound no matter how hard he tries. At the end of the dream, he sees a blank space. Michael wakes up, his mouth still wide open, breathing heavily with his heart pounding as he lies in his urine-soaked bed."

Brenda listened intently as the psychiatrist described the events of Michael's recurring dream. "What did you make of this dream, doctor? I mean, how did you interpret it so that it shows relevance to this case?"

Dr. Evans wiped his brow and leaned forward.

"Interpreting Michael's dream required a discussion between the two of us to determine the meaning of the symbols and how they affected his behavior on the night of August sixteenth. That information would enable me to determine his state of mind, but it would take time for me to explain it to the court."

"Go ahead. Take all the time you need," Brenda said, opening her palms.

Dr. Evans took a sip of water.

"It was a dream about fear. Both Ilona and Michael could not hear anything when they tried to scream. They were so paralyzed with anxiety that no sound could come out of their mouths.

"I asked Michael who the man was. The professor just shrugged. Then I asked him why the man was dressed in black, wore a black mask, and had a black cape. His face was even dark. He said he didn't know. At this point I knew he was not capable of having any input into his dream. Too much was buried in his unconscious and he had no clue, so I helped him.

"I explained to Michael that his dream disguised events and feelings in his unconscious mind, making it difficult for the conscious to figure out the symbols that contributed to his behavior on the night of August sixteenth. He did not perceive that the man in the black clothes and the postman were the same person, Hans Stern.

"It was Stern who jumped onto the patio dressed in black. He had black hair and dark skin, the *opposite* of Stern's real appearance. Stern was blond and fair. The black mask was a dead giveaway. People use them at masquerades to disguise their faces. When I explained how our dreams are coded by disguising people in the dream with looks *opposite* to the real person, his eyes widened and his jaw dropped. In that moment, it came to him and he understood that the man in the dream *was*, in fact, Stern."

Brenda glanced at the jury. "Dr. Evans, can you tell the court if Michael Ross found anything significant about the double doors?"

"He said he saw the wrought iron gate as if it were in a horror movie on a dark, stormy night with lightning bolts shooting into the ground and where bad things were about to happen. When I asked him what the gate meant in his dream, he instantly said, 'Auschwitz.'"

Brenda stroked her jaw and walked closer to the

witness stand. "So, the gate had some sort of relevance in the dream? Why was it significant?"

"Objection! Leading," Weisman called out. "The defense is assuming relevancy and there is no foundation."

"Please rephrase your question, Ms. Coleman."

"Dr. Evans, When Michael Ross answered 'Auschwitz,' what was your interpretation of his response?"

"It was the meaning *he* attached to it and I agreed. Then I asked him why there were *two* doors and if he felt they had any significance in his dream. He thought it was related to Auschwitz but didn't know why.

"With my help, we talked about it further. I reminded him that the outer door on the patio was a metal gate and the inner door was made of wood. This represented the two entrances to the camp that Michael had to go through at Auschwitz. The first was a wrought iron gate and on top were the German words, *Arbeit Macht Frei,* work will make you free. The inner wooden door symbolized the entrance to the barracks, where Ross slept."

"Did you discuss these symbols further with Michael Ross?"

"Absolutely. It was the most important thing for him to understand. After Hans Stern forced his way in, his disguise quickly changed to elude the conscious again, which is why he was dressed in the gray uniform of a postman. SS officers wore uniforms that were close to gray.

"The idea of Stern forcing his way in through both doors on the patio symbolized the constant fear and anxiety Michael felt while as a prisoner in Auschwitz. It can also be a reference to how the Nazis barged their way into the homes of Jews and others, arrested them, and sent them to concentration camps. However, when I questioned Michael about its importance, he shook his head. I told him there is a deeper meaning to why Stern was dressed as a postman."

"What was it, doctor?" Brenda asked.

"Once inside, Stern's vile, basic nature surfaced, but he kept it hidden by dressing as a postman."

"Why a postman's uniform, Dr. Evans?"

"Because a postman is normally accepted in the community and is trusted. He's someone you may see every day. Stern is certainly the opposite of a friendly postman. Once Stern is in his postman's uniform, he becomes credible as a trusted person, which makes it easier for him to trick Michael and Ilona to do his bidding. Now, Stern takes advantage of them, just as the Nazis tricked the Jews when the Jews first came to Auschwitz and were immediately led to the gas chamber under the pretense they would be showering.

"The postman in the dream can now perform his evil deeds. He attacks Ilona and pulls her toward a large room with beds, which symbolize the place where prisoners slept. As she was dragged there, her arms come out of their sockets and Michael sees her as a broken woman."

"And the wall, doctor. I'm sure the jury would like to hear its meaning. What did it signify?"

"When I asked Michael about the wall, where all the blocks were wired together, I had no idea what it represented, but knew it was something that created fear in him, so I asked him what it meant. Michael surprised me with his answer and said it was a barbed wire fence. He was able to break through its disguised meaning and it was something *only* he could have known because it was connected to a tragic event in his life. His wife had taken her life by intentionally running into an electrified barbed wire fence."

"It appears that psychiatrists can't always figure things out on their own." Brenda smiled.

"No, there are times when we need the patients help." Evans smiled back.

"Dr. Evans, how important is the issue of a blank space in Michael's mind? It has often come up during this trial. Would you please elaborate on its significance and how it might shed light on Michael Ross's mental state on the night of August sixteenth?"

"Yes, of course. It is an important point. Michael's recurring dream always ended with a blank space, and that had a major bearing for me to arrive at my final diagnosis. I asked him what this space looked like. He said it was like being in a movie theater, looking at a lighted screen with no images on it."

Doctor Evans paused and took a deep breath.

"Basically, the blank space represented a gap in time for events buried in the unconscious to reach his everyday mind—his conscious. During those minutes, time was non-existent for him. Michael didn't remember that he'd killed Stern until he arrived in town fifteen minutes later. He would be considered insane during that gap in time."

"Thank you for your interpretation, doctor. Would you tell the jury your final conclusion about how your lab tests, talk sessions, and dream analysis came together in a meaningful way for you to make a conclusion?"

"After Michael Ross was arrested, he had this dream repeatedly. At the end, there was always a blank space where nothing happens. Even after he awakens, some time must pass before he can remember the tragic events of that night. It's an example of extreme fear and depression, where he is controlled by a tragic happening resulting in a memory lapse. I explained the reasons earlier.

"After spending a good deal of time with the defendant, I was convinced from the moment Michael Ross realized the man sitting in his house was Hans Stern, he acted uncontrollably, as dictated by his unconscious mind. He killed Stern, then came the space that lasts about fifteen minutes. By that time, he's in town. There was no way that Michael could ever remember killing Stern. His mental state was strongly compromised to the degree that, at that moment, he was temporarily insane, and that nagging blank space blocked any remembrance of what happened in the garage until later, when he got to town."

David Weisman leaped to his feet and cried out, "Objection, Your Honor. This is a long, drawn out narrative and it's only a dream."

Brenda looked toward the judge. "It's his professional opinion, Your Honor."

Judge Jordan replied, "Overruled. He is an expert

witness. Continue, counselor."

Brenda walked back to the defense table and looked at her notes. Then she turned toward the witness.

"Dr. Evans, to sum up, you said in your testimony that Professor Ross's action was uncontrollable. Is that your expert opinion?"

"Yes, it is," he answered with assurance.

"It was uncontrollable and not uncontrolled?"

"Absolutely. There was no way that Ross was capable of any type of cognition. He acted out of impulse."

"Would you say it was an irresistible impulse?"

"It was," Dr. Evens said.

"How can you be so convinced, doctor?"

"I have gained experience after treating several of my patients with the same issues. They could not remember the terrible deeds they had done until afterward. One of the patients, instead of seeing a blank space saw total darkness before he was aware of what he had done. Another saw the blue flame of a pilot light. Why these images? I don't know."

"You have diagnosed these cases before?"

"Yes, but not often. In Michael Ross's case, he could not resist the impulse he felt. It consumed him. It was irresistible and he acted uncontrollably. That was it. There was no question in my mind."

"The defense rests, Your Honor."

"Will the prosecution offer a rebuttal?" Judge Jordan asked.

David Weismann stood. "We will, Your Honor."

"In that case, we will adjourn this case until 10 a.m. tomorrow morning."

Michael returned to his cell.

Chapter 29

The events of the past months had drained Michael's spirit. He fortified his resolve to honor his family by making an example of the evil crimes of one SS officer who, like other Nazis, inflicted torture and death on millions of innocent people. Many of those who died would have contributed so much to the world of science, medicine, literature, and music, but they're dead and the families that could have come after them were never born. One third of the entire Jewish population were killed by the Nazis. There were so few Jews in the world, which made it a greater tragedy.

The case was important to Michael. The Holocaust must never be forgotten. The Nazis could have been stopped if people were alert and paid attention. World War II didn't have to happen, but human beings are just that, human, and busy with their own lives.

Michael feared that the incomprehensible insanity that the Nazis unleashed on the world would be trivialized by future generations. It would be unimaginable, but it's possible that some might say that the Holocaust never happened. New enemies could one day terrorize the world and hatred would raise its ugly head again with even greater force, and, like a snake, empty its venom upon humanity.

Was what Michael did legal? He knew it wasn't, but he couldn't report Stern to the authorities as a war criminal because the lessons of the Nuremburg trials told him that, while a few were hanged, most of them went free after a short sentence. He couldn't take a chance on Stern serving a year or two in prison, then being released and free. He had no choice but to end Stern's life. When Stern was on trial in Michael's garage, it was Stern's turn to listen to Michael's false promises that he would be freed, Stern's turn to suffer sitting in his own excrement. It was Stern's turn to be humiliated and Stern's turn to know what it was like to be gassed the way so many millions of innocent people were by people like Stern.

There was one important reason that Michael wanted to be freed, only one. Maybe there would come a time when he would be able to meet Erika and see Ilona in her eyes.

***

Michael didn't like the idea of stretching the truth in court. He was an honorable and caring person, but he rationalized that there must be times when people must strike out against evil in their own way, like the way Israel made an exception when they excluded Eichmann from Israel's law against capital punishment. Those who did those evil deeds so long ago had to be punished using extreme measures. All they were able to do was hang him, an easy death with no suffering. Michael was only able to do the best he could by gassing Stern. Stern paid a small price, considering all the years he spent as a free man. Michael tried to be hard on him by making him sit in squalor and keeping him handcuffed, but that was not enough torture. Then again, he could never be like Stern. Michael could never be an evil person no matter how much he tried with Stern.

He needed to be taken away from his thoughts and be with Ilona.

Michael sat on his bed with his back up against the cement walls of his cell and turned off the world.

***

My dearest wife,

I long for you so much. My daydreams are filled with memories of our love. The years are piling up on me, and it won't be long before we will be together again. I have never talked to you about Auschwitz because I would never want you to relive those agonizing times and feel the pain of losing our little girls in that lunatic asylum. Those years will haunt me forever, along with the guilt I feel for surviving.

I can only imagine the pain you must have felt when you had to give in to Stern. I know you; you are a beautiful and loving woman. Please don't feel that you have betrayed me. Prisoners in concentration camps are capable of understanding those things. If I ever have the opportunity to lay my eyes on Erika, I will only see you.

You are my beautiful wife. Not just for now, but for all eternity, and we will share our lives again for always. And yes, I'll keep your feet warm on those cold nights. I love you.

Chapter 30

Sheets of rain cascaded from the dark sky as crowds pushed their way into the courthouse, their umbrellas crashing against each other. Newspaper headlines blasted in large print:

Trial May End Today!

A few neo-Nazi skinheads paraded outside the courthouse carrying rain-soaked signs that read, "GUILTY," but they were soon run off by the crowd. The court session began at 10:30 a.m. Dr. Evans was re-called to the stand and advised he was still under oath.

Judge Jordan turned toward the prosecutor. "Counselor, your witness."

Weisman began his questioning.

"Dr. Evans, the defendant, Professor Michael Ross, is an intelligent man and has had a brilliant teaching career. He has written several books on complex topics and has never demonstrated any behavior that would indicate any type of insanity.

Would you agree? Yes or no?"

"I cannot answer based on the limitations of a yes or no," Evans replied.

The Judge turned toward Evans and asked him to answer the question. "Did he or didn't he?"

Evans hesitated, "Yes, it's true. His general behavior may not have shown a departure from his normal conduct but extreme emotional circumstances could alter his mental state significantly."

"Wouldn't you say that could be true for everyone?"

"Of course, but it was different for the professor. His feelings of guilt created periods of insanity within him."

"Dr. Evans, you claimed that Ross acted as a result of irresistible impulse and that his actions were uncontrolled. Is that correct?"

"No, sir. I said his action was *uncontrollable,* which means he acted out of impulse and had no choice with respect to what he did. If his action were merely *uncontrolled,* it would mean he had the choice of exercising the act or not. In other words, *uncontrolled* involves a decision-making process. *Uncontrollable* means he acted without conscious thought."

Weisman scratched his head, shrugged, and paced back and forth in front of the witness stand, then turned toward Evans. "So, you're saying that Ross acted on some kind of *uncontrollable* impulse?"

"I am. He acted in a way that was consistent with an irresistible impulse, which resulted in the demise of the victim."

"Dr. Evans, you described a recurring dream that the defendant had during psychoanalysis. It was rich in detail. Did you keep a record of the dream?"

"I did. I made a recording of it in the patient's own voice on a Teac reel-to-reel tape recorder and listened to it several times in order to capture the nuances and emotions in his voice. A written record would state only the words he said on paper. That kind of record would have limited meaning for a psychiatrist because there would be no emotion associated with it. The tape was significant because it was an account of what he said combined with the emotions he felt. Under those circumstances, a psychoanalytic psychiatrist would be able to interpret it in a more meaningful way."

"How can you be so sure that your interpretation of his dream has the meaning you attributed to it?"

"I have had advanced training in psychoanalysis and dream interpretation. When a patient has a dream, I teach him how to interpret its elusive symbols and how they relate to repressed events in his conscious behavior."

"I see," Weisman replied, looking at his notes. "Is it possible that another psychiatrist would come to the same conclusions as you did with respect to your interpretation of Michael Ross's dream?"

"Yes, and highly probable if he had in-depth training in psychoanalysis."

"So, it would also be possible for another psychiatrist to arrive at an entirely *different* conclusion with respect to the same dream."

"Yes, it's possible."

"Is it possible *many* psychiatrists would come to different conclusions?"

"It would be highly unlikely," Evans answered. "Perhaps they would disagree on a few points, but at the end there would be a consensus."

"But it would still be possible?"

"To some degree, yes."

David Weisman took a deep breath and interrupted his questioning of Evans. He walked past the jury, his hand on his chin, and appeared to be in deep thought. Then he turned toward the witness.

"You know, Dr. Evans, I have a feeling that your testimony was contrived by the defense to try to show that the defendant was insane at the time, taking advantage of a subset of the insanity defense which relates to irresistible impulse. The idea that he did it without thinking is absurd."

Brenda Coleman leaped to her feet and, in an authoritative voice, cried out, "Objection, Your Honor. No foundation, prejudicial, and an expression of the prosecutor's personal opinion. Move to strike."

The judge turned to the jury. "The jury will disregard the comments made by Mr. Weisman." Judge Jordan looked at Weisman. "You're an experienced lawyer. Please don't do that again."

Weisman continued his interrogation. He walked closer to the stand and faced Evans.

"Doctor, do you think that what Ross did was planned in advance? Didn't it have to be premeditated?"

"Absolutely not! After examining the defendant,

I concluded that Professor Ross's actions were definitely not planned in advance and were in no way premeditated." Evans looked directly at Weisman as he answered.

"Based on your therapy sessions with the defendant, doctor, isn't it possible that the defendant *could have* had a well-planned scheme to murder Harry Sanders, which continued over a number of days prior to the victim's death?"

"Based on my examination of Professor Ross, it would be unlikely. He was too impulsive to devise a long drawn out plan to kill Stern. His basic nature wouldn't allow it."

"Is it possible that the defendant might have been lying in wait to take Harry Sanders prisoner and kill him?"

"No!" Evans cried out. "It was impulsive."

Weisman paused. He had a slim grin on his face.

"Are you aware of previous testimony that indicated that the handcuffs, *owned* by Michael Ross, were found on the wrists of the victim and attached to a strong pipe?" Weisman stared into Evans' eyes.

"I do know about the handcuffs."

"Would that information be consistent with your conclusion that the defendant acted as a result of irresistible impulse? How impulsive could it be if he took the time to lure the victim to the garage, find the box where the original owner had placed the cuffs, handcuff the victim to a pipe, start his car, and leave it running? With all the time it took to perform those actions, would it be rational to believe it could be done impulsively, without thinking?"

"I maintain it *was* impulsive. Mr. Ross's basic nature was that of a non-violent man, so the act of killing someone had to be repressed into his unconscious. In his mental state, time had a different dimension and that blank space in his mind could have lasted anywhere from a few minutes to an hour. When he arrived in town, his mental status changed, and he was once again connected to his conscious mind and remembered what he had done."

David Weisman paced and shook his head.

"Dr. Evans, did you ever consider that Ross *did* plan to kill Harry Sanders because he held him responsible for the death of his family, of which there is no proof? Isn't it reasonable to think that this was a crime of revenge, pure vengeance, and that Ross *was* lying in wait to commit this crime? He lured Sanders to his home, took him to the garage, handcuffed him, turned on the car engine, and left him there to die.

"Ross had the motive to murder Sanders and he had plenty of time to do it. There were too many time-consuming events that had to take place. Would you say that a person's state of mind, in a murder case, should be judged by only one man?"

"I don't know about only one man, but in this case, the evidence is obvious."

"Obvious, Dr. Evans? Tell me, is psychiatry an exact science?"

"You know it's not. Why even ask the question?"

"The witness will answer," the judge intervened.

"It's not a quantitative science, but the findings of psychoanalysis can be meaningful and are accepted universally."

"Thank you for your opinion, doctor. No further questions."

Judge Jordan asked, "Ms. Coleman, a rebuttal?"

"Yes, Your Honor." She approached the witness stand. "Dr. Evans, could you please summarize your findings for the jury?"

"Ms. Coleman, I have spent many hours with Michael Ross. My copious notes relating to his mental state have been submitted to the court. Based on Professor Ross's numerous therapy sessions with me, there was no question that the victim *was* Hans Stern, an SS officer in the German army.

"When Michael first met Sanders at the pharmacy, he was not able to make the connection. However, when Sanders entered Ross's home for a planned game of chess, the man's laughter triggered a response from the professor. He now saw Sanders as Stern, an evil man who pointed the way to the gas chamber for his young daughters and was responsible for the death of his wife at Auschwitz.

"Then his mind went blank and stayed that way until he arrived in the town of Oneonta. Through psychological testing, Ross showed that he is not a violent man, but in that volatile emotionally charged moment with Sanders, he demonstrated an uncontrollable response and killed who he believed was the Nazi SS officer, Hans Stern."

Brenda looked directly at Evans, then glanced at the jury.

"Is it possible that Michael Ross, without realizing what he was doing, went through the process of handcuffing Sanders to a pipe and gassing him? Wouldn't that take time?"

"It did take time, but his actions were motivated by passion and an obsession to lash out at this man. He was driven and moved at lightning speed and had no memory of what he had done. The notion of time itself has a different value when a man's mind is compromised. When he reached town, he remembered he had killed Stern."

"Well, how do you know that Professor Ross's actions hadn't taken place over several days?"

"That would be highly unlikely. I examined Mr. Sander's medical records. They showed that he took several heart medications. They were all in his system at the proper levels when he died. The records also showed that residuals of the longer acting drugs were in his body for several days. I can't believe that anyone planning to commit murder would think of those incidentals. Mr. Sanders had to be taking these medications on his own."

"Dr. Evans, Professor Ross is a pharmacologist and a pharmacist, an educated man. Why *wouldn't* he think of giving Sander his prescription drugs every day so that they would show up in his lab results?"

"As I said, tests showed that the medications had been taken consistently for several days prior to the victim's death. I agree with the cardiologist's report that Sanders had severe cardiovascular disease and died as a result of a heart failure with no indication of undue stress. His body just gave way as it would if he had died in his sleep."

"Objection, Your Honor. The witness is not here to determine the victim's cause of death."

"Objection sustained. The jury will disregard the witness's reference to the cause of death. Continue with your questioning, Ms. Coleman."

Brenda took a deep breath. "It is a fact, doctor, that you are *not* here to determine the victim's cause of death, only to provide a psychiatric evaluation of the defendant with respect to his mental state at the time of the deceased's death. During your early testimony, you indicated you have another specialty in addition to your license to practice psychiatry?"

"I do," Evans replied.

"And what are your specialties?"

"I am a board certified cardiologist and psychiatrist in the states of New York and Massachusetts."

"Was your cardiology training a valuable asset in evaluating patients with mental disorders?"

"Yes, indeed. There is a clear association between depression, other compromised mental states, *and* heart disease."

"Thank you for enlightening me, Dr. Evans. If you remember, Judge Jordan intervened and admonished Mr. Weisman when he briefly alluded to the idea that you and I entered into some kind of scheme to create events that were false in order to delude the court into believing that Professor Ross was insane at the time. Is it true that you and I had this kind of understanding?"

"Absolutely not. We had no contact other than

you informing me by subpoena that I would be called as a witness. With respect to Michael Ross's state of mind at the time of the victim's death, Mr. Ross was insane based on his inability to control his action."

"Dr. Evans, would you please connect your conclusion of Ross's mental state to the amount of time it would take for him to prepare for his action."

"Yes, of course. Irresistible impulse means that his response that triggered his action had to take place immediately, but something compelled him to require Mr. Ross to gas the victim just as his daughters were gassed in the concentration camp. It would be symbolically important and would take no time. Just turn on the engine.

"As I have said previously, time is viewed differently when a person's mental state is compromised, just as in dreams. When we remember our dream, we think it took place over a long time, when it only took less than a second. People who are not medically trained may have difficulty understanding that point. For Ross, what he did was simple and fast. It took several minutes. Then he forgot what happened and forgot that he had forgotten it. That's a phrase some psychiatrists use to explain the unconscious."

"Thank you, Dr. Evans. You're excused. The defense rests."

"Mr. Weisman, are you ready for your summation?" The judge asked.

"I am, Your Honor."

Weisman stood in front of the jury. "Ladies and gentleman, allow me to thank you for your service in this case. You provide an important contribution in our justice system. The prosecution has conclusively proven its case through testimony and evidence that Michael Ross is guilty of killing Harry Sanders, an innocent man.

"In addition, the prosecution has established beyond reasonable doubt that the insanity plea argued by the defense has no basis in fact. What is a fact is that the defendant signed a sworn admission that he committed this crime.

"The defendant will have you believe that he acted out of an irresistible impulse. How could that be? Do we really know that the handcuffs appeared as a result of a house sale? The bill of sale for the transaction did not itemize every item, and there is no proof that a pair of police handcuffs were conveniently left behind. Did he buy them a day before the murder? A week before? Where were they at the time of the murder? In a box somewhere? Didn't he have to go looking for them, or did he already know *exactly* where they were? Wouldn't that take time? The circumstances don't fit the requirements of an insanity plea. It could not have been an impulsive act. It had to be planned because there were too many time-consuming events that had to be put in place before Michael Ross killed Harry Sanders, an innocent person.

"Direct testimony by the witnesses for the defense were filled with a series of guesses and conjecture about the defendant's state of mind. It's difficult for me to imagine that dream analysis could possibly have any validity in a murder case. It's far from an exact science, and the search for hidden meanings within dreams leave us only with speculation.

"An expert witness indicated that the blood tests showed that Sanders's heart medications were at the proper levels. Perhaps the defendant gave Sanders his medication over several days, anticipating this court case? If he was smart and cunning enough to commit the willful murder of an innocent man, why wouldn't it be reasonable to believe that this intelligent man planned ahead and either gave or forced him to take his heart medications? It would be very clever, indeed.

"The bottom line is that Michael Ross carefully planned the murder of Harry Sanders, took the law into his own hands, plotted the act in advance, and took several days to torment and murder the victim.

"Please do not allow your emotions to get in the way of making a true and just decision. Although many of you have remembrances of World War II and Nazism, they are not on trial here. Your obligation to justice is to follow the law and I ask you to find the defendant guilty of murder in the first degree.

"Thank you."

The judge looked toward the defense table. "Ms. Coleman?"

* * *

Brenda walked past the jury and took the time to look at each one of them.

"Ladies and gentleman, thank you so much for your time, effort, and patience for serving on this jury. When a trial draws to the end, each and every one of you *are* the law because your decision is final and determines the fate of the defendant.

"The strong evidence and expert testimony the defense presented in this case proves, far beyond a reasonable doubt, that Michael Ross had no choice when he responded uncontrollably to cause the demise of the victim.

"In the same sense he, too, was a victim. His mind was not his own after he discovered that Harry Sanders and Hans Stern were one and the same. As a result, he was driven by a powerful force over which he had no control. How would you feel if you committed a criminal act that conflicted with your basic nature and had no memory of doing it? After all, you're all law-abiding citizens. Would you be able to appreciate what you'd done? Those questions would only bring more questions, and rarely answers, because the truth is, ladies and gentlemen, there would be *nothing* you could do if your action was uncontrollable.

"Expert testimony has proven that Professor Ross was literally and emotionally detached from his conscious brain and driven by an unconscious force, over which he had no control, when he caused the death of the victim. A renowned psychiatrist testified to the fact that Michael Ross lacked the substantial cognition to appreciate the outcome of his action, and, as a result, the defendant acted with irresistible impulse. The defense has shown, with facts, that Professor Ross's action was *legally* consistent with the definition of irresistible impulse, and you, ladies and gentlemen, must be guided by the law.

"A person who acts as a result of this specific impulse does not have the choice or the time to think about what he must do or not do. He acts without thinking and it's not his fault. When someone has no control whatsoever of an impulse that causes harm, the law makes allowances for that. Irresistible impulse was written into the law for good reason. There *are* circumstances when we must act as an understanding and forgiving society when someone has no control of his actions. That's what makes us human and allows a person's state of mind to be a consideration in determining guilt or innocence. For these reasons, Michael Ross should not be held criminally responsible.

"I ask the jury to take into account that the defense has also called into question the cause of Harry Sanders's death. A board certified cardiologist has concluded that Sanders's death was caused by heart failure.

"Michael Ross knew instantly that he was facing a killer, an evil Nazi SS officer who had killed his family. He was compelled by a powerful emotion emanating from his unconscious, driving him to kill this man. What *was* he thinking? What was he feeling? We could never know, and neither could he. That's what 'uncontrollable' means. There was no choice for him to act otherwise.

"Committing murder is wrong, and it's a punishable crime. No one should ever take the law into his own hands. We are a nation of laws, but because we have human feelings, we have included in our law certain exceptions. Lawyers and judges expanded the legal definition of insanity to include more cognitive elements, not merely that a person knew right from wrong, but whether they had uncontrollable impulses, which might cause them to commit a crime such as murder.

"The defense has focused on two points. One is that we have contested Sanders's cause of death and showed, with expert testimony, that he died as a result of an existing heart condition, separate from stress, carbon monoxide, or other events. Second, further testimony proved that Michael Ross displayed an *immediate* response in that split second when he realized that the man facing him was the killer who destroyed his family. He acted in a way consistent with irresistible impulse, which was in line with the definition described in the New York State Penal Code. These two facts alone call for reasonable doubt.

"You see, ladies and gentleman, the law *does* allow for human, extenuating circumstances, and your duty is to make your judgment based on the existing law. I ask you to find Michael Ross not guilty. Thank you."

Chapter 31

Newspapers screamed out the headlines. The Oneonta *Daily Star* reported:

Nazi Killer's Case Goes To Jury.

The *Albany Herald* proclaimed:

Deliberations in Ross Case End, Waiting For Decision.

It took the jury three days to come to a verdict. Brenda, Jeff, and Michael stood and faced the jury as the bailiff handed the small white paper to the judge. Weisman sat at the prosecution table, leaning forward, his hands folded over a legal pad, his eyes on the jury.

The court was filled to capacity. Everyone was silent. Michael's entire body trembled. His lips tightened. He needed to be with Ilona for only a quick moment before the verdict. It would give him peace.

***

Ilona, I just have a minute. The case is over and I'm waiting for the decision. Any outcome will be easy for me to accept because you will be with me wherever I am. Maybe the things people share should not be measured in time. For us, it was not about how long we had together, but how our beautiful love unfolded in the time we had. In the scheme of things, our time on Earth is just a snap of the finger, but the snap we shared became our lives and filled our hearts.

The trial is over. The judge is reading the verdict. I feel calm inside. I killed a monster, someone who never should have been born. It had to be done.

Oh, did I tell you? I might see Erika. She lives in New York City and is a ballet dancer. I wonder where she got those genes? I may try to see her if it's possible. I would only see you in her face, but you know, I was thinking, maybe she is my daughter too. My own flesh and blood and not Stern's. We both know it was possible. That would be a laugh, Stern keeping her alive and bringing her to America, thinking she was his. I'm smiling now at the thought. And not only that, but Hilda brought her up, not realizing that Erika's real father would be the one who would control her and her husband's lives. It would make a good story, but it's really not so much about who Erika's father is. It's only about you, Ilona, her mother. It will be you that I see if I meet her. I have to go. I love you.

The jury announced the verdict on the morning of November 16. All eyes were on the jury.

"In the case of *The People versus Michael Ross*, case number 70-CR3210, we, the jury, find the defendant, Michael Ross, not guilty."

The roar of those in the crowded courtroom filled the air. Everyone applauded and looked toward the defense table. David Weisman shook the hands of the defense team, put some papers in his briefcase, and left.

"Oh my God!" Michael exclaimed, his eyes filled with tears. He turned toward Jeff and Brenda, who looked up at him bright-eyed and smiling. The three of them hugged and Michael's heart raced with joy.

"Thank you both." Michael shed tears as he kept his arms around both of them. "I can't thank you enough. Brenda, can I keep the suit? I've gotten used to it and it fits perfectly," Michael joked.

"It's all yours, Michael. I'm glad we won, but I think this will be my last murder case. Way too much stress. Maybe I'll start practicing real estate law and do closings on property transfers. Boring, but a breeze after this case."

"Real estate law for you? I wouldn't go that far. Never!" Michael said, overwhelmed with joy. "You're an outstanding lawyer. Stick to crime." He laughed. "In your case, crime pays! I thank you so much."

"You're welcome. I'm happy for you, but don't do anything like this again. Next time, you get charged double. You still owe me for cleaning out your refrigerator." Brenda smiled.

"Next time?" Michael shook his head. "Never. Thank you for giving me my life back."

They walked out through the back door of the courthouse to avoid the crowds. Brenda drove Michael home and reminded him that the key was still under the mat.

Michael entered his house. An hour earlier, he didn't know if he would ever be able to return. The ring of the phone startled him. He wasn't sure if he paid the bill, but Dan must have taken care of those things while Michael was away. It was Brenda.

"So, Mr. Free Man, how do you feel?"

"I'm still a little numb. You were amazing."

"Yeah, I'm one amazing lady." She laughed. "I even got a big hug from my husband, and as a reward for winning, he's taking me out to Blackbeard's Cove tonight for dinner. They have the best seafood anywhere and tonight is lobster night, so thanks to you, I'll be having a romantic candlelight dinner."

"I'm happy for you. Make sure you wear a bib," Michael said, smiling into the phone. "Eating lobsters together isn't quite a romantic moment."

"One more thing I wanted to cover, Michael. The money you asked me to give to Albert Chisholm's lawyer for his defense fund is already in his hands. Mr. Chisholm has been told that Tom Kennedy is acting *pro bono* on his behalf. Between you and me, Michael, Tom really *does* pro bono cases anyway, and when expensive lawyers, like Tom, do *pro bono* work, the judges appreciate it. I think having Kennedy lead his defense will give Mr. Chisholm a great advantage. He's one helluva lawyer, the best."

"Except for you."

"Yeah, except for me." She giggled. "Talk soon."

Michael hung up, but kept his hand on the phone for a moment, thinking. Then he went into the study, shook his head, and smiled. *Animal Farm* was still open on his desk. He poured himself a cognac, Polignac VSOP.

***

It's over, Ilona. All went well. Erika was another reason I wanted to stay free, so I could meet her, look into her eyes, and see you. It would be such a gift for me, but it's a little scary. I don't know how she'll react or even if she would want to meet me. I'll think about it.

Anyway, I'm not sure that meeting her is even a possibility. I don't know. My head is all mixed up now. Will think about it later. Love you. Kiss!

***

Michael walked the short distance to the garage. Only he knew the truth of what happened there. He was free and, in a way, so was Stern. He no longer had to live in squalor. Perhaps he knew all along that justice would find him, and it did. Those in concentration camps, who were gassed and thrown into the ovens, found their freedom too. It's strange how "freedom" takes on different meanings depending on the circumstances. Michael lived with guilt, but Stern had none. Guilt only plagues a man of conscience.

I learned a lot from Albert. He was a good human being, thoughtful and kind. Because of him, I can never feel imprisoned wherever I am. My freedom will always be within me.

***

The lock was still knocked out on the garage door, so it was easy to roll it up. He walked inside and felt as if he were in another world, another time, a place from long ago. He looked at one section of the pipe and the stains in front of it. The firefighters had moved things around, but his Chevy remained where it was, except the windows were open and there were white stains all over the seats.

Michael sat with his back against the front fender and looked straight ahead, to where Stern had sat. He still remembered his cries. *Was macht du?* A moment later, he saw an image of Stern in front of him as a broken man, his eyes open, staring, and his mouth closed. The dead prisoners in the concentration camp had the same look. Now Stern was like them.

Michael peeked in the box, which previously held the handcuffs. There was also a gas mask.

I could have worn it and stayed in the garage with Stern, eye to eye, and watched him die as he looked at me in terror. His eyes would've been filled with ultimate fear and I could have watched him struggle for air until he was dead, but I have no reason to think like that anymore. It will take time for me to put my time with Stern behind me.

Michael's thoughts were elsewhere. He had a life to live and many more years to go. He went back to the house, sipped a glass of Hungarian Tokoi wine, and thought, once more, of the day he first laid his eyes on Ilona at her father's vineyard. She was so shy, but when she looked at him, her smile gave her feelings away and he knew she cared.

Michael drank another glass of the syrupy, amber wine and drifted off to a deep sleep in a real bed.

Chapter 32

When Michael awoke the next morning, he was startled by his surroundings. His cell had become his home for too long. He breathed a sigh of relief, happy that he was in his real home. Shopping for food was high on his list of priorities, but there were also phone calls to be made. One in particular. He wasn't sure he could summon the courage to do it.

What would she say? What would I say?

The sudden, shrill ring of the phone startled him. It was Dan.

"Michael, congratulations. I'm so happy for you. I knew you were innocent. You would never do anything like that. They mentioned the verdict on WSKG this morning. I'm glad the jury found things your way. We must celebrate."

"Thank you for saying that, and I can't express my gratitude enough. Thanks for keeping an eye on things."

"You're back home just in time. The Catskill Symphony Orchestra is doing an all-Mozart program tonight. I would love to go with you."

"Thanks, Dan, but I'm not up for that yet. You enjoy it. We can make it another time. By the way, the store is yours. I wouldn't put it in anyone else's hands. You're a good man and it's time for me to leave The Chemist's Shop and take a new direction. Maybe write a book."

"Make it a memoir. You've got a lot to tell. Is it okay if I come over to your house tonight after work? It's been a while, and I'd rather see you than go to the concert."

"Of course, I would love it. I miss our talks. We'll have some wine and relax. Looking forward to it."

Michael put down the phone, but left his hand on the receiver for a moment and stared at it. Then he dressed and turned on the TV. News about the trial was on, so he turned the TV off.

He sipped a cup of black coffee as he sat on the couch, thinking. Then he walked to the phone and dialed her number. A woman answered. Michael cleared his throat.

"Hello, is this Erika?"

"Uh, yes," she said in a soft voice, "but I don't use that name anymore. Who is this?"

Michael paused. "Eva?"

"Oh, yes. Are you calling me from Avery Fisher Hall about the rehearsal?"

"No, Eva, my name is Miklos Rosen and I'm calling because I knew your mother."

"I see. Did you know my mother died a few months ago?"

"Yes, I do know that, and I'm sorry. I'm a pharmacist and had a pharmacy in Oneonta. Your mother filled her prescriptions there, and I learned from one of the staff that she has passed away. It's a little late, but I'd like to offer my condolences."

"Thank you so much, that is very kind of you. I'm sorry, I don't want to be rude, but I'm expecting a call about my rehearsal. Was there anything else?"

Michael felt rushed. "Well, I did know your mother, Hilda Sanders, but I also know that you were adopted, and I knew your birth mother. I don't know what you know about her, but I knew her very well, and I thought you might like to know more about her."

"Can you tell me her name?"

"Yes, it was Ilona."

"Oh my God, this is so real and unexpected! Yes, of course, I'd like to know more about her. How did you know her?"

"Well, it's a rather long story. Are you getting ready to go out? If this is not a good time to talk, I can call another time."

"Oh, no, my other call can wait. Please, I would like to know more."

Michael heard her breathing rapidly into the phone. There was a long pause.

"This is so strange," she said. "I don't know what to say. Did you know my father, Hans? They lived in Oneonta. To be honest, I was not close with him or my sister. How did you get my number?"

"Yes, I knew him, but not very well. Your mother, Hilda, had given me information about you. Can you tell me what you know?"

"Oh yes, absolutely. I know I came to America as a child. I had an Italian passport. I still don't know why, but I have an American passport now. Things must have been so complicated back then. It was just after the war. Can you let me know more about my mother, my real mother? I was told she died in childbirth while she was having me. I feel so sad for being responsible. Tell me, how did you find me? I'm sorry I am rambling."

"Finding you wasn't difficult. Hilda told me you were a ballet dancer in New York City and your name was Erika. I took a chance that you still kept your last name. I checked the ballet companies for Erika, but there was none. Then I saw 'Eva Sanders's in the list of dancers at the ballet company and I knew it was you. I was glad you didn't have an unlisted number. So, what else do you know about your beginnings?"

"My father told me I was born in Germany, and my birth mother's name was Ilona. My real father was killed in action and Hilda and Hans adopted me."

"Yes, you know quite a bit, Eva. I love your name."

"I like it better than Erika, Mr. Rosen. That name sounds so hard, so harsh, but Eva flows smoothly, like music. I use my middle name as my stage name."

"I always wondered how young women were able to dance on their toes."

"For me, it's more natural than walking, although I do have to have my ballet slippers custom made because my right toe curves outward."

Michael paused before he spoke. *So does mine.* "Did you have an injury?"

"No, I was born that way. It's a genetic trait, probably from one of my birth parents."

Michael felt his heart beating faster. *Could it be?* "Did you always want to be a dancer?"

"Yes, always."

"And if you couldn't be a dancer, what else would you be?"

"Nothing else. I started dancing when I was young. I only wanted to be a dancer."

"Thank you for telling me that." Michael smiled. "I feel I know you after so short a time on the phone. Your voice is so much like your mother's."

"I wish I could have heard her voice, or that I had a picture, something. How did you know my mother?"

"Ilona and I fell in love when we were twelve and we—"

"Oh my God, twelve? That is so beautiful."

"I can see you're a romantic, Eva. It was *love*, even at twelve, and we kept those feelings for many years. We even planned to marry, but our lives were interrupted by the war. What is your life like? It's a pleasure for me to be talking to someone whose mother was the love of my life. I hear Ilona's voice when you speak. It makes me feel good and sad at the same time."

"To tell you the truth, I live a quiet life. Dancing is my passion and that's where *my* love affair lies. It's my most precious gift and when I'm not dancing, I practice, so I have little time to myself. I don't even read newspapers, magazines, or watch TV."

"Are you married? Do you have someone special

in your life?"

"I'm not married and don't have a boyfriend like most of the other girls who perform. I hope someday I will meet someone, get married, and have a family. I love music and dancing and that fills my life. I think the good genes in my body brought me to the world of music and dance. I sense, deep inside, that it must have come from my mother. I often wondered what she was like. I wish I had a picture."

A single tear flowed over Michael's cheek. "I can give you a picture of your mother in words, little Eva. Maybe that will help."

"Little Eva, no one has ever called me that. Please, tell me everything, Mr. Rosen. I'll sit here and listen. Let me know more about my mom. You're the only one in the world who really knew her in a special way. I can hear how much she meant to you in your voice. Please, take her out of my imagination and bring her to life for me."

Michael took a deep breath. *What will I say? I can't tell her everything. It will only hurt little Eva.*

"Okay, but my thoughts are scattered. I'll tell you what she was like as it comes to me."

"That's fine, Mr. Rosen. Thank you so much."

"I met your mother when we were both very young. And, yes, even at twelve, it was love at first sight for us. It's not that we weren't sure. We both knew it, but we were way too shy to tell each other. Do you believe it was possible for us to have felt that way, so young?"

"Oh, yes, I do," Eva said excitedly. "The best love is love at first sight at *any* age."

Michael smiled, took a deep breath, and went on. "We lived in a small town and shared our feelings together for many years. We went to concerts with our families, listened to music, and had picnics in the countryside, where we danced in the sunshine. My father provided the music on his accordion."

"It sounds so idyllic and sweet," Eva whispered into the phone.

"It was. Our families were close, and they envisioned that we would marry and have a happy life together. When we were seventeen, we talked about getting married and knew it would happen when the right time came.

"Your mother worked in her father's winery and I was a student at the university. We made our plans, but Hitler was coming into power, and my family moved to America to escape the war. I had to leave the university and the beautiful young girl who owned my heart. I still love her, and I felt terrible when I heard she died."

"It's such a beautiful story. I'm so sorry. I understand how you feel. She meant so much to you. It would make a wonderful ballet. Love and tragedy go well together."

Michael smiled. *She's so much like Ilona. The same voice, the same feelings, everything.*

"When we arrived in the United States, I continued my education and became involved with academia and teaching, but I never forgot your mother, never. She is still in my heart. Hilda told me you were a ballet dancer. I'm happy for that. It was the most important information that led me to you."

"Yes, I'm happy too, Mr. Rosen. What did my mother look like?"

"She had dark hair, a creamy complexion, high cheek bones, and sparkling brown eyes. Anything like you?"

"Everything like me. I don't believe it. It's so good to know that I look like her. It makes me feel she's still alive inside me."

"From what I can tell from your voice and your passions, you're very much like Ilona."

"Hilda was kind to me, but she had a difficult life with my father, and I don't have good feelings about him. Is it wrong to hate your father?" She sounded so innocent. "I wanted nothing to do with him, and when my sister told me he died, I was glad."

"It happens, Eva. Put those thoughts behind you. You can't change people and you can't change the past. Get on with your life and do the things that fulfill you.

"I do know a wonderful young man who, I think, would love to meet you. His name is Dan Berman, and I've known him for many years. Interested?"

"I'm still a little on the shy side, but, you know what? You bring something refreshing to me. Yes, coming from you, I would like to meet him."

"I think you would have a lot in common. I know he likes classical music. Does he have to love the ballet?"

Eva giggled into the phone. "No, he just has to be a good and kind person. Oh, and with a nice smile."

"He is all that! Even the smile. Let me know

when you'd like to arrange it. He's a sensitive, caring person with a wonderful sense of humor. Oh, he's nice looking too. I think you both would get along well together. Actually, he said he would come over to my house tonight for some wine and cheese. We haven't seen each other for a while. I'll tell him about you, Eva. You never know what can happen." Michael smiled.

"I like the mystery of it all. Let's just see what happens if we can meet."

"Good. If it's all right with you, I'll give him your phone number and I'll give you the pharmacy number where Dan works."

"Thank you. It's good that I'm able to reach him too. I'll try not to be too shy."

"Just be yourself. You're a lovely young lady. Do you think we can meet sometime?"

"Oh, I would love that. I knew you were for real when you knew the name of my mother who gave me life. No one knew her name except for my parents. It would be wonderful if you could come to one of my performances. We are performing *Swan Lake*. I will be playing the lead, Odette, the swan queen. Do you know this ballet?"

"Yes, I know it quite well and I can see you in that role. You were probably dancing around the house when you were a little girl."

Eva laughed. "That was me. Does tomorrow night work for you?"

"Yes, it's fine."

"Good, I'm so excited. I can leave a ticket for you at the box office, and if you want to bring your wife..."

"Oh, I'm not married."

"I see, okay. I will leave an orchestra ticket for you and after the performance, we can meet backstage."

"I think backstage might be a little busy. Could we meet outside, near the theater?"

"Yes, of course, the fountain at Lincoln Center, and afterwards, we can go to this wonderful Hungarian restaurant. It's on Second Avenue near Eighty-Sixth Street. It's a cute place that serves great goulash, stuffed cabbage, and homemade strudel you will die for.

"It's owned by an older Hungarian man named Laszlo. The two of you would have a lot to talk about, although I learned from a friend that he was in a concentration camp and lost some of his family. He never talks about it, but maybe it would be different with you."

"I'm sorry to hear that. It must have been terrible for him."

"Yes, I'm sure, but he's very upbeat and full of life. There is also a violinist at his restaurant who plays sad, tearful gypsy melodies...melodies to cry with, then livens it up with some Czardas music. I always feel like getting up to dance when I hear it, but I will just sit and listen as you tell me everything about my mother."

"You know, being in a Hungarian restaurant, eating stuffed cabbage, would be a special experience for me. Your mother was Hungarian, as you may know."

Eva didn't say anything and Michael held his breath as he waited for her to speak.

"You mean she wasn't German?"

"No, she was Hungarian. We met and fell in love in Szentendre, a small village in Hungary. Ilona was a lovely country girl and the daughter of a winemaker."

"Oh, Mr. Rosen, that makes me so happy. I don't know why. It just does. We have so much to look forward to when we meet."

Michael's heart was filled with joy. "Yes, that will be great. It will be nice to drive down to the city. I haven't been there for a while. Okay, so it's tomorrow, Lincoln Center, at the fountain, after the performance?" Michael wrote the details on his notepad as he spoke.

"How will you find me?" Eva asked.

"Trust me, Eva. I'll know you." Michael smiled. "You won't have to wear a red carnation."

"Good, I can't wait."

She was so pure, so innocent, nothing like Stern. How could that be? His mind drifted to Ilona's last words before they were taken from their home.

"Remind me to tell you something, Miklos."

"Tell me now."

"No, it's a surprise for the whole family."

They hung up. Michael was elated.

She's my daughter!

He checked the phone book for a florist and added it to his notes under Eva's name and her phone number.

He ordered a dozen red roses to be sent to her on stage at the end of the performance.

Every ballet dancer should be taking her bows with flowers in her arms.

Michael had some food delivered from the local grocer. As he enjoyed his lunch, he thought of Eva, little Eva. She sounded exactly like Ilona. *It was wonderful to hear Ilona's voice once more.*

He couldn't wait to be with Eva. The gypsy music at the Hungarian restaurant would be a gift from heaven. Ilona would be with him once more tomorrow night. What more could he ask?

***

Michael was more exhausted from the trial than he realized but was relieved and relaxed after his conversation with Eva. A heavy emotional weight had been lifted from his shoulders and now he had a special event to look forward to the next night. After lunch, he enjoyed a peaceful, dreamless nap until it was dark.

A loud knock on the door woke him.

It's Dan. I'll tell him about Eva.

Michael hurried to the door, and, smiling, he opened it.

But it wasn't Dan.

In the dim light stood a man, bald, with a small swastika tattoo on his head. His hard, hate-filled eyes held Michael's as he raised a sawed off shotgun and fired.

The blast pierced the stillness of the night. Then all was silent again.

ACKNOWLEDGMENTS

First and foremost, my deepest respect, thanks, and love go to my wife, Carol, who has provided me with the inspiration, insight, editing, and patience I needed to write this book. Thanks to Judy Ratto, an in-depth researcher who checked some of the facts. Sincere appreciation and gratitude go to my friends and scholars, Roy Wolff, Roy Sanders, Rabbi Dennis Math, and Norman Oksman, who provided their time, wisdom, and constructive input. I am indebted to Rosa Sophia, an established author and good friend who has been a constant source of encouragement. Special thanks to my young nieces, Daniela Brumer and Victoria Brumer, for listening to my story and offering feedback. I am especially thankful to my critique group, Writers of Abacoa: Joseph Alcock, Edee Corrias, Judy Ratto, Fred Lichtenburg, Stan Leeds, Judy Lucas, Ellen Seacrest, Linda Van Dyck, David Yates, Patricia Benedetto and Allen Balogh. My thanks to Tiffany T. Cole for her efforts in editing my book.

ABOUT THE AUTHOR

Richard Brumer grew up in the Bronx and now lives in Florida with his wife, Carol. For many years, his passions were skiing, sports car racing, and sailing, including sailing solo in the South Pacific.

As a retired pharmacist, he turned his hand to writing and has written several novels and short stories.

Books by this Author include:

The Last Sunrise
Gelt without Guilt
Meeting Max

Facebook:
https://www.facebook.com/RichardBrumer

Twitter:
https://twitter.com/BrumerRichb816

Website:
http://richardbrumer.com/